THE GUILD CODEX: SPELLBOUND / SEVEN

LOST TALISMANS
AND A TEQUILA

ANNETTE MARIE

dark owl
fantasy

Lost Talismans and a Tequila
The Guild Codex: Spellbound / Book Seven

Dark Owl Fantasy Inc.
PO Box 88106, Rabbit Hill Post Office
Edmonton, AB, Canada T6R 0M5
www.darkowlfantasy.com

Cover Copyright © 2020 by Annette Ahner
Cover and Book Interior by Midnight Whimsy Designs
www.midnightwhimsydesigns.com

Editing by Elizabeth Darkley
arrowheadediting.wordpress.com

ISBN 978-1-988153-49-0

MORE BOOKS BY ANNETTE MARIE

STEEL & STONE UNIVERSE

Steel & Stone Series

Chase the Dark

Bind the Soul

Yield the Night

Reap the Shadows

Unleash the Storm

Steel & Stone

Spell Weaver Trilogy

The Night Realm

The Shadow Weave

The Blood Curse

OTHER WORKS

Red Winter Trilogy

Red Winter

Dark Tempest

Immortal Fire

THE GUILD CODEX

CLASSES OF MAGIC

Spiritalis
Psychica
Arcana
Demonica
Elementaria

MYTHIC

A person with magical ability

MPD / MAGIPOL

The organization that regulates mythics and their activities

ROGUE

A mythic living in violation of MPD laws

LOST TALISMANS
AND A TEQUILA

DRUIDS AND WITCHES are not the same thing.

I mean, I knew that already, but seeing the differences firsthand was a whole new experience.

"So, uh," I began, eyebrows arched, "are you sure this is ... strictly necessary?"

Kaveri looked up, her long brown hair swinging over one shoulder. Balancing a bag of dark soil on her palm, she frowned. "Of course. Is something the matter?"

"It's just ... the first time I did this, it was different."

She straightened, and several feet away, Delta also turned toward me, holding a bundle of fresh-cut flowers. The two witches gave me looks that were part "then your first time was wrong" and part "are you serious right now?"

With a deep chuckle, Philip walked past the two witches. He carried a large tree branch, dead leaves still clinging to it. "I'm guessing your previous experience involved a druid?"

Kaveri and Delta pulled faces as though he'd uttered a nasty swear word.

I made a face back at them. Was there any point in denying it? Considering my entire guild thought I'd had *relations* with a notorious rogue druid, it wasn't exactly a secret.

"Yep," I declared unapologetically. "And it was a snap, gotta say."

Delta sniffed. "And probably a weak bond."

Kaveri glanced away, a faint flush tinting her warm tawny skin. She'd never admit it, but she totally had the mythic version of a bad-boy crush on said druid.

"Unfortunately," Philip said, "we only know one way to join a witch and her fae familiar. It's slower, but equally effective."

"I wasn't complaining," I clarified. Okay, maybe a little bit of complaining. "Just … you know, making sure I understand."

Not that I understood anything about the weird nature circle the three witches were setting up around me.

Philip had chosen a cluster of trees in a park only a few blocks from the Crow and Hammer for the fae-familiar ritual. It was a nice spot, sheltered from passersby, and I could almost forget we were in Vancouver's disreputable Downtown Eastside. The mood was only a little ruined by the fact that, three months ago in this same park, I'd participated in a five-way confrontation between a team of demon hunters, a demon mage, an unbound demon, and a contracted demon, plus me, Aaron, and Kai.

There'd been a lot of demons.

But the witches didn't know about that incident, and I had no plans to mention it.

I hitched a pleasant smile onto my face as Philip, Delta, and Kaveri bustled around me, setting up their fancy dirt circle with leaves, flowers, dried herbs, seeds, a dish of water, and a wax candle. Philip used his stick to scratch incomprehensible markings in the hard-packed earth. Considering I was supposed to *be* a witch—according to my mythic registration paperwork, at least—I should probably know more about the Spiritalis class and their unique magic.

While they worked, I curled my arms around the warm critter in my lap. Hoshi watched the witches with curious fuchsia eyes, her long silver tail looping behind me. Her spiny, insect-like wings were tucked against her back, but her long antennae bobbed in my face, the crystalline tips glowing faintly.

She perked up when the three witches took positions around the circle and began a songlike chant. The sylph weaved her head side to side as she listened, huge eyes blinking.

Repairing my bond with Hoshi was high on my to-do list, but as the chant went on, I couldn't stop my thoughts from wandering. Fresh in my mind were too many traumas, the memories crowding each other as they fought for my attention.

A week ago, Kai and I sneaking onto a plane and flying south to Los Angeles. Breaking into an MPD precinct to rescue Zak and destroying the building on our way out.

That night, Zak and I returning to the ruins of his farm. Grieving together over what he'd lost. His hatred-fueled need for revenge.

Had it only been three days since we'd planned our attack on Varvara Nikolaev, her rogues, and her inexplicably powerful golems? Only three days since Zak had betrayed me, Ezra had lost control, and I'd destroyed all my magic to save him?

"Tori?"

I jolted. Philip was crouched beside me, a narrow stick of charcoal in his hand.

"Where would you like the familiar mark?" he asked.

Untangling my arms from Hoshi, I unzipped my leather jacket and shrugged it off. The late January cold bit into my skin as I rolled up the sleeve of my thin sweater. I wanted it in the same spot as last time.

Philip held my upper arm steady as he began to draw. I twisted my mouth at the scratchy tip of the charcoal, thinking wistfully of Zak's pragmatic eyeliner pencil. That probably wasn't natural enough for a witch.

It took the witch a few minutes longer to complete the complex design, but he didn't need a reference for it, which impressed me. He lowered the charcoal and surveyed his work.

"Excellent," he said. "Now, we begin the formal ritual of exchange, where I'll invite the fae to—"

Hoshi stretched out her neck and bumped her nose against the mark on my arm. Heat flashed through my body—followed by a wave of swirling color in my mind.

"Hoshi!" I gushed delightedly, sweeping her into a squirmy hug. A rainbow of pink assaulted my mind's eye as she buried her face in my chest, tail flicking.

"Or we can skip that part," Philip said drily. "You have a strong bond with your familiar without any magic at all, Tori."

"Probably because she's my friend," I said, giving the sylph one more squeeze. "Are we done?"

"I guess so."

As I pushed to my feet, I glanced across at the elaborate nature circle, then at my arm. I almost asked if we *really* couldn't have skipped to the familiar mark part, but instead, I grinned at the witches.

"Thanks for your help. I'm so glad to have Hoshi back."

They smiled happily, and Delta even looked misty-eyed over the sylph's dizzying dance, her serpentine body undulating excitedly as she circled me. Her language of color was pinging in my head so fast I couldn't follow, but I wasn't worried about that. We had lots of time to catch up.

As Philip and Delta tidied the circle, Kaveri wandered over to me. She watched Hoshi settle behind my back, her paws on my shoulders.

"Thanks again, Kaveri," I said more quietly. "I really appreciate it."

She nodded. "It wouldn't have worked, you know."

"Huh?"

She pointed at my bare arm, the charcoal lines dark against my pale skin. "If Philip had drawn that without the ritual, it wouldn't have worked. Don't you remember what I told you?"

"Uh ... which thing that you told me?"

"About witches versus druids. Druids can manipulate natural energies directly, but witches can't do that. We need the ritual."

"Oh." Right. No need to admit I barely recalled that conversation. The arrival of the actual druid we'd been discussing had distracted me immediately afterward.

"I would've liked to see the Crystal Druid perform a familiar ritual without ... the ritual. It would've been interesting to witness." She gave me a sidelong look. "I don't suppose he'll be back to visit you?"

A heavy weight settled over me, pressing on my lungs. "No. He's long gone."

"But aren't you two frien—"

"No." The word came out harsh and clipped. "We were never friends."

She glanced down at her feet. "Sorry."

Hoshi nudged the back of my neck. Shaking myself, I stooped to grab my jacket and pulled it on. Beneath the black markings on my arm would be a faintly glowing replica of the design that would fade in a few days. Kind of a shame, as the pinkish blue magic looked pretty damn cool.

As I zipped up my jacket, Philip slung his duffle bag of witchy supplies over his shoulder. "Shall we head back?"

I nodded, and Hoshi spun a final circle around me before fading from sight. The three witches glanced up to watch her fly away—or that's what I assumed was going on. They could see the sylph when she shifted into the fae demesne, but my lame human eyes couldn't detect shit.

Oh well. Having glimpsed the secret fae world, I was cool with nice, predictable human reality.

As we followed a quiet street back toward the guild, I let the witches draw ahead of me. My thoughts were wandering again, rushing forward to what came next—to the impossible task I had to accomplish and the obstacles piling up in my path. I'd fought mages, sorcerers, witches, fae, and demons, but my new enemy was undefeatable and unstoppable: time.

When you wanted it to hurry up, it slowed to a crawl. When you desperately needed more, it rushed ahead. Time was such an asshole.

As the cube-shaped guild came into view, a gray SUV rolled through the intersection and slowed, its signal flashing. It turned into the parking lot.

"I'm going around the back," I told the witches. "See you inside."

Waving, Kaveri followed Philip and Delta to the front door. I veered toward the sidewalk, and as I entered the lot, the SUV door slammed shut.

Not realizing he had an audience, Aaron stood with his shoulders hunched, keys clutched in his hand. The sight of the pyromage alone, when just a week ago it had been rare to see him without one or both of his best friends at his side, made me ache.

At the crunch of gravel under my shoes, he glanced up. His shoulders went back and he flashed a grin—but it didn't reach his dull blue eyes.

"Hey," I said. "You're here early."

"So are you." He reached out, and I stepped into his arms. He hugged me tight. "How'd the familiar reunion go?"

"All done!" I said brightly, arms around his broad shoulders. Our sentimental hug wasn't strictly necessary—it'd been less than a day since we'd seen each other—but we both needed it. "Hoshi and I can talk again."

"Awesome."

I peeled myself from his hold and headed for the guild's back door. "What about you? I didn't know you were coming in today."

"I want to check with the officers if there's anything I can help with. Maybe I can cover Felix's shift or something."

Zora, Felix's sword-wielding sorceress wife, was still in critical condition after the battle against Varvara's forces. We were all waiting anxiously for good news from the guild's healers.

Holding the door for Aaron, I didn't point out that he could've called Girard or Tabitha instead of showing up at the guild. It was second nature for most Crow and Hammer members to return to the guild during times of uncertainty. This place was their safe haven.

"That's considerate," I began, nervousness shooting through me as I followed him into the narrow kitchen, "but instead of volunteering for shifts, maybe—"

I broke off. Almost too quiet to hear, someone sniffed wetly. Aaron frowned, and we both looked toward a nearby door, open a crack. Another sniffle sounded. Was someone crying?

Stepping sideways, I swung the door open to reveal Clara's office, her desk piled so high with folders that it resembled a model of Manhattan's skyscrapers.

The assistant guild master jumped when the door bumped the wall. She whirled on her chair, holding a handful of crisp white papers. A courier envelope lay in her lap, the top torn open.

"Oh!" She wiped hastily at her face. "Tori, Aaron! Good morning! Or—oh—afternoon, I guess. Good afternoon!"

"Clara …" I took in her rumpled brown hair and trembling mouth with concern. "What's wrong?"

"Nothing!" She clutched the papers to her chest as though trying to hide them. "I'm fine."

She ruined her firm declaration with another sniff.

Aaron pointed at the papers. "What's that?"

"Nothing. You shouldn't be back here, Aaron. Kitchen staff only."

"Okay, but what are those papers?"

"Paperwork, and it's none of your concern."

"Clara." I gave her a gentle but firm stare. "What's wrong?"

All the fight went out of her, and she slumped miserably in her chair. "I guess you two already know anyway."

She held out the papers, and Aaron took them. I leaned close as we scanned an official document, the MPD logo filling the top left corner.

"It's just so sudden," Clara mumbled, tearing a bit of cardboard off the stiff courier envelope. "No one so much as mentioned …"

The title at the top of the page burned into my brain: *Guild Transfer Request.*

"He never said anything … then to just … so sudden …"

Aaron's fingers bit into the papers, crinkling the crisp white surface, but even as the packet shook with the force of his grip, I couldn't miss the name on the form.

Kaisuke Yamada.

Ripping more pieces off the envelope, Clara sighed heavily. "I just can't imagine the Crow and Hammer without Kai."

"He's transferring out?" I whispered. "He's leaving the guild?"

Clara's head snapped up. Her face paled as she took in our expressions. "You … you didn't know?"

The documents crumpled in Aaron's fist, then he shoved them at me. Turning on his heel, he swept out of the small office. I held the form, fighting the urge to tear it up.

"I—I'll call him," I said unsteadily. "Convince him to—to wait."

Tears welled in Clara's eyes. "The transfer is already done, Tori. That's the signed paperwork for our records."

I flipped to the last page. There at the bottom was Kai's sharp, slashing signature. Below it was Darius's scrawled autograph, and beneath that, a loopy name. The signatory: Makiko Miura, Acting Guild Master, MiraCo.

My jaw clenched so hard pain built in my teeth.

Tossing the papers toward Clara, I rushed out after Aaron. She half-heartedly called me back, but I continued through the empty kitchen and shoved through the saloon doors.

Aaron sat on his usual stool at the bar, elbows braced on the countertop and forehead resting on both hands as he stared at the scuffed wood. Aside from him, the pub was deserted, the neatly arranged chairs waiting for the dinner rush. I stopped across from him, breathing hard as I fought to calm my emotions.

"I should've expected it," Aaron muttered. "They want to bury him in that guild as deep as they can. Of course they'd transfer him."

I pressed both hands to the bar top, fingers splayed.

"We joined together." He slid his hands up into his hair. "I've never been a member of the Crow and Hammer without him. I've never been a member of *any* guild without him."

"He'll be back," I whispered. "He said he'll figure it out. He promised."

Aaron didn't reply, his fists clenching in his copper hair. After a long moment, he dragged his head up. "I need a drink."

I slapped my butt, searching for my phone so I could check the time, before remembering I'd left it at home on Philip's orders. No electronics allowed during my witchy nature ritual. But even without my phone's clock, I knew it was nowhere near four, when the pub officially opened.

With a quick look at Aaron's morose pallor, I decided to ignore that. "What do you want?"

"Tequila. Lots of tequila."

I got out a pair of shot glasses and fetched a bottle of silver tequila off the back shelves. After pouring two shots to the brim, I slid one to him.

He didn't pick up the glass. "What the hell are we going to do? Kai's left the guild, and Ezra is ..." He swore, his voice hoarsening. "What do we do?"

I took hold of his hand and pushed the shot against his palm. Then I lifted my glass to my lips and stared at him until he raised his. In unison, we tossed the liquor back. I swallowed against the burn.

"Aaron." I set my glass on the bar and picked up the tequila bottle. "You can't volunteer to take Felix's shift."

He watched me refill our shot glasses. "Why not?"

"Because we have something else to do." I slid his shot over and lifted mine. The cold glass pressed against my lower lip. "I don't know what we can do for Kai right now, but Ezra needs our help."

Aaron's fair skin lost what little color it had left, and he threw back his shot like it was the only thing keeping his stomach down—which made no sense to me. Tequila had the opposite effect on my stomach.

His glass thudded against the counter. "There's only one thing we can do to help Ezra."

I poured the tequila down my throat, then slammed my glass down beside his. "Bullshit. I know you and Kai looked into it years ago, but neither of you has connections to the world of black magic. Zak did—or does." I grimaced. "Whatever. What I mean is I asked him about it."

"What did he say?"

"He said whatever the MPD knows about Demonica—or what they admit to knowing—is the kid-gloves version. It's the basics and nothing more. Zak said that summoners are like druids, and that master summoners guard their secrets, never revealing them to anyone but their chosen apprentice."

Aaron clenched and unclenched his jaw. "Zak is a lying bas—"

I raised my voice over his. "I also talked to an ex-summoner from Odin's Eye, who told me there's no standard method of creating a demon mage, and each summoner who does it has a different technique."

Pressing my hands to the counter, I leaned across the bar. "To unmake a demon mage, we need to know how he was made. We need to dig into the dark magic of Demonica—the scary, illegal shit that MagiPol doesn't want anyone to know about."

"And how will we do that?" he asked with a mutinous scowl, like I was suggesting we cancel Christmas.

I exhaled harshly through my nose. "I get it, Aaron. You don't want to hope. You already tried everything, and you've been steeling yourself for this for years. It'll just hurt more to try again and fail."

"If you understand, then why—"

"Because I won't ignore a chance, no matter how slim. I don't care if the odds are one in a million. I'm going to try everything before I let you or Kai or Darius end Ezra's life."

He absorbed my vehement words, then huffed. "I'm not doing anything about Ezra without Kai, but Darius knows what happened. You can't stop him from—"

"I can. I already did."

Aaron's eyes widened.

"I talked to him. He's going to wait. He even cleared my shifts so we can leave immediately."

"We—leave? What? Where?"

I splashed more tequila into my shot glass and raised it in a toast to no one. "We'll go first thing tomorrow. I just need to arrange a few things, and talk to Kai ... and Ezra."

"Go *where*, Tori?"

Knowing he wouldn't like my answer one bit, I tossed the shot back and smacked the glass down. I met his demanding glower with a steady stare.

"We're going to Enright."

2

THANKS TO A COLD WALK HOME, I was sober enough to hesitate as I swung open the door to my basement apartment. Poised at the top of the steps, I listened.

Silence.

And that was all kinds of wrong.

My hand went to my back pocket, where for eight months I'd carried the Queen of Spades. But my trump card was no more, and I hadn't replaced any of my magical defenses. I didn't even have my phone on me.

Well, if trouble was waiting for me, I'd just have to improvise. With my fists.

"Hoshi," I whispered.

A silver shimmer. She appeared behind me, paws resting on my shoulders and nose bumping my cheek.

"Are there any fae or druids down there?"

She cocked her head, then sent me a blip of dark red. Negative. Thank goodness.

I opened the back door then slammed it shut to make it seem like I'd left the house again. With Hoshi trailing behind me, I tiptoed down the stairs, skipping the squeaky fifth step. Heart thudding with adrenaline, I crept to the bottom, crouched, and peeked down the hallway toward my living room.

There *was* someone in my apartment. A man sat on my sofa, his back to the hallway, but I recognized that brown hair and those broad shoulders.

The tension left me all at once. I sucked in a deep breath—then let it out in a furious shout. "*Justin!*"

My brother started violently and whipped around.

"What the hell are you doing in my apartment?" I snarled, my post-adrenaline-rush temper riled real good. "Did you *break in*? What's wrong with you?"

"I didn't break in," he spluttered, shoving to his feet. "You gave me a key!"

My stomping steps faltered. Oh right. I *had* given him a key—back when we'd been speaking. Before I'd killed a mythic in self-defense and Justin had unilaterally decided I was a criminal in a magic street gang.

He scrabbled for something on the sofa cushions, then straightened, a cell phone in his hand. "I called you about six times. Why did you leave your phone at home?"

I strode over and snatched my phone from his hand. "Why are you here? In case you forgot, we haven't talked since before Christmas, when you shouted at me that we weren't family anymore and stormed out."

He flinched.

"And," I added, summoning more anger to hide my hurt, "you didn't even respond to my Merry Christmas message."

He stared at the floor, arms hanging limply at his sides.

Heaving a sigh, I headed into the kitchen. "So? What do you want?"

He stopped beside the breakfast bar as I opened the fridge. "I'm sorry, Tori. For what I said ... and for everything else."

I straightened so fast I almost clipped my head on the inside of the fridge and goggled at my brother. He wasn't the apologizing type.

"It isn't an excuse, but I—I haven't been coping well with things." He sat heavily on a stool. "Back in August, when you were arrested and I found out you ... you'd joined that guild ... Sophie had left me a couple weeks before that and I felt like I'd lost both of you."

He scrubbed at his short beard, unable to meet my eyes. "I did a lot of thinking while I was away over Christmas, and I realized I'd handled this all wrong."

Eyebrows scrunched, I pulled cheese and butter from the fridge. "Want a grilled cheese sandwich?"

He smiled weakly. "Sure."

Grabbing a loaf of bread and a cutting board, I started laying out slices. Surreptitiously, I studied my brother. His brown hair was cut shorter than I remembered, the beard I'd convinced him to grow neatly trimmed, but despite his well-groomed appearance, there were dark circles under his hazel eyes.

"You've been a massive asshole," I told him bluntly, slathering butter across the bread.

He nodded.

"I tried to explain things to you, but you wouldn't listen. I tried to introduce you to my friends, but you didn't want to meet them."

Another nod.

"And you've changed your mind about all that?"

"Yes. I want to know everything."

Dropping my gaze to the cutting board, I cut slices of marble cheese and stacked them beside the bread. My chest ached, old wounds and more recent ones reopened by his presence. Part of me wanted to run around the counter, throw my arms around my big brother, and tearfully unload all my pain and fears on him.

Before Christmas and our fight, I would've done exactly that. But now, after so much had happened, I wasn't pouring my heart out to anyone with the potential to add to the beating it'd already taken.

"Well, I'm not explaining anything." Pulling out a frying pan, I set it on the stovetop and turned on the burner. "Not anymore. I gave you a chance—several chances—and you threw it all back in my face. I want things to be right between us again, but I'm done justifying my choices to you."

"How am I supposed to understand if you won't tell me anything?" he asked stiffly.

I spooned a blob of butter into the warming pan, fighting a fresh wave of anger. "Are we family, Justin?"

"Of course. Tori—"

"Then you don't need to understand anything. You just need to be my big brother."

He put his elbows on the counter. "You can't expect me to pretend nothing has changed. I need to know what's really going on."

"Why?" I demanded.

"So—so I can …"

"So you can decide once and for all if I'm a mythic crook?" I pointed my spatula at him. "Is that why you're here? So you can judge me some more?"

"No! I want to fix this, Tori."

I tossed the buttered bread into the pan and let the slices warm. As I flipped them and layered cheese on, Justin watched me, his brow furrowed and jaw set with stubbornness.

I closed up the sandwiches and flipped them again. When the outsides were golden brown and crispy, I slid them onto two small plates and set one in front of Justin.

"Then be my brother," I told him. "Not the moral police."

He looked down at his sandwich, a breath rushing through his nose. "All right."

We ate in silence, weighing each other with our gazes. Justin and I knew each other very well, but our adult selves kept running face-first into our past expectations. He was wondering how hard he could push this grown-up Tori, and I was wondering how far I could trust my once-hero brother with my poor, battered heart.

I shoved the last corner of my sandwich into my mouth. "I'll be busy until next week at the earliest. When I'm free, we should get coffee on your lunch break like we used to."

"What are you busy with?"

I narrowed my eyes, warning him not to go all "interrogator" on me. "A friend needs help. I'll be busy with him."

"Is there anything I can do?"

Yeah, he could not twist up my emotions when I already had so much to deal with, but I wasn't mean enough to say that. "Thanks, but no. I'll send you a message next week."

Recognizing his dismissal, Justin scooted off his stool and stood. He hesitated, then held out his arms hopefully. I circled the bar and stepped into his hug. He squeezed me tightly.

"Missed you, Tor," he murmured.

"Missed you too," I sighed. "Please don't be a dick this time."

He huffed a laugh.

I saw him to the door, shaking my head as he climbed into his shiny, dark blue Dodge Challenger. My brother and his muscle cars. I should've noticed it parked on the curb.

Grinning at the memory of him teaching my seventeen-year-old self how to do a burnout in his old Mustang GT, I hurried back inside. As I hopped the last step, a bush poked up from behind the sofa, followed by a pair of huge chartreuse eyes.

"The human is gone?" Twiggy asked in his high voice.

"Just left." I swept into the kitchen and turned on the tap. It'd need to run for two minutes before I got any hot water. "I'm surprised you didn't scare him off."

"I tried, but he wasn't scared."

I almost dropped the plates I'd picked up off the counter. "You did? What did you try?"

"Spooky noises first." Twiggy walked along the sofa cushions, head bobbing as he searched. "I made the lights go on and off, and the shadows move, but he didn't run away."

He stuffed a long-fingered hand between the cushion and armrest and pulled out a TV remote. Turning to the screen, he pressed a button. The television came on with an ear-splitting blare of sound—an audience cheering.

"Turn it down!" I yelled, dunking the plates in the sink. "What else did you do to Justin?"

Twiggy dropped the volume by a few notches, his eyes glued to the spinning wheel on the screen as the game-show announcer described the prizes on the line for contestants. The faery didn't react to my question, all thoughts of Justin gone from his leafy head.

Rolling my eyes, I finished up the dishes, headed into my room, and pushed up my sleeves. Aaron and I were hitting the road tomorrow, and I needed to pack.

Problem was, I wasn't sure *what* to pack.

Combat gear, for sure. I hauled it out of my closet and tossed it on my bed. What else? I might need to blend in, so street clothes of several varieties. I rifled through my closet, selecting likely contenders. Crouching, I dug through my shoes, tossing the occasional pair over my shoulder. What else?

Toiletries, I supposed.

When I opened my bedroom door, another blast of sound hit me. A screeching woman on the screen was jumping up and down in hysterical excitement as three beautiful models posed beside the powerboat she'd won. Shaking my head, I wondered if the woman even wanted a powerboat. Did she live near water?

In the bathroom, I pulled out my toiletry bag and loaded it with the usual hygiene supplies. Zipping it shut, I opened my makeup bag and pondered its contents for what I might need. Fake eyelashes? Yeah, no. Been there, done that, and never doing it again.

My fingers drifted past a tube of mascara to a round powder compact. I picked it up, brushed some pink dust off the top, and flipped it open. My pale face frowned back at me in the tiny mirror as I lifted the spongy applicator puff.

Dark metal glinted beneath it.

The demonic amulet lay in the compact, neatly nestled on top of its chain. A ring of creepy sigils encircled a larger symbol in the center—a symbol that matched the one etched into the breastplate of Robin Page's demon.

Vh'alyir's Amulet, Eterran had called it. All I knew was that it could interrupt a demon contract. How the spell worked, why a demon had been carrying it, what the sigils meant, how it was connected to Robin's demon—I had no answers. I'd spent a month searching for answers and found nothing.

Maybe the amulet could save Ezra, or maybe it would give Eterran full control of his body. I didn't know, but if I couldn't find answers in Enright, I would try it. How could I not? Ezra would die anyway. If there was even a tiny chance this could save him …

Replacing the puff, I snapped the compact shut and returned it to my makeup bag. With the two bags tucked under my arm, I walked out of the bathroom—and heard the faint ringing of my phone.

Twiggy's game-show audience let out another eardrum-rupturing cheer as I dove for the counter where my phone sat, the screen alight with an incoming call from an unknown number.

"Turn it down," I called as I fumbled for the phone. The volume didn't change, and as I hit the answer button, I whirled toward the sofa. "Twiggy, turn the TV down before I throw your green ass out the window!"

With a rebellious scowl, he lowered the volume by half.

Returning his glare, I slapped my phone against my ear. "Hello?"

"Tori?" a female voice inquired with a distinct note of uncertainty.

"Who's this?"

"Robin."

"Oh." Why on earth was the petite, mysterious demon contractor calling me? "How are—"

As I spoke, the cheering of the audience swelled.

"*Don't you dare turn that up again!*" I bellowed at the faery, belatedly pulling the phone away from my face. "Wait until I'm off the phone. Geez!"

Shoulders hunching, Twiggy hit the pause button. The room went blissfully silent.

"Sorry, Robin," I said into the phone as I stalked over to the breakfast bar. "Roommates, I tell ya."

Twiggy shot me a half-pouting, half-pleased look over the top of the sofa. Despite his annoyance at my television tyranny, he loved it when I called him my roommate. It made his little green day every time.

"I just have a quick question, if that's okay," Robin said, her sweet alto voice hollowed by the phone connection.

"Sure. What's up?"

"When we were meeting with Naim at Odin's Eye," she began, "you, um … you had some MDP cases in your folder. I noticed a photo in one, and I was wondering … could I get the case file?"

"Oh?" I murmured, sliding onto a stool. I knew exactly what she was talking about. Our ill-fated appointment at Odin's Eye—which had ended in fire, steel monsters, and getting more up close and personal with her demon than I would've liked—had begun with a friendly interrogation of ex-summoner Naim Ashraf. I'd bluffed him with a folder of MDP cold cases, and as I'd flipped through the printouts, Robin had gone all gaspy over a particular page of photos.

"Sure," I told her. "On one condition."

A wary pause. "What condition?"

"You tell me what's special about that photo."

Another longer pause as she decided what she wanted to tell me. "One of the men in the photo looked like the mythic who summoned my demon."

That wasn't the answer I'd been hoping for. "It doesn't have anything to do with that ancient amulet thingy?"

Ancient amulet thingy—by which I meant the very same amulet hidden in my makeup bag. She'd shown up to our meeting with a perfect drawing of it, claiming it was a medieval infernus she was researching.

"No," she replied firmly.

Too firmly?

"Hm. All right, give me a moment." I hopped up and returned to my room. Where had I left that folder? I wasn't actually investigating any of the files and I probably should've thrown it out, but that would've required a level of organization I didn't possess right now.

I shuffled through a stack of mail on my nightstand. As I opened the drawer, I stepped on a shirtsleeve hanging off my bed. It and my toiletry bag tumbled to the floor. Swearing under my breath, I nudged the makeup bag into the middle of my mattress before it fell too.

"Sorry," I told Robin, pinching my phone to my ear with my shoulder. "I'm in the middle of packing and my place is a mess. I think I buried the folder."

"Are you moving?"

"Huh?" I dug into the drawer, but it was frustratingly folderless. "Oh, no, not that kind of packing. I'm going on a trip."

"Where to?"

Oh, nowhere. Just Enright—you know, the infamous location where the largest group of demon mages in modern history were found and brutally exterminated.

"South," I said, turning toward my closet. "We're leaving soon, so I need to—" As I stepped over my suitcase, my foot caught on the handle and the suitcase landed flat on its face, spilling all three things I'd managed to pack so far.

"Shit." I picked it up, tossed the now *un*folded clothes on my bed, and faced the closet again. "What was I ... right, the folder."

"Are you going with your friends?" Robin asked. "The mages?"

"Yeah." I shoved a heap of shoes aside, revealing a brown folder lying on the floor. "Aha!"

I remembered now. I'd decided the papers should be shredded, not thrown out, so I'd put them somewhere "safe."

"Got it. Let's see ..." I sat on the edge of my bed and opened the folder. "It was a photo of two dudes, right?" I flipped through cases until I found a photo with a pair of men talking. "Here it is. Case 97-5923."

"Thank you."

"No problem. So, you think your demon's summoner is skeevy?"

"I *know* he's skeevy. Just not sure how much."

Oh, interesting. Did that imply her contract might be on the skeevy side too? Her demon *was* kind of strange. "Hope that case has some juicy details for you, then. Let me know if you need any help. I owe you one for taking me to see Naim."

"He wasn't any use."

"Yeah, but you still shared your lead with me." My gaze turned to my makeup bag, sitting innocently beside me. Robin was researching the amulet too. Had she found answers I hadn't? What did she know?

When I'd first seen her drawing of it, I'd decided that pressing her for information was too risky—but after Ezra's dip into madness three days ago, the time for caution was well and truly over.

"Robin, can I ask you something?"

"Okay."

"That amulet." I gripped my phone more tightly. "Do you know what it does?"

A pause. "No ... I'm trying to learn more about it."

"If you find out anything, will you tell me?"

"Have you seen it, Tori?" Intensity sharpened her voice. "Do you know where the amulet is?"

Shit. I'd said too much. "I have to go." I hesitated, then added, "I'll talk to you when I get back, okay?"

Before she could say anything else, I ended the call. I had no choice anymore. If we didn't find answers in Enright, then Robin and I would be having a chat. She knew something about the amulet, and I'd find out what.

How I'd force information out of the shrimpy contractor was a challenge I'd tackle when the time came. Robin wasn't as timid as she seemed, and she had an unstoppable weapon in the shape of an abs-tastic demon to protect her.

I pushed to my feet and surveyed the disaster that my room had become. Enright and its mysteries first. Then Robin and her unknown knowledge of the amulet next.

One way or another, I would save Ezra.

3

"WHO WANTS PIZZA?" I singsonged as I waltzed through the front door of Aaron's house, three large boxes held dramatically above my head.

Aaron appeared in the doorway that separated the hall from the living room. Hands tucked in his jeans pockets, he arched an eyebrow. "You mean the pizza I ordered?"

"Don't let the boxes fool you," I declared loftily, breezing past him. "I made these pizzas with my own two hands."

He followed me into the dining room. "Tell me you at least paid the delivery guy."

"What, you think I tackled him and stole the food? I'm not the Hamburglar." I slid the boxes onto the table and flipped the top on the first one. "Ham and pineapple?"

"With extra pineapple." Aaron flashed a grin. "Might as well get our fill before Kai is back to discriminate against our topping selections."

I set the first pizza aside and opened the second box. "Deluxe pepperoni with …" I shot Aaron a disbelieving stare. "With *pineapple?*"

Aaron's grin widened.

Pushing that box out of the way, I flipped up the third lid. "Chipotle chicken with—"

"*Pineapple,*" a smooth voice whispered in my ear.

I shrieked and my hand mashed down into the hot pizza. I yanked it back, my palm coated in sauce and cheese. "Ezra!"

He stepped around me, his fingers brushing my waist—a brief touch, there and gone. Matching Aaron's grin, he held his phone above the table. The flash went off.

"Did you just take a picture of the pizzas?" I asked bemusedly.

"No," he lied, straight-faced as his gaze turned to his phone, thumbs already whizzing across the screen. "And I'm not sending any photos of our extra pineapply pizzas to Kai, either."

"*Pineapply* isn't a word."

Aaron picked up a slice of pineapple-pepperoni. "Make sure to tell him that the chicken one is messed up because Tori stuck her hand in it."

"Hey! That wasn't my fault." I held my cheese-smeared hand out like it was contaminated with radioactive waste. "Ezra, don't—"

"Oops. Already hit send."

I stomped into the kitchen to wash my hands. When I returned, Ezra and Aaron were perched on chairs and already on their second slices. I grabbed a ham and pineapple slice before they ate it all. How could they pack away an entire pizza each and still look that freakin' good?

Ezra had one bare foot propped on his chair, his messy curls damp from a recent shower. If I had to guess, he'd only just stepped out of the shower and pulled on a t-shirt and sweats before sneaking upstairs to scare the crap out of me.

Yeah, that was exactly what had happened.

Trying not to think about him in the shower—if only I'd arrived a few minutes earlier—I took a big bite of pizza. Delicious, but not as good as Ezra-in-the-shower would've been.

His phone chimed, and he slid it off the table without shifting his pizza slice too far from his mouth. Peering at the screen, he let out a whoop of laughter—and choked on his mouthful.

Coughing, he shoved his phone at me and grabbed for the can of soda Aaron was holding out to him. He took a long gulp.

I blinked down at the screen. Kai had replied with a photo of his own—a selfie of the dark-haired electramage himself, staring disapprovingly into the camera while taking a sultry bite of his pineapple-free pizza.

Laughing, I passed the phone to Aaron and stuffed more food into my mouth. He chortled over the image, amusement brightening his eyes for the first time in days.

"Wednesday night pizza triumphs!" His delight faltered as he studied the photo. "But shit, look at that place. Where is he?"

Ramming the last of my slice between my teeth, I snatched the phone back and looked again. I'd been so focused on Kai's face—and pizza choice—that I hadn't noticed the background of the photo. He was sitting on a white sofa with curvy lines, and behind him stretched a massive suite with two-story-high windows in place of walls, the glowing lights of Vancouver ending at the dark water of the ocean. Aside from the designer sofa, everything in the room seemed to be made of glass or white marble.

"Is that a *glass staircase*?" I muttered, peering at the spiraling structure descending from the ceiling. "That's terrifying. Do you think it's slippery?"

Ezra reclaimed his phone and typed a reply. When his eyes, sparkling with mirth, darted to me, I made a wild grab for the phone again. With his stupid demonic reflexes, he spun in his chair and I ended up lunging into his back.

"Sent!"

"What did you type?" I growled, leaning over his shoulder.

Aaron leaned in from the other side to read the screen.

Ezra's reply glowed beneath Kai's photo: *Tori wants to know if you've fallen down those stairs yet.*

The phone chimed and Kai's response appeared: *Yeah. I think I cracked my tailbone.*

My forehead scrunched. "Is he serious?"

"Good question," Ezra muttered. "Should I ask—"

Another chime. Kai had added to the message: *Makiko spilled a glass of water. They were slippery.*

I pulled my arms from around Ezra. "Wait. Are they staying in the same suite?"

"You mean," Aaron corrected, "are they staying in the same bedroom?"

Dropping back into my seat, I clenched my hands. "He better not be sleeping with that woman."

"He wouldn't."

"He's slept with tons of women."

"And none of them were part of his life, which was the whole point." Aaron took another slice. "Well, that and the sex. Maybe the sex was more the point."

I snorted. "Okay, but—"

"If he *is* banging her, then it's all part of his escape plan."

"Sleeping with the enemy, huh?" I muttered, avoiding thoughts of Izzah, who was head over heels in love with Kai and had no idea why he'd dropped her like a nasty river rock covered in algae slime.

"The important question here," Ezra said, staring grimly at his phone, "is whether he really fell down the stairs. Because I think he didn't but I'm not sure, and the fact I'm unsure means that whether he fell or not, he still wins."

"Wins what?" I asked.

Ezra and Aaron looked at me with identical expressions of disbelief.

"Never mind." I chose another slice of pizza.

When most of the pizza had been devoured and the remaining slices arranged in one box to form a new Frankenpizza, we retired to the living room and played a dozen rounds of Aaron's favorite racing game. We laughed and razzed each other and drank through a six-pack of beer, and it was almost like normal.

Almost like normal, except for the empty spot on the sofa.

Almost like normal, except Ezra lost every other round, too exhausted—or distracted—to leverage his superior reflexes.

Almost like normal, except I couldn't stop thinking about my suitcase, packed and waiting in my apartment for tomorrow morning.

"I'm done," Ezra decided after the twelfth game, tossing his controller onto the cushion between us. "I need to stop now before I lose my reigning champion title."

"Chicken," Aaron taunted, waving his bright-red controller. "This is the most I've won since I first introduced you to the wide world of console gaming."

"Yeah, right." He stretched his arms over his head, back arching. "I lost nonstop for the first couple of months. You refused to go easy on me, even though I'd never touched a controller before."

Never? I knew Ezra had been homeless for a couple years before meeting Aaron, but I hadn't realized his childhood before that had been devoid of luxuries like console games.

"You wouldn't've learned anything if I'd gone easy on you," Aaron declared. "Besides, I knew you'd be stomping me in no time."

A smile flickering over his lips, Ezra pushed off the sofa. He glanced at me, humor softening, sadness lurking. Silent, he disappeared into the kitchen, and the bathroom door clacked shut.

"Wanna watch a movie, Tori?" Aaron asked.

"Sure. Your pick."

He switched modes on his huge TV and began scrolling through the action flicks. Two minutes later, Ezra reemerged and headed toward the stairs.

"Night, Tori." He tossed a grin at Aaron. "Night, loser."

"Oh, ouch. Harsh, man."

They both laughed at Aaron's "I'm so wounded" act, then Ezra traipsed up the stairs. I listened for the sound of his door, but he closed it too softly for me to hear.

I glanced at the clock glowing on the PVR under the television. Barely past ten, but it'd only been three days since the Carapace of Valdurna had devoured all his magic. It'd be days more before his stamina fully recovered.

A movie began with a swell of music, but I hadn't seen which title Aaron had chosen.

"Have you talked to him yet?" he asked quietly.

"Not yet."

"We're leaving in the morning."

"I know. Are you packed?"

"Yeah. My bag is in my room." He settled deeper into his recliner. "What about Kai?"

"I called him this afternoon. He's as excited about my plan as you are. He said he'd work on Makiko to get her to loosen his leash for a few days, but he couldn't make any promises."

Aaron nodded. "You sure about this, Tori?"

"As in, am I sure this will be anything but a huge waste of time? No. But I'm damn sure we're doing it anyway."

"I just don't understand what you expect to find after eight years."

My gaze rose to the ceiling where Ezra's bedroom was. "I know what I'm looking for ... and I know where to look for it."

"How?"

"Insider information." I pushed to my feet. "I'm going to see if Ezra is asleep yet. Don't wait for me."

I could feel his questioning gaze as I left the room, but I didn't look back. My mind was made up. My preparations were complete. And before we left tomorrow, I needed to hammer out the details of our plan.

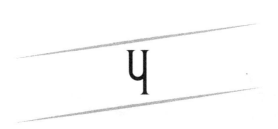

4

AT THE TOP OF THE STAIRS, I halted in front of Ezra's door. A dim light shone through the gap underneath it. I tapped on the wood.

A muffled sound answered me, and I pushed the door open. Ezra was halfway between sitting on his bed and rising to his feet, and three things registered in my brain all at once: that muffled response hadn't been permission to enter, he was shirtless, and he was holding a tan folder.

He blinked at me, then sank back onto his bed. "Come in?"

Why, *why* was he so gorgeous? His bronze skin stretched taut over hard muscles—and my god, I needed to touch this man. His sweats clung to his hips, revealing the waistband of his boxers, and his shirt lay on the foot of the bed; he must've started to strip down for bed before getting distracted.

And now I was the one distracted.

Shaking myself, I offered a guilty smile. "Sorry, I thought that's what you said. Do you mind?"

"No, it's fine."

I shut the door, then crossed his room, glancing wistfully at his guitar on my way past. He'd only played for me once. Should I ask if he'd play for me again?

As I sat on the mattress beside him, I tried and failed not to glance curiously at the folder he'd tucked halfway out of sight on his other side—but, of course, he noticed. Sighing, he slid it onto his lap. His fingers disappeared inside, then he withdrew a photograph, marred by creases but still glossy.

Guilt stabbed me. It was the photo I'd found in his dresser eight months ago while searching for a t-shirt. Snoopy me had taken a good long look at the image of young Ezra and a blond girl before hiding the picture back in the folder.

"I told you about her," he murmured.

I studied the girl's beaming smile, full of joy. How long after this photo had she become a demon mage, spiraled into madness, and almost killed Ezra before being killed herself?

"This is the last photo I have of us before I became a demon mage ..." His voice roughened. "I was excited. I'd been *chosen*. I felt so goddamn special."

He reached into the folder again, and this time, he handed me the photo—an even older one. An olive-skinned man and woman grinned at the camera, a laughing boy between them. Ezra took after his mother's side of the family; his father had a blocky face and heavy jaw, his head shaved. His eyes, however, were the same warm chocolate brown as Ezra's.

"I always liked this photo," he murmured, gazing at his parents. "Things were never easy for us, but my parents were just happy to be together. That changed after ..."

I waited, then prompted gently, "After you became a demon mage?"

"No ..." His hand curled into a fist. "After they joined the ... group."

He tugged the photo of his parents from my fingers and returned both pictures to the folder. Before he could stand, I touched his arm.

"Will you tell me about it?" I asked softly.

The air rushed through his nose. He stared at the folder, avoiding my gaze.

"I hate thinking about it." His eyes closed, deep creases in his forehead. "I hate how naïve they were. I shouldn't blame my parents, but sometimes I do. Especially now."

I slid my hand down his wrist and entwined our fingers.

His shoulders hunched. "I was seven when my parents met some new people. My parents were poor, unregistered mythics and didn't trust easily, but they spent more and more time talking to their new friends, and that summer, we moved. Our new home ..." He shook his head. "I know now that it was a commune, but I was a kid. All I cared about was that there were a few other kids my age."

"A commune," I mumbled, my fingers tightening around his.

"My parents started attending ... *meetings* every week with the other adults, and they ... changed. And they wanted me to change too."

"They were being brainwashed?"

He stared at our entwined hands. "When you're a kid, your parents' approval is everything. And in that place, everything revolved around the leaders and *their* approval. I don't even remember if I resisted it. The leaders and my parents and the whole group said I should be honored to be chosen as a 'protector,' so that's how I felt."

"A *protector*? Against what?"

He sighed bitterly. "I don't even want to tell you the twisted garbage they filled our heads with. I don't think my parents were stupid, but they fully bought into it—how we were special and enlightened, and how the outside world wanted to destroy us."

"Didn't your parents realize they wanted to turn you into a demon mage?"

"Oh, they knew. But I wasn't becoming a *demon mage*. I would be a 'protector,' wielding a demon's magic like a weapon, empowered by the group's moral ideology. As long as I was strong in my faith, I would have unwavering power over the demon."

"What?" I exclaimed angrily. "They thought you could control a demon with *faith*? That's—"

"Bullshit. Yeah. But even once I became a 'protector,' I could never admit that controlling my demon was difficult. They would've said the demon was testing my faith and if I was struggling, it's because I was weak. I believed that."

I gripped his hand so hard my fingers ached. I wanted to teleport back in time and punch every member of that group—especially their leaders.

"The group didn't even call them demons. They were *Servi*." He rubbed his thumb across the back of my hand. "It's ironic, you know? I didn't doubt anything I'd been taught until Eterran started poking holes in my beliefs. He'd given up on forcing control by then and was trying to break me down in a different way."

"But you probably thought that was another 'test,'" I guessed.

He nodded. "Everyone I knew and loved was part of the group. I couldn't imagine life outside it, so I refused to question anything."

"What about …" I hesitated. "… the girl?"

"Lexie," he revealed heavily. "She saved me, in a way. After they killed her, they said she'd failed because her faith had been weak. But I knew that wasn't true. I'd seen her struggle. She'd tried so hard. If they were wrong about Lexie, what else were they wrong about?"

I leaned against his shoulder, increasing the contact between us as old grief settled over him. "What did you do?"

"I ran away. I ended up in Portland. They were searching for me, and I wouldn't have lasted a day on my own, but …" His jaw clenched and unclenched. "Eterran also wanted answers. He helped me, and I was desperate enough to listen. We evaded the people searching for us and found other mythics, got in with them, asked careful questions … got the answers we needed.

"It took just over four weeks. I finally knew what I was and how they'd used me, and I went back. I was going to explain everything to my parents, and we would escape. Together, we'd find a way to get the demon out of me."

A heavy, ominous weight settled in my gut.

"I think it was my fault," he whispered. "The people searching for me weren't careful enough and they caught the attention of the Keys of Solomon. The guild followed the trail back to the commune, and …"

"Ezra, it wasn't—"

"I came back to ruins." He didn't seem to hear me. His voice was devoid of all emotion. "Everyone had been killed. Sixty-eight people. Only ten were demon mages. I was the eleventh. Lexie was supposed to be the twelfth, but she was already dead."

My lungs didn't want to inflate properly. "The Keys killed *everyone*? How—how was that allowed?"

"Harboring a demon mage is a capital crime. There should've been a trial, but what did the Keys care about that? They'd gotten the hunt of their lives."

I'd already hated the Keys of Solomon, but my hatred was rapidly transforming into white-hot loathing.

"Everyone I knew was dead," he mumbled. "I had nowhere to go, so I went back to Portland. I didn't know if the Keys realized they'd missed a demon mage. I couldn't trust anyone."

Only fifteen years old, with half his life spent isolated from society. Every mythic a potential enemy, and his worst enemy of all living inside him.

What depth of resilience did it take to lose everyone you loved in a single day and keep going? What kind of resolve did it take to suppress the demon inside you, day after day after day, and keep going? How much tenacity did it take to face a life of loneliness and secrets that would end in death and madness, and *keep going?*

"Those years were pretty terrible," he admitted matter-of-factly. "Then I ran into Aaron. Saved his idiot life, actually."

"You saved him?"

"And then he saved me. He dragged me home, made a place for me in his guild, and didn't let me run off—though I tried quite a few times that first year. He and Kai put up with a hell of a lot from me." Humor softened the hard lines of grief around his mouth. "I wasn't what you'd call *socially adjusted*. I broke Girard's nose once."

My eyes widened. "You did what?"

"He came up on my blind side when I wasn't paying attention." He grinned. "Luckily, I don't startle as easily nowadays."

"You *are* quite difficult to startle, but I've managed it a few times," I told him, puffing my chest out with pride.

He laughed quietly. "You're highly startling, Tori, in a lot of ways."

My amusement faltered as his gaze settled on mine. The air between us thickened, electric with things unsaid and feelings unacknowledged. My pulse drummed a slow, steady beat in my ears.

All of a sudden, I was intensely aware of his shirtless state, my arm still linked through his, our fingers tangled.

I won't lose you. I couldn't say the words. They would just hurt him.

I need you to survive. I couldn't say that either. More words that would wound him.

I almost lost you already and I can't bear it again. Still no.

Though I wasn't speaking the words, my thoughts must've touched my face, because his gaze dropped. He slipped his arm free and picked up the worn folder. Crossing to the dresser, he tucked the remnants of his past at the bottom of a drawer, slid it closed, and turned to me.

Sitting on the bed, I watched him approach, my mouth dry.

He stopped between my knees, staring down at me with an unreadable expression. Hands rising, he gently cupped my jaw and tilted my face up. There were so many things I wanted to say to him that I couldn't—and his eyes were full of unspoken words too.

He leaned down. Our lips brushed in a whisper-soft touch.

He inhaled. His mouth returned to mine. A brief, hungry press of his lips. He pulled back and breathed again as though debating, as though torn, drawn, doubting.

His mouth covered mine.

I grabbed his wrists and held on as he kissed me urgently. His mouth opened against mine, and I answered with parted lips. The hot slide of his tongue pierced me with heat, and air rushed from my lungs.

The bed dipped, his knee on the mattress between my thighs. My hands ran up his arms, fingertips dragging across taut muscles. Our mouths moved ceaselessly, lips and tongue, hard and insistent. Edged with need.

Edged with desperation.

I didn't know I'd tipped backward until my back hit the blankets. He followed me down, elbows braced beside me, hands in my hair, mouth locked on mine. His body covered me, strong and hot and irresistible—and god, I'd wanted this, wanted to be under him so badly for so long.

I raked my hands across his bare shoulders as I pulled myself up into him. My legs wrapped around him, stronger than my arms, squeezing our bodies together.

A near-soundless groan rasped in his throat, and his weight pressed me into the bed. As his mouth closed over my neck, wet and ravenous, his hips rocked against mine, igniting my core. I tore my mouth from his to bite my bottom lip, stifling a moan. Need had reached an inferno pitch inside me, months of buildup combined with days of fear and anguish and the desperate drive to have all of him before … in case …

I dragged his face back up and kissed him again. More fiercely. More urgently. The empty ache between my legs intensified, the hard press of him through our clothes not enough—not nearly enough.

Our frenzy of kissing and roaming hands slowed. Deepened. His mouth savoring. The grind of his hips sweet, slow torture.

"Ezra," I moaned in a faint, breathless whisper. "Can we ... please?"

His lips softened, and he sucked gently on my lower lip before he lifted his head. "We ..." His breath caught, voice hoarsening. "Not ... not now. I can't ..."

I didn't understand why he couldn't or what was holding him back, but I didn't argue. "Okay."

We stared at each other—and I couldn't stop myself from pulling his mouth back for one more inferno-stoking kiss. His weight came down on me in a fierce press of strength, muscle, and desire, and I locked my legs tighter around his hips, needing just a little more, *a little more*.

Braced against me, he pushed his face into my neck. "Shit, Tori."

I squeezed my eyes shut, panting for air. With effort, I unclamped my arms and legs. Letting him go felt all wrong.

He pushed off me, stared insatiably at my heaving chest, then turned away. Shoulders moving with his own deep breaths, he sank onto the floor. While he leaned back against the bed, I remained sprawled across the mattress. Minutes slid past as my heart rate gradually calmed, my lungs slowing their greedy panting.

When we'd both recovered, he stood up. I scooched over, making room as he flipped the blankets back and slid into bed.

He settled his head on his pillow, and I stretched out beside him, on top of the blankets where I couldn't misbehave.

He'd left his sweatpants on. Pretty sure he didn't normally sleep in them, but I could guess why he wasn't removing them.

I swallowed hard, trying not to squirm against the slow heat rolling through me. I wouldn't press him for more, or for an explanation. He was the one going through hell right now, and I wasn't going to push his boundaries.

There were other things we needed to talk about—badly—but a soft silence that had fallen between us and I didn't want to disturb it. The things I needed to tell him wouldn't be fun, and I needed just a little longer.

Just a little longer before I faced the consequences of decisions I'd made weeks ago.

5

"TORI. *Tori.*"

A hand roughly shook my shoulder, and I jerked my head up with a jagged inhale, bleary eyes scrunched. Had I fallen asleep?

Ezra was sitting up in bed beside me, the blankets pooled in his lap. My attention caught on his bare chest, delaying the moment when I got my gaze up to his face.

Burning crimson eyes stared down at me.

Fear jolted through my gut, and I sat up with a curse. "Crap, sorry. I didn't mean to drift off."

Eterran's mouth thinned with displeasure. "We don't have long. He isn't sleeping deeply—too restless. I wonder why?" he added mockingly.

"Butt out. You might be sharing his body, but you don't need to be a perv about it." I straightened my shirt, reminding myself to keep my voice low and soothing so Ezra didn't wake up.

Eterran watched me, too still and predatory, his glowing stare devoid of Ezra's warmth. I hated seeing the demon in his face.

"All right," I whispered in a businesslike tone. "Our plan. Two parts—the amulet and the summoner."

"The amulet may be all we need."

"But it might not get your body back," I countered fiercely. "That's our goal. Not to give you control of Ezra's body, but to free you both. To do that, we need to know how you two are bound together—*exactly* how. And we need to know *exactly* how that amulet works."

His jaw tightened.

"After our last talk," I told him, "I spoke with Darius. He's going to wait to act. So are Aaron and Kai. You and Ezra just need to focus on keeping calm and levelheaded while we figure this out."

"Are we leaving soon?" The faintest shadow of fear touched his cold expression. "Every day counts."

"Tomorrow morning." I rubbed my hands together nervously. "You said last time that the summoner who turned Ezra into a demon mage died during the Enright extermination."

"Along with all the others."

"But you're sure the summoner's grimoire is still in Enright?"

"I am not sure." He rested his elbows on his knees, hunching forward. "I was summoned first into a circle, and during that time, I observed everything. There was a hidden room beneath the ritual area—the summoner's lair. I could hear faint noises through the ground. When we returned after the extermination, that hidden place hadn't been uncovered."

"But that was eight years ago."

"Why would anyone excavate the ruins?"

"Good point. But would the summoner have left anything down there?"

"The *group*," Eterran sneered, "treated summoning and rituals as performances. Their leaders shared a large, ornate grimoire. It contained all their rituals and spells."

I puffed out a breath. "So it wasn't a personal grimoire. There's a good chance, then, they stored it in the 'lair.'"

"That is my thought. If it isn't there, you may find other information."

"We'll need your help to find the hidden room. And that means …" I steeled myself. "I'm going to tell Ezra everything."

"No."

"He needs to know before we—"

"*No.*" Eterran bared his teeth. "He won't believe that I would help him—help *us*—without betraying him."

"You two worked together once before, didn't you? Ezra told me—"

"After his parents and everyone he knew were slaughtered because *he* ran away, he turned all his guilt and self-loathing on me. He hates me down to his soul."

"They weren't killed *because* Ezra ran—"

"If he hadn't run, they wouldn't have searched for him and the Keys of Solomon would never have found his family." Eterran made an impatient rasp in his throat. "Humans cannot accept the senselessness of death. They need *reasons* for death. The only reason he can find is his own choices."

His hand closed around the back of my head, and he dragged my face close to his.

"Understand, Tori," he growled. "There is only one thing Ezra cannot bear. He will endure any pain or suffering himself, but he will *not* allow his family to die because of him—not again."

I stared into the demon's burning lava eyes, my throat too tight for words.

"If he finds out I have this level of autonomy, he will find a way to die—immediately. I will have no choice but to fight him for control, and that could destroy us both."

Swallowing back nausea, I gripped his wrist. "Let me go."

He opened his fingers. "You cannot tell Ezra."

"I can't *not* tell Ezra. He's way too smart to believe any half-baked cover story about why we're going to Enright, and as soon as we need your help in locating that hidden room, he'll find out that—"

"Then we wait for him to sleep."

I set my jaw stubbornly. "I'm not lying to him anymore."

"*Zh'ūltis!*" he snapped. "Worry about his forgiveness after you have ensured his survival! We cannot—"

His eyes went wide, his arm shuddering in my grip. "He's—"

He jerked, throwing his head back. It hit the wall with a thud. Gasping, he buckled forward, tearing his arm from my grasp as he pressed both hands to his face. His shoulders heaved.

He slid his hands down, revealing Ezra's human eyes staring blankly ahead as he panted.

My hammering heart lodged in my throat, muffling my voice as I whispered, "Ezra?"

He jolted as though my whisper had been a slap. His wide-eyed stare shot to me, whipped across my face, and stopped on my hand still hovering in the air.

Lowering his hands from his face, he looked at his wrist. The one I'd been holding.

"You were talking to me ..." he muttered hoarsely.

"I—" Panic rushed through me, and I blurted without thinking, "I was telling you to calm down. You were having a nightmare—"

"You were talking to *him*."

My voice died.

His eyes regained focus. "He was—he was talking—but I was—wasn't I sleeping?" He sucked in a lungful of air and expelled it in a rush. "I was sleeping and he was—and *you* were—"

Shit, shit, *shit*. The decision about when to tell him the truth was no longer up for debate. "Ezra, I need to—"

"What happened? Was Eterran in control? What—" His frantic questions cut off. Mismatched eyes swept across my face. "Why are you so calm?"

I reached for his arm. "I can explain. Just—"

"Explain?" He jerked away from my hand. "Didn't Eterran just take control while I was sleeping? How could you possibly explain that? How ..." He broke off, his face losing what little color remained. "Wait. No. *No*."

He flung the blankets aside and rolled off the bed. As his feet hit the floor, he clamped his hands to the sides of his head. "My insomnia in December. It's not—he wasn't—was it *him*?"

Panic bled into his voice, and my anxiety ratcheted in response. Ezra's usual levelheadedness was rapidly losing out to the realization that one of his worst nightmares had come true.

He whirled on me. "What do you know?"

I slid to the edge of the bed and swung my feet down to the floor. "Ezra, please calm down. It's okay. Let me explain."

"My demon controlled me in my sleep! How is that *okay*?"

"I'll explain it," I replied, keeping my tone even despite the fear clogging my lungs. "Please, Ezra. Just sit down and let me talk."

His chest heaved as he fought to bring his emotions under control, and I shivered from the tension gripping me. Too dangerous. This was way too dangerous for him. The lethal feedback loop of emotion that had almost destroyed him a few days ago was too close.

I held my hands out, imploring, "Please, Ezra."

He stared at me. "You said I was having a nightmare. You lied to me."

"I—I didn't want to freak you out the second you woke up."

"Eterran was talking to you." His voice rose. "What did he say to you?"

"Ezra, please just—"

"*What did he say to you?*"

This time, he shouted the question, and I recoiled, clenching fistfuls of blankets.

Footsteps thudded up the stairs. Aaron whipped the bedroom door open. "What's wr—"

"Tell me, Tori!" Ezra yelled.

"*Ezra!*" Aaron barked, aghast. "What's—"

"This wasn't the first time, was it?" Ezra snarled. "You're too calm. How long, Tori?"

Aaron took an angry step into the room. "Ezra—"

"*How long have you been talking to my demon?*"

I cringed back. Aaron's mouth hung open, and his disbelieving stare jerked to me.

I had to swallow before I could speak. "Since we went to the Sinclair Academy, but it's not what you think. It was—"

Ezra stepped sharply back, bumping into Aaron. "The werewolf attack. I couldn't remember what happened."

"All that destruction at the alchemist's house," Aaron muttered, his attention darting between me and Ezra. "That was *his demon?*"

"Yes, but guys, please listen. Eterran helped me because—"

"*Helped* you?" Aaron interrupted, anger igniting through his disbelief. "You mean the demon that's almost killed me and Kai several times each—"

I shoved to my feet. "Yes, that demon! And if you'd both shut up for half a minute, I could explain why I didn't tell you!"

Aaron raked his hands through his hair. "I'm listening."

I looked at Ezra, but he was backing away, his shoulders moving with short breaths. His stare had lost focus and he was gripping his hair again, knuckles white. The room was far colder than it should've been.

Aaron put a hand on Ezra's arm. "Come on, man. Breathe. Whatever's going on, we'll figure it out."

Ezra sucked in air. Slowly, his hands unclenched and he lowered his arms.

Keeping a grip on Ezra's shoulder, Aaron looked at me, his anger banked but not gone. "Spill it, Tori."

I folded my arms. This was not how I'd wanted to have this conversation. "You two remember the demonic amulet, right? The one I used to free Burke's demon?"

"Yeah," Aaron said shortly. "The demon disappeared with it."

"No. I kept it."

His eyes widened.

"Eterran knows I have it. He figured out how to stay awake while Ezra is sleeping, and when we were staying at the academy together, Eterran paid me a visit one night. He wants the amulet to break his contract with you, Ezra. He thinks it will free both of you, but—"

"Wait." Aaron stared at me. "Eterran can act independently when Ezra is *sleeping*? And you knew this? And you didn't tell us?"

I gripped the sides of my shirt, arms still crossed. "If I'd told you, you might've decided Ezra had to die immediately and—"

"You didn't tell us Ezra's demon could freely walk around at night while we were all asleep? In my home? With *my parents?* He could've killed them!"

"But he didn't want to kill anyone! He wanted the amulet, and I wasn't going to help him if he—"

"Help him?" Ezra whispered.

I glanced at his frozen stare, my heart constricting, then looked back to Aaron. "I made Eterran agree to stop controlling Ezra at night while I figured out the amulet. There's a chance it could—"

Ezra turned away from me, pulling his shoulder from Aaron's hand. He was breathing hard again, fighting for control. He pressed both hands to the wall, head bowed.

I watched the white puff of his breath for several seconds before realizing how much the temperature had dropped. Frost crept across the windowpanes.

"Tori ..." His quiet voice shook. "Get out of my room."

My body went colder than the icy air. "Ezra—"

"Get out."

"Let me explain—"

"*Explain!*" The word burst from him in a shout. His hands balled into fists, knuckles grinding against the wall. "Explain how you let me walk around *for weeks* knowing that any night,

Eterran could take over? You let me sleep in the same house as the *only people I love!* He could've killed you or Aaron or Kai at any time!"

"Eterran wasn't going to hurt anyone. I made him promise—"

"You have no idea!" He whirled around to face me, his shoulders hitting the wall and his face contorted. "Do you know why he's tried to kill Aaron and Kai so many times? *To hurt me!* To punish me for being his prison! He *enjoys* making me suffer!"

I stepped back, my legs bumping the bed. "Eterran wants—"

"I know what he wants, and I know how manipulative he is, and you have *no idea!* He could've turned on you at any time!" A crackle of red power sizzled up his arms. "I promised myself I wouldn't put any of you in danger. I can't live with that, don't you get it?"

My heart hammered in my ears, as loud as his rising voice.

His hands balled into white-knuckled fists. "It's already hard enough when one slip of my control could mean your death! And now it turns out Eterran's capable of *this?* For *weeks?* You *knew* about it and you didn't say a word to—"

"I didn't tell you so I'd have a chance to save you, Ezra!" I cried, eyes stinging. "There's a chance—"

"There's no chance!"

"Why are you so determined to die?" I screamed, terror and pain and panic spilling into my voice. "Why won't you fight for yourself the way you fight for your friends? Don't you realize how much we love you?"

"Of course I do!" he shouted back. "But not every fight can be won! Not every problem has a magic solution, and you should know that by now—but the only thing you've learned about being a mythic is keeping secrets and telling lies!"

"I was trying to protect you!"

"I've been trying to protect *all of you!* Three days ago, I almost killed you! It's only luck that you had the one magical item that could stop me!"

"Then maybe all we need to save you is a bit more luck, but you won't even *try*—"

"Saving me shouldn't mean endangering you!" His hands clenched so hard muscles rippled up his arms and across his chest. "I have to listen to Eterran's bitterness and hate every single day, and the only thing I have to balance that is you and Aaron and Kai. Without you three, it's not worth it!"

My hands had formed into tight fists too. "Your life is worth—"

"Nothing!" he roared. "I don't have a future, but you three do!"

I reeled back, bumped into the bed, then set my feet so I wouldn't retreat.

He bared his teeth furiously. "Protecting the three of you is the most important thing to me—and you went behind my back to give my worst enemy the chance to hurt you!"

"I took a *calculated risk*. To *save you*. And you can tell yourself all day long that your life is worthless, but as long as your friends love you, that's just a bullshit excuse!"

He recoiled.

"You can make all the excuses you want, but I'm not afraid to fight this battle. Neither is Eterran, and if that means I have to get his help instead of yours, that's on *you!*"

His eyes widened—and crimson veins streaked up his wrists. A spasm wrenched his limbs, and he whirled with blinding speed, his fist swinging for the wall.

He pulled back at the last second, and his knuckles hit the drywall with a dull bang instead of smashing right through. He panted as he fought for control. The temperature dropped until the air burned my face.

"Tori, go."

I started, my frightened stare jumping to Aaron.

"You've said enough." He took a cautious step closer to Ezra. "Go and wait for me at the car. *Now.*"

I staggered backward, then spun on my heel. As I sped out the door, Aaron put his hands on Ezra's shoulders, murmuring quietly, talking his friend down from the spiral of emotion dragging him deeper and deeper toward madness.

I hardly saw the stairs, the empty living room with Aaron's movie still playing, the kitchen where I'd once cooked a casserole for the guys before blurting out something stupid that had sent Ezra running into the arms of his enemies.

The winter chill hit me as I slammed through the back door. I ran the length of the yard, hauled the gate open, and stumbled to a stop on the gravel pad at the back, where Aaron's gray SUV was parked. Kai's motorcycle was tucked in the corner with a black cover over it.

My breath caught in my chest, hitching with each gasp. I stumbled to the fence, slumped back into it, and slid to the ground. As my butt hit the uneven gravel, the tears finally fell.

He will not allow his family to die because of him—not again.

The one thing Ezra couldn't bear was endangering his friends, and I'd let it happen. But if I'd told anyone, they might've killed Ezra. What was I supposed to have done? Doubts whirled around and around in my head, and fear circled my heart, ripping at it with every pass. Uncertainty and hurt battered me, unrelenting, and I regretted every word I'd shouted at Ezra. What was wrong with me? Why had I done that? Why hadn't I kept my cool?

Minutes dragged by while I shivered in the cold, my face buried in my folded arms. The rumble of an approaching vehicle brought my head up, and I squinted as bright headlights hit me. A sleek black SUV pulled into the gap beside Aaron's vehicle.

The engine cut off, but the headlights continued to blind me as the driver's door opened. Footfalls crunched on the gravel as a man walked toward me. When he cut across the lights, I got a proper look—and terror seized my chest.

"Darius!" I jumped up, stumbling with stiffness, and realized I was shivering violently. "What are you doing here?"

The GM glanced at the house, his face grim. "Aaron called me."

I grabbed the front of his leather jacket, pushing into him so he couldn't advance. "You promised! You promised to wait!"

"I'm not here for that, Tori."

I hesitated but didn't release him. "Then why did you come?"

"Aaron said the two of you need to leave immediately, and Ezra shouldn't be left alone." Gray eyes searched my face. "What happened?"

My fingers shook. I tightened my grip on his coat to stifle their trembling. "Ezra found out … about his demon and … all the stuff I was hiding from him."

He sighed. "That was inevitable, wasn't it?"

"But it happened all wrong," I whispered. "I think he hates me."

"You went against everything important to him," Darius said bluntly.

I cringed as my heart split down the middle.

"But would you rather he die loving you, or live hating you? You made this decision already, Tori."

My lungs struggled for breath and I gasped in the chilly air. "Y-yes."

He put his hands on my shoulders. "You and Aaron have a job to do. Make it worth it."

A flitter of memory scraped me. *Was it worth it, Zak?*

I shuddered. Zak had betrayed me and my friends for his own ambitions. I was trying to save Ezra's life—and save Aaron's and Kai's happiness, which Ezra's death would destroy.

Closing my eyes, I pulled the shredded vestiges of my determination around me. Eyes opening, I released the GM's jacket. "Please take care of Ezra while we're gone."

"I will." Passing me, he pulled the gate open. "But Tori … I think you'll find that Ezra, who's survived more than he'll ever tell us, doesn't need protection. All he needs is a reason to fight."

Arms wrapped around myself and teeth chattering, I watched Darius cross the small yard and let himself in through the back door.

A reason to fight.

The amulet. The summoner's grimoire. I would find answers—and give Ezra the reason, and the hope, he needed.

6

I stared out the windshield at the pavement flashing past beneath the SUV's headlights. Everything was black, the trees on either side of the highway barely discernible against the night sky.

"Give me the whole story," Aaron ordered. "From the beginning."

Drawing in a deep breath, I collected my thoughts. This time, I told him the sequence of events in order, explaining each decision I'd made. How I'd made a deal with Eterran to buy time. How the demon had proved himself semi-trustworthy when he'd helped kill the shifters instead of slaughtering everyone—including me—and escaping. How Eterran had pulled Ezra back from their shared mental collapse at Varvara's hands.

"We talked the night after," I revealed. "We discussed the amulet and what I'd learned about demon summoning, and whether it was feasible to unmake a demon mage."

"You discussed it ..." Aaron muttered, gripping the steering wheel with both hands. "Eterran has taken control several times in front of me and he's never spoken. He's just tried to kill us."

"He wants out of Ezra's body. He thinks there's a chance we can do it ... and I think so too. He told me about the Enright summoner who turned Ezra, and that the summoner's grimoire might still be there."

"*That's* why we're going to Enright?"

"My plan had been to tell Ezra everything—in a calm discussion, not a shouting match. He would've come too, and Eterran would've helped us find the grimoire."

Eyes on the road, Aaron exhaled slowly. "Do you know what happened in Enright?"

"Some of it."

"Ezra's last memory of that place is discovering everyone he ever knew had been massacred. I don't think he should ever set foot there again."

My body chilled. "You think it would be too much for him?"

"In his current state, yes." Aaron breathed out again, and the air trembled from his lungs. "Ezra's in bad shape, Tori. If something doesn't change soon, we're going to lose him before we can save him."

"That's why I did this. All of this."

He nodded. "If we find the summoner's grimoire, what then?"

"We use it to find out how Ezra was turned into a demon mage. If we know the details of the contract magic—if there is any—we'll have a better idea of whether the amulet will work to break it."

"And if the amulet won't work?"

"We'll cross that bridge when we come to it," I muttered.

The vehicle rumbled along the highway, the pavement empty of other vehicles. I stared into the darkness, steeling myself against the heartache building in my chest. Ezra would understand. He would forgive me.

And if he didn't, at least he would be alive.

"While I'm spilling secrets," I said abruptly, "there's something else you should know."

Aaron's blue eyes darted toward me, his face lit by the dashboard's glowing display.

"I'm in love with Ezra. We kissed under the mistletoe at Christmas. We've made out a few times."

Silence.

I couldn't make myself look at Aaron, my gaze fixed on the road ahead. "I didn't realize I had feelings for him until months after you and I broke up. Ezra and I aren't dating or sleeping together. I should've told you sooner, but I didn't know if this thing between me and Ezra was even going anywhere."

Aaron said nothing for a long, torturous minute, then sighed heavily. "Hell, Tori. You don't have much faith in me, do you?"

I shrank in my seat.

"Did you think I would forbid you from seeing Ezra like a possessive boyfriend? I love you both. Why would I want either of you to be unhappy?"

I shrank a little more, feeling about two inches tall. "I'm sorry."

"Anything else you've been keeping to yourself?"

My nose scrunched. "Um ... I never slept with Zak. He implied I did, but he was just being a prick."

"When isn't he a prick?" Aaron muttered, then settled back in his seat, his hold on the steering wheel relaxing. "You should get some sleep. I'll wake you up when we reach Seattle, and we can switch."

"Sure." I reclined my seat by a few degrees. "Aaron?"

"Yeah?"

A tear slipped down my cheek, leaving a cold trail. "I'm really, really sorry. I should've trusted you from the start."

The rush of tires over asphalt filled the quiet between us. Miserable and aching inside, I shuffled my limbs, trying to get comfortable.

"It might be better that you didn't tell me," Aaron whispered. "Kai and I promised Ezra … No matter what you'd said, I'm not sure we would've waited."

I stared at him, my chest tight, then closed my eyes, knowing it would be a long time before my thoughts calmed enough for me to sleep.

***

"I DON'T GET MOTION SICKNESS," I told Aaron as I pressed the brakes and guided the SUV through a turn, the tires roaring over the packed gravel-and-dirt track. "But this is the windiest road I've ever driven on, and I think I'm getting motion sickness."

Clutching the handhold on his door, Aaron kept his unblinking stare on the road. "You could slow down. That would help."

"We're already going so slow," I grumbled, following another tight bend. "We've been driving on this crap road for, what, forty minutes? Fifty? How much farther?"

"A few more miles. But Tori, there's snow on the road and you should really go a bit slower."

"This little dusting? Aaron, I grew up in Ontario. I know how to drive in the snow."

He pressed his lips together so hard they turned white. Bet he wished he was driving. Grinning, I kept the SUV's speed steady.

Aaron had taken the first three hours of the drive, and in Seattle, we'd switched so he could get some sleep. Seattle to the Oregon border had been a breezy two-hour drive down a straight highway, but then it had gotten unpleasant.

Don't get me wrong, the Oregon Coast Range was beautiful. Thick forest covered the low slopes, and the winding roads followed wide, snaking rivers bordered with white snow. But therein lay the problem: *winding* roads.

Our progress had slowed, and by the time the morning sun had lit the mountains, Aaron's GPS had directed us from a two-lane highway to a wide single-lane road with no center line and a lot of potholes. No sooner had I complained about the shit road conditions than the asphalt had transformed into dirt. And maybe it was just me, but the road seemed to worsen the farther we drove.

It was truly the middle of nowhere. Aside from the occasional house right off the nonexistent shoulder, I hadn't seen a single town or village. Not even one of those teeny hamlets with twelve houses and a general store. If I were going to hide a collection of brainwashed mythics and underage demon mages, yeah, this would be a great spot. Frankly, I was surprised the Keys of Solomon had ever found it.

"All right," Aaron muttered, shuffling through printouts of routes and maps I'd prepared yesterday. "Which one of these ... Here's the map for Enright, but—"

"But we're not going to Enright." Which Google Maps didn't know how to reach by vehicle anyway. "You want the directions from the Wheelie Wanderer blog."

Enright wasn't really a town. It'd been one once, but now it was just a stretch of abandoned train tracks and rusting equipment. Our destination was a nearby private property.

Aaron found the instructions to access Enright—provided by dirt-biking enthusiasts—as well as the information I'd dug up, with a little help from Darius, on the property where the demon mages had been found. I slowed the vehicle as we began searching for the turnoff.

Guess how excited I was when we finally found the turn and it put us on an even narrower, dirtier road?

I clutched the steering wheel as the vehicle bounced over the uneven ground. Luckily, the weather had been mild lately. Though a few inches of snow lingered in the sheltered forests, the roads bore only a thin layer that didn't obscure its borders.

"Who," I growled as we bounced, "would want—to live—here?"

"People who don't want to be found," Aaron replied grimly.

We followed what I assumed was a logging road past a clear-cut patch of forest, then turned onto another track that wound along the side of a mountain. We descended into a valley, and our view of the peaks disappeared as winter-bare trees hemmed in the road, so close that the occasional branch slapped the SUV.

It took another fifteen minutes to find the correct driveway, obscured by overgrown trees. The road, winding into the forest, was little more than two strips of dirt where tires had packed down the earth.

"This is it," I muttered. "Let's do this."

I turned onto the track—and discovered the true and bone-shaking meaning of "bumpy."

The wheels dipping and suspension rocking, I steered along the road at a crawl. I couldn't tell if it had been maintained since the "extermination," but at least it was clear of debris. Fallen branches and tree trunks lined the sides, but nothing blocked our route.

We bounced along for almost ten minutes, rounded a bend, and there it was.

Ezra's former home. The twisted prison he and his parents hadn't realized they'd fallen into. The scene of a massacre where sixty-eight people had died, including the summoner who'd doomed Ezra.

I shifted the SUV into park, cut the engine, and threw my door open. Cold air rushed into the vehicle as I jumped out into an undisturbed inch of snow. Despite being deep in the mountains, the temperature hovered just above freezing—not bad for late January.

Before its destruction, the commune had covered the gentle slope of a mountain in several tiers, with a large building at the base and several rows of housing beyond it. A dilapidated fence encircled an overgrown field to the west, and near the ridge at the top, one more structure had stood, but I couldn't guess its purpose.

All the buildings were rubble now.

I studied the community center at the bottom of the slope, trying to imagine what it had looked like. I tried to imagine adolescent Ezra standing in this same spot when he'd first arrived with his parents seventeen years ago. I tried to imagine the Keys of Solomon storming through, armed and eager to do battle with rare demon mages—the ultimate trophy kill.

The SUV's hatch slammed shut, making me jump. I turned to find Aaron zipping his coat over his protective vest. Sharpie, in its black case, was slung over his shoulder.

"We're out in the sticks," I reminded him. "I don't think you need your sword."

"No sense in taking chances."

Okay, sure. I could get on board with paranoia. Exaggerating my gestures, I pointed the key fob at the SUV and pressed the lock button. The vehicle emitted a short beep as its alarm engaged.

Rolling his eyes, he held out my combat belt. I automatically reached for it, but as my hand closed around the leather, my throat constricted painfully.

The belt, which had once been loaded with all my artifacts, held only alchemy supplies—my paintball gun, an extra magazine of sleeping potions, and a handful of alchemy bombs. With such limited magic, would I be of any use as Aaron's back up?

Shoving down my doubts, I took the belt and peeked in the back pouch. Hoshi, in orb form, was nestled in the leather, probably dreaming sylph dreams—or avoiding the cold. Who knew, but at least I could count on her help.

Buckling the belt on, I straightened my shoulders, took a deep breath, and started forward. "Let's do this."

We approached the community hall first. Three of the four walls were in various stages of "crumbling to dust," and the ceiling had caved in. A small forest sprouted from the rubble, the saplings patiently waiting for spring.

"They probably had gardens and livestock," Aaron mused, leaning over a broken wall to peer toward the back end of the hall. "Communes like this try to be self-sufficient."

"Yeah," I agreed. "They wouldn't want to draw attention with massive grocery orders. Besides, who'd want to make the drive out of here more than once a month?"

We poked around in the ruins for a few minutes, then I shook my head. "Eterran said the rituals were treated like performances. Based on that, I think our destination is there."

I pointed up the slope to the ruins at the top, and Aaron nodded.

Together, we traipsed up the wide path through the center of the community, our breaths puffing white. Cold, sorrowful weight gathered in my chest with each step, and I steeled my emotions against the sights.

Two children's bicycles had been abandoned in front of a house, tires deflated and chains rusted. Gardening tools lay in the dirt, long handles snapped. A quad with its front crushed, as though it'd run into something, sat between two houses with a helmet beside it, a dead weed poking through the broken visor.

Signs of lives cut short were everywhere, belongings forgotten and homes empty. One day, the people here had been living in relative peace. Twenty-four hours later, the Keys of Solomon had killed them all.

"These families weren't criminals," I said, my voice quiet but the words harsh in my throat. "They were victims. How could the Keys slaughter them and get away with it?"

"I don't know." He stepped over a two-foot-deep rut in the earth. "But it doesn't look like the demon mages went quietly to their deaths."

He gestured toward another fissure splitting the ground, and I studied my surroundings again. The damage had weathered, the years softening it, but now that I was searching for the signs, I could see deep tears in the soil and rubble thrown twenty, thirty, even fifty feet from the demolished structures.

Ezra alone had blown apart a building. What would it have been like to face *ten* demon mages working together to protect their home?

Aaron and I continued up the slope to the rubble at the top. Huge chunks of stone lay all around a wide, empty circle made of flat concrete. Untouched snow blanketed the floor, which hadn't suffered damage despite the rest of the structure being reduced to crumbled rock.

I kicked at a short, cylindrical stump at the circle's edge. "What was this?"

Crouching, Aaron brushed snow off the top of the stump, revealing broken concrete. "I think … these were pillars. This was a temple, sort of like the ancient temples in Rome."

I rubbed my cold hands together. "I guess this is the ritual location, then. The hidden room is underneath this, according to Eterran."

In unison, Aaron and I peered around.

"Well," he muttered, "this might be difficult."

"There's got to be a way in that doesn't involve digging." I walked onto the flat, round floor. "Maybe if I step in the right spot, I can trigger a door."

"Or a booby trap."

Wishing Eterran had given me better instructions, I wandered across the disc-like platform. Was this where Ezra had been turned into a demon mage at fourteen?

"Tori … look."

He was pointing at my footprints in the snow. Where my boots had uncovered the floor, dark lines crossed the stone.

Using one foot, I swept a larger patch of snow aside, then squatted to touch one of the black markings.

"Silver," I realized. "It's tarnished silver inlay."

I started back toward Aaron, tapping on the pouch at the small of my back. With a rush of pale light, Hoshi uncoiled from the pouch. Her eyes glowed with pink radiance as she swirled around me, sniffing at the crisp mountain air.

"Hoshi, could we get a little wind?" I waved at the snow-covered floor. "Can you blow this clean?"

Her fan-like wings snapped open and closed. Rising above me, she flicked her long tail back and forth.

A breeze stirred my hair—then a tornado-like gust blasted across the stone circle. The snow billowed upward, and as the wind died, it fluttered back to the ground twenty yards away.

Aaron stepped up beside me, and we studied the newly uncovered temple floor. The silver inlay marked three fifteen-foot-wide circles set in a triangle, each one adorned with spiraling lines, geometric shapes, and hundreds of runes. Some I vaguely recognized from glimpses of Arcana, while others were spiky, twisted, and oddly disturbing.

"The circles aren't quite the same," Aaron observed, voice hushed. "But they look a lot like summoning circles."

"They seem completely untouched. Why is this the only place that isn't damaged?"

"I don't know, but leaving this intact can't be a good idea. It—"

Beep beep beep!

Aaron and I whirled around as the noise reverberated through the valley. At the bottom of the hill, the SUV's alarm blared, its lights flashing. Even from our high vantage point, I could see no sign of whatever had triggered the alarm.

I fumbled the keys out of my pocket and hit a button. As the vehicle went silent, I flicked a glance at Aaron.

Without a word, we both broke into a jog. Hoshi trailed after us as we ran down to level ground, adding another set of footprints to the snow. Ten feet from the SUV, I stopped. Aaron slid to a halt beside me.

"Uh." I blinked a few times. "Are you seeing what I'm seeing?"

Our SUV, which I distinctly remembered parking on a totally normal, flat patch of ground, was now sitting in a shallow grave. A perfect rectangle of earth had sunk two feet, taking our vehicle with it.

Swearing, Aaron swung Sharpie's long black case off his shoulder and grabbed the zipper.

"Aaron?" I began. "What—"

The earth trembled, and the ground in front of me erupted.

A WALL OF EARTH shot upward, spraying me with dirt. I recoiled, arms shielding my face. The ground heaved as a tearing sound deafened me.

"Tori!" Aaron yelled.

I spun unsteadily and saw three more walls of dirt rising around us to form a prison.

With no time to get his sword out of its case, Aaron shoved the weapon into my hands and leaped at a wall as it surged past his head. He caught the top, heaved himself over it, and disappeared on the other side.

"Quick!" he called. "Throw me—"

A crack of breaking rock interrupted him, and he swore.

"Shit shit shit!" I panted, slinging the sword over my shoulder. I ran at the ten-foot wall and sprang upward. I grabbed the dirt top, but it crumbled under my fingers before I could pull myself up.

With a silvery flash, Hoshi appeared behind me. She grabbed my coat and hauled up, her tail lashing. I scrambled over and dropped, landing on my feet—only for the earth to shudder under me. A few yards away, Aaron yelped as the ground threw him.

Yeah, the ground. It *threw him*. I didn't know how else to describe the way it'd heaved under his feet like a bucking horse.

"Aaron!" I yanked Sharpie from its case and flung it toward him. As he shoved back to his feet, he caught it out of the air and ripped the blade from its sheath.

"Lie flat, Tori," he ordered as fire burst across his hands and ran up the steel. "Now!"

I dove for the ground as Aaron's face tightened with concentration. He whipped his blade in a wide, horizontal arc and a sheet of red-hot fire swept out in an expanding ring at waist height. It whooshed over me and blasted across the nearby buildings. The quaking earth stilled.

Aaron grinned fiercely. "Got you, you bastard."

As he leaped over the cracked ground, I shoved up. "Got who?"

"The terramage!" he yelled, charging toward the crumbling community hall. "They're over here!"

Terramage? I glanced at the fun new hole our SUV was parked in. An earth mage. That made sense—but I sure as hell didn't like it.

Unholstering my paintball gun, I sprinted after Aaron as he vaulted over a broken wall and into the building ruins. Not being an athletic machine like him, I slowed before doing a one-handed hop over the rubble. As I landed on the gritty floor inside, the ground heaved again—but now I could see the source of the mini earthquakes.

Inside the derelict building, our adversary waited for us. Nearly six and a half feet tall with powerful shoulders, their breadth enhanced by his sturdy leather jacket, the man held a wooden quarterstaff with steel-tipped ends. His tanned complexion stood out against the snow-dusted wall behind him, his dark brown hair shaved on the sides with a messy fauxhawk on top.

Fire burst across Aaron's forearms as he swung Sharpie, sending a wave of flame at the terramage. The man smacked the butt of his staff into the ground, and a thin sheet of soil shot upward, forming a wall in front of him.

Aaron's fire burst against it, and the wall crumbled as the terramage whirled his staff with easy grace. He swung the end around and pointed it at Aaron, thirty feet of empty space and scorched saplings between them.

The ground under Aaron's feet shattered. As he staggered, the terramage flipped his staff in another swift, deliberate motion. The butt end hit the earth.

A four-inch-wide column of concrete and clay burst out of the dirt in front of Aaron. It shot upward and slammed into the pit of his stomach, lifting him a few inches off the ground.

He crashed down on his back, eyes bulging, unable to breathe.

"Shit!" I gasped again. I was saying that way too much.

The terramage's eyes snapped to me, and that staff began to spin again. I didn't wait to see what earthly terror he was about to inflict. I sprang forward, dodging saplings.

The quarterstaff swung to point at me. The ground in my path burst into ankle-breaking fissures. With a shriek, I leaped over them, landed on an unbroken patch, and jumped again with flailing arms.

"Asshole!" I yelled furiously. "Hoshi, smack that piece of shit in the head!"

The terramage braced, eyes darting as he searched for whoever "Hoshi" was.

The sylph appeared above him. She spun in a tight, violent circle and whipped her tail into the side of his skull with a loud *thwack*. As he thrust his staff up to knock her out of the air, I leveled my gun at him and pulled the trigger.

Pop pop pop pop!

Yellow potion burst everywhere—except on the terramage. All my shots had caught on the tangle of wussy little sapling branches between us.

"Goddamn it!" I snarled, my grip tightening on the gun. I had nothing else to fight with. The paintball gun was the only offensive weapon I had left!

Orange light flared across the crumbling walls. A fiery orb the size of a beach ball expanded on the tip of Aaron's sword, and it blasted toward the terramage.

A whirl of that staff and another shielding wall of dirt rose in front of the mage, catching the fireball. As the barrier crumbled, I reached for a smoke bomb. My fingers curled around the cool glass orb, but I hesitated. A smoke shield would hide us from the terramage, but it would also hide him from us and maybe I shouldn't—

The terramage whirled his staff in a new pattern and slapped it down.

The concrete beneath me and Aaron shattered, and we both fell. The soil around me heaved up in a bowl shape with me in the center, and a load of loose earth was dumped on my lap, burying my legs.

Another swing of that staff and the earth bucked under Aaron, throwing him back down to his knees as he tried to stand.

The terramage's staff blurred as he spun it. He slammed it down one more time and another narrow column of rock launched at Aaron—this one shooting toward his skull.

I had one second to realize Aaron was about to take a possibly fatal blow to the head, and it was my fault for hesitating.

Aaron reeled back—and the earth went still, the rocky end of the column inches from his face.

The terramage pitched forward with his arms and legs vibrating. Two shiny wires ran from his back to the taser gun in the hand of another man, who was crouched in the rubble five feet behind the mage.

I stared, my mouth hanging open and my brain fizzing worse than the electrical current immobilizing the terramage. For a long, agonizing moment, I couldn't speak. Then my voice returned—in a full-volume bellow of furious disbelief.

"*Justin?*"

* * *

"I HATE FIGHTING TERRAMAGES," Aaron growled, brushing at the grit clinging to his jacket.

I shot him a glare. He was barely smudged, whereas the terramage had straight-up buried the lower half of my body. I had dirt in my underwear.

In. My. *Underwear.* Aaron had nothing to complain about.

My glower skimmed across the terramage, now unconscious with yellow sleep potion splattered over the side of his neck. While he'd been down from Justin's taser, I'd wrenched myself out of the dirt and made it over in time to shoot him.

"A terramage," Justin muttered, arms crossed and feet set wide in a cliché policeman stance. He was dressed in civvies, with a blue toque and warm leather gloves.

My furious glare veered in his direction, but I forced it back to Aaron. If I spoke to my brother now, I'd end up screaming like a lunatic.

"What's wrong with terramages?" I asked Aaron.

"Nothing *wrong* with them," he admitted begrudgingly. "They're just hard to beat, especially when they're as good as this guy. It's the most defensive order of Elementaria.

"Yeah, kinda hard to kick his ass when we couldn't get near him."

"That's usually the terramage strategy."

My temper cooled as curiosity took over. "What's the counter strategy?"

"Exhaust them," Aaron answered, flashing a tight grin. "Which I was working on. Terramages don't have great endurance."

"Ah." I nodded in understanding. That explained why Aaron hadn't tried any of his flashier moves. He'd been conserving strength while wasting the terramage's. A good plan—except for the part where he'd almost gotten brained by a pillar of stone. Maybe he'd been counting on me to pull my weight as his combat partner.

Which I'd completely failed to do. My gaze flicked to the splatters of sleeping potion everywhere. Some help I'd been.

Aaron seemed to be thinking along the same lines, because he grimaced at the downed mage. "I should've roasted him with discorporate ignition, I guess, but I didn't want to use that kind of force when he didn't seem to be trying to kill us."

Discorporate ignition—the technique of igniting magic away from the mage's body. Aaron was very, *very* good at it. And so was the terramage, seeing as how everything he'd done probably fell under the same label.

"Who attacked who first?" Justin asked.

My temper flared white-hot in an instant. "Butt the hell out, Justin. Also, it's who attacked *whom*." I jabbed him in the shoulder with a stiff finger. "I don't want to hear a single word from you until I'm ready to discuss how you followed me across an international border and two states!"

Yeah, I was angry. Stalking was not cool, especially when it was your overprotective, extra-judgmental big brother.

"Let's deal with rocks-for-brains first," I told Aaron, pointing at the terramage. "Ready to wake him up?"

Nodding, Aaron helped me heave the terramage up and lean him back against a cinderblock wall. Justin had obligingly handcuffed the mage, so we only had to kick his staff out of reach before I dug out a small vial of Wake The Hell Up potion from my belt.

That wasn't what it was actually called, but that's what it did, so I was sticking with the name.

I dribbled a few drops on the man's face and recapped the bottle.

He woke with a groggy snort. Dark mahogany eyes cracked open, and he tipped his head back to take in the three people standing over him—one of them holding a big-ass sword and the other longingly caressing the paintball gun on her belt. Did I mention there was dirt in my undies?

His gaze flicked across us, then he grimaced. "Well, shit."

My eyebrows rose.

"That about sums it up," Aaron agreed flatly. "Wanna explain why you attacked us?"

"Sure," the terramage replied in a deep voice. "But if you'd rather leave now, you can probably get away before my team arrives."

"What team?"

The terramage tilted his head, his hair flopping over his forehead. "My Keys of Solomon team. Heard of them? They're always happy to tag a few rogue scumbags."

Aaron and I exchanged frowning looks.

"Dude," I said. "We aren't rogues."

"Sure."

I rolled my eyes. "No, seriously. We're here on an investigation."

He leaned back against the wall. "You're eight years too late for an investigation. I know why you're really here—for the same reasons as everyone else who shows up."

Aaron threw me another confused glance, and I had to agree. I had no idea what this guy was going on about.

Stepping closer to the terramage, Aaron crouched. "Got any ID on you?"

The mage's eyes narrowed.

"Look, man. Either you tell me which pocket your wallet is in, or I have to grope around all of them."

"Inner jacket, left side."

Aaron stuffed a hand down the mage's jacket and pulled out a wallet. He flipped it open.

"'Blake Cogan,'" he read as he pulled out his phone and hit a speed-dial number, then put the cell to his ear. "Hey Felix.

Can you pull up a mythic profile for me? ID number 85-02-554309."

Blake blinked at Aaron in surprise as we waited.

A faint voice emitted from the phone, and Aaron nodded. "Okay. Yep. Got it. Thanks." He pocketed his phone and said to me, "He *is* a Keys of Solomon member."

"No way." I glanced at Blake. "I thought *you* were the rogue—though as a Keys member, you're one in everything but name, in my unbiased opinion."

Blake snorted. "You must not have met many rogues, then."

"I have, actually. And most of them would never murder families and children like the Keys did here eight years ago."

The terramage gazed up at me with an unreadable expression. "Is that what you're here to investigate?"

"No, we ..." I hesitated. Not having expected to encounter a single soul in or around Enright, I hadn't prepared a cover story to explain our presence. "We believe the summoner who created the Enright demon mages is still alive."

Liiiiar, I sang in my head. But hey, it was a good excuse to excavate the area in search of a summoning grimoire.

"Unlikely," Blake said. "There are questions about how the people here died, but *who* died isn't a mystery."

"What questions?" My voice sharpened with rising anger. "The Keys slaughtered everyone."

"Not even close." He arched his eyebrows. "Uncuff me and I'll give you an exclusive tour of Enright's mysterious and extremely disturbing demon mage cult."

8

"**WE KNEW WHAT** we'd be facing," Blake revealed as he strode out of the community center's wreckage—now significantly more wrecked by our battle. His long gait had an odd hitch, his left step shorter than the right.

"You were here?" I asked in surprise, following the terramage. He looked about thirty-five to me. Eight years ago, he would've been on the young side for an elite bounty hunter, but no younger than Aaron was now.

The pyromage was walking at my side, while Justin trailed after us, listening intently. I disliked that this would be my brother's first major exposure to mythic crime and justice, but short of shooting him with a sleep potion, I couldn't make him stay behind.

My hand drifted toward my paintball gun. That was kind of tempting …

"A team had already captured a cultist in Portland and interrogated him," Blake continued, facing the center path that led to the temple ruins. "When they found out what was going on in Enright, they called in the entire guild. Teams rushed in from across the continent, and eighty demon hunters assembled in Portland."

"Eighty?" I repeated, appalled. "Against sixty-eight non-combat mythics?"

"Against eleven demon mages." His face hardened. "And I'll tell you now: only sixty-three Keys made it home. My team was among the seventeen who died."

His voice deepened hoarsely on the final words, and I almost felt bad for him—except he was a Keys hunter and had helped slaughter families victimized by a cult.

"If all eleven demon mages had teamed up against us, our casualties would've been catastrophic." Putting his back to the mountainside, Blake faced the overgrown road. "We spread out in a half circle, coming through the forest. The terrain was a nightmare, but the demon mages were forced to split up to meet our advance on the commune."

His gaze swept the winter woods. "We killed five in the forest, but the others didn't come for us. We assembled here, and by then, all the houses were empty. The families had gathered in the temple."

Turning toward the hillside, he pointed. "Five of the remaining six demon mages were lined up in front of the community building, waiting for us. If you didn't already know how screwed up this place was, three of them were teenagers."

My gaze skidded across the faded destruction. A slight twist of fate and Ezra could've been one of those five.

In his uneven gait, Blake headed up the hill. "It was the ugliest battle I've ever seen. The pure destructive power of demon magic—it was worse than I could've imagined."

We passed the first row of houses.

"We killed two, and the other three were giving ground. We could see they'd gone all demon—nothing human left. The demons were fighting for their survival, and they're more brutal than any human."

We passed the second row of houses.

"My teammates were already dead, and I was down. I never made it past this point. The remaining teams went for the fifth one. That demon was the most powerful—his magic seemed endless."

We passed the last row of houses.

"It took five contractors sacrificing their demons to kill him." Blake approached the temple ruins, steps slowing. "There was only one demon mage left, and the teams suspected he was hiding among the cultists in the temple."

The terramage stopped a few yards from the temple.

"The teams approached with caution, and the cultists just stood there. Men, women, some children. Maybe they thought they were safe in the temple. They didn't even try to run, and then …"

Blake gazed at the destruction before turning toward us, his face like stone. "And then the temple lit up with red light, and a blast of demon magic more powerful than anything we'd witnessed yet obliterated the entire cult."

Lightheadedness swept through me. "What … what do you mean?"

"The last demon mage killed everyone in the temple, including himself. I don't know if it was the man or the demon who did it." He looked from me to Aaron. "We assume the last demon mage was also the cult leader. It's happened before—the leader killing everyone when a cult is threatened—but we'll never know for sure why he did it."

I swallowed against the sickness in the back of my throat. "You found the bodies of all eleven demon mages?"

"Only the ten we killed. The bodies in the temple were ..." He shook his head. "The MPD cleanup crew did a body count, though. All cultists were accounted for. Every single one dead."

"What about the original cultist?" Aaron asked. "The one interrogated in Portland?"

Blake grimaced. "That one is my guild's fault. They were holding him at headquarters, and supervision wasn't sufficient. He hanged himself."

Holy shit. Ezra really was the only survivor of Enright.

"So," Blake concluded, "there's nothing to investigate. The cult leader is dead, along with everyone else who was involved."

"Then why are *you* here?" Aaron asked bluntly.

Blake folded his arms over his broad chest. "I live on a bordering property, and I have cameras set up everywhere. I saw you drive in."

"Okay, that explains why you're here right now." I cocked an eyebrow. "Doesn't explain why you'd want to live next door to a former cult where so many people died."

"I'm here because rogues are lazy idiots." He waved at the temple ruins, the three summoning circles cleared of snow. "Why build your own summoning circle when you can borrow an even better one? Rogue summoners think this place is abandoned, and my guild makes sure those rumors keep circulating, even this many years later."

Aaron blinked, then laughed with a note of grudging appreciation. "*That's* why no one destroyed it. It's a honeytrap for rogues."

"I tag a dozen or more a year. When I get sick of the deal, I'll destroy the circles before I go. Until then …" He shrugged. "It works for me. I like living out here, and I don't have to chase down my tags."

Just when I thought he wasn't twisted enough to be a Keys member, he admitted to *liking* it out here? Yeah, he was crazy.

Blake started back down the slope, and Aaron fell into step beside him, the fit pyromage looking a tad scrawny next to the heavyweight terramage. Their quiet conversation trickled back to me as I followed a dozen paces behind, but I wasn't paying attention. My gaze slid across the destroyed houses as I absorbed Blake's story.

While the terramage limped into the community hall ruins to get his quarterstaff, Aaron, Justin, and I reconvened at the car. Pointedly ignoring my brother, I leaned close to Aaron.

"The Keys killed ten demon mages," I whispered, "and claim the eleventh slaughtered the cultist families. But"—I dropped my voice even lower—"we know the eleventh demon mage wasn't there."

"Then who killed the cultists? Was it demon magic, or is that a cover story?"

I tapped my chin thoughtfully. "Honestly, I'm inclined to believe Blake—at least in that a demon mage killed everyone. Maybe it was an unaccounted-for one. Could the summoner have created a new demon mage in four weeks?"

My mistrust of the Keys aside, the terramage's story seemed sound. It didn't make sense for the Keys to murder unresisting families. I mean, yeah, a Keys of Solomon team *had* tried to kill me, Aaron, and Kai, but we'd deliberately and obnoxiously put ourselves between them and Ezra. Different situation entirely. Even a shithead like Burke would've thought twice about butchering families, right?

But if a cultist had committed the crime, the big question was … why?

Uneven footfalls, accompanied by the thud of a staff hitting the ground with each step, announced Blake's return. He gave us an assessing once-over.

"You don't seem to be packing up."

"Because we aren't," I said brusquely. "We didn't drive all the way out here to turn right around and go home. We're going to poke around for a bit. You can head on back, though. Tell your team or whatever to head back too."

"I was bluffing. I never called my team."

"Oh, well, you can just go, then, can't you?"

His eyes narrowed stubbornly, and I sighed in annoyance.

Our unwelcome supervisor waited as we opened the hatch. Surprise flicked over his features when Aaron pulled out a pair of shovels and a pickaxe, purchased in one of the towns along the way. With Eterran's tip about an underground lair, we'd come prepared to excavate the ruins.

I was *so* excited to dig holes in the half-frozen ground.

"You aren't planning to exhume bodies, are you?" Blake asked as Aaron handed me the equipment. "Because there aren't any here."

"Good." Turning, I dumped the shovels into Justin's unprepared arms. "I don't want to dig up any graves, on purpose or by accident. Since you're butting in," I added to my brother, "you can make yourself useful."

Scowling, he opened his mouth, then glanced at the terramage and said nothing.

With Aaron, Justin, and I carrying the gear between us, we headed back up the slope. Blake trailed after us, slowed by his gimpy leg. At the temple ruins, I rammed my shovel into the hard ground and surveyed the area, trying not to think about all the people who'd died in this very spot—including Ezra's parents.

"Okay." I rubbed my cold hands together, wishing I'd thought to grab my gloves from the vehicle. "Aaron, let's see if we can find the access point. If it survived the damage, that'll be the easiest way in."

"Got it. I'll start over here."

"Justin and I will take this end."

As Aaron started toward the far side of the temple, I grabbed Justin's arm and dragged him in the opposite direction. We walked into the rubble beyond the edge of the untouched summoning platform.

"All right, spill it," I hissed, my fingers digging into his wrist. "What are you doing here?"

"That's my line." His hazel eyes, so similar to mine, flashed angrily. "A cult? *Demons*? Dozens of people killed in this place? What are *you* doing here?"

"Did I not explain to you yesterday how I'm done justifying my actions?"

"And I was okay with that—until you skipped town in the middle of the night."

Seething, I dropped into a crouch and brushed snow off some rocks. What would the entrance to a secret underground lair look like? Hidden, but presumably easy to get at, right?

"Look," Justin muttered, squatting beside me. "I was worried, okay? I didn't know if you were running away because of me, or if you were in trouble, or what."

"Yeah, but Justin." I glowered. "You shouldn't have known I was leaving town in the first place. How did you follow me?"

I hadn't noticed any suspicious vehicles on the drive, which meant he'd been far enough behind us to stay out of sight. That suggested ...

"You hacked my phone," I growled.

"I didn't hack it. I unlocked it with the same passcode you've been using since you were sixteen."

Damn it. I was changing that code ASAP.

"That's illegal," I snapped at him. "You're a cop. You can't—"

"Are you going to report me?"

I glowered. Again.

He shuffled sideways and brushed at the snow coating a hunk of concrete that might have once been part of the temple roof. "What are we looking for?"

"*I* am looking for the secret entrance to the secret underground lair of the evil bastard who ran this secret cult—and killed everyone in it."

"And ... *why* are you looking for it?"

"None of your damn business. But feel free to go home and leave me to it."

His jaw tightened—the same way mine did when I was digging in my heels with all the bullheaded stubbornness that fueled my cranky redheaded soul.

"Like you said, I didn't drive all the way out here to turn right around and go home."

I clenched my jaw right back at him. We glared at each other.

"Are you two searching or what?" Aaron called from the other side of the ruins, an annoyed bite in his voice. "We have an underground bunker to find, remember?"

Realizing the sum total of my and Justin's efforts was brushing away a bit of snow, I pushed to my feet, angry at myself for being distracted and at Justin for—

"*That's* what you're looking for?" Leaning on his quarterstaff, Blake stood at the edge of the ruins, halfway between Aaron and me. "An underground bunker? Beneath the ruins?"

"Yeah," I admitted, even more annoyed. "So if you don't mind—"

"Get over here, then."

"Huh?"

He waved at us to join him. "I'll prove you're on a wild goose chase so we can all go home. Unless you'd prefer to search the hard way."

I headed toward him, unconvinced and suspicious. "Prove it how?"

"I'm an earth mage and you're looking for a hole in the earth."

My eyes widened. I glanced at Aaron, who also looked surprised. He broke into a jog, heading for Blake, and I hurried to join them.

"You can detect underground spaces?" Aaron asked.

"Easily." Blake raised his staff in both hands. "I've always avoided shifting the earth up here to preserve the summoning circles, but checking for an open space shouldn't damage them."

He jammed the butt of his staff into the ground—and the earth vibrated as though he'd struck a huge stone bell. The booming toll rippled outward, making the thin layer of snow shiver and dance.

Blake gripped the staff, his eyes hooded with concentration. His breath caught. "Well, I'll be damned."

"What is it?" I demanded.

"There *is* an open space." He pointed to the hillside that rose toward the mountain's peak. "It isn't under the temple, but just behind it."

"Oh man," I gushed. "You just saved us so much time. Where's the entrance?"

"No idea, but we don't need one. Come on."

Resisting the urge to clap delightedly—I *really* hadn't wanted to dig—I followed on the terramage's heels. He crossed the summoning platform and stopped at the edge. Taking a moment to ponder the rocky hillside, he raised his staff. A complex twirl, then he tapped it lightly against the ground.

A three-foot-long crack split the earth. With a hideous grinding noise, the edges of the fissure peeled back, dirt rolling away from the widening gap. Impressive—and creepy. This guy would make the world's most efficient grave digger.

At the thought, my hand slipped toward the holster at my hip.

The tremors quieted. A new, almost perfectly square hole in the ground awaited us, the inside as dark as pitch.

"Nice!" Aaron exclaimed, unslinging a duffle bag from his shoulder. He pulled out two flashlights. "Shall we see what secrets await?"

"We shall," I agreed in the same grand tone. "Just one thing first."

As the three men looked curiously toward me, I raised my paintball gun and fired a shot into Blake's face.

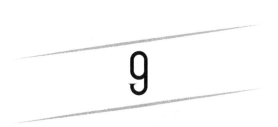

9

OKAY, NOT QUITE his *face*. I wasn't that mean. I shot him in the muscular side of his neck. It would leave one hell of a bruise, but that was it.

Aaron caught Blake's shoulders as he keeled over backward. He eased the heavier man to the ground, almost dropping our flashlights in the process.

"Tori!" Justin gasped. "Why did you do that?"

I holstered my weapon. "Lesson one for the mythic world, Justin. Don't trust random mages who could bury you alive in the grave they just dug."

He glanced nervously at the hole.

Flicking my ponytail off my shoulder, I faced the scary darkness. "Blake can take a little nap while we investigate. Right, Aaron?"

"Yep. Also, Tori?"

I glanced back at him.

He grinned. "You're seriously hot when you take out mages twice your size."

"Aw, thanks, babe." I kept my reply flippant, hoping he didn't notice the slash of despondent guilt that iced my chest. Without any artifacts, shooting mythics with sleeping potions was the extent of my usefulness—and look how much good it had done in our earlier fight against Blake.

I approached the opening in the hillside. "Got those flashlights ready?"

Joining me, Aaron passed over a flashlight. As he turned his on, Justin stepped up on my other side, his expression vacillating between an annoyed scowl—directed at Aaron—and an uneasy frown—directed at the hole.

Turning on my light as well, I directed the beam into the pit. Hmm. Did mine eye spy a dirt-dusted stone floor?

"Are you both going in there?" Justin asked.

"Yeah, but maybe you should wait here. I don't think we should all go in."

Aaron pursed his lips. "I've got to agree."

Pulling out my paintball gun, I extended it toward my brother. "If Blake starts to wake up, shoot him on bare skin and he'll lose consciousness again."

Justin hesitantly took the gun. "All right ... but only if you actually explain all this to me afterward."

"Fine," I grumbled.

"And keep calling to me. We should stay in earshot in case anyone else shows up. If they're ... a mythic ... you'll need to get out immediately."

My brother was many things, including smart. I should've thought of that myself.

"Good idea. Okay, Aaron. Into the villainous lair of evil we go."

Snorting in amusement, he passed me his flashlight, sat on the edge of the hole, and dropped in feet-first. He landed with a thud, the top of his head five feet below ground level.

I handed both flashlights to him, then jumped in. My boots landed on gritty stone, and musty staleness assaulted my nose.

"We need a canary," I muttered to Aaron as I retrieved my flashlight from him.

He pulled a blocky electronic device from his pocket. "Or a gas monitor?"

"Oh, yeah. Much better."

He switched the monitor on and clipped it to his belt, then we both lifted our flashlights to see what we were dealing with down here. My beam landed on a wall directly across from us, where a pair of eyes glared angrily above a toothy, snarling snout.

"Well, that's creepy," I muttered.

I flicked my light around, finding more snarling gargoyles carved into the thick stone pillars supporting the ceiling. Aaron and I stood at the edge of a decent-sized room, the ceiling and floor both made of stone.

"We're going farther in," I called to Justin.

"Okay."

Dust puffed away from my boots as I moved deeper into the room, moldy cobwebs hanging from the corners. I rubbed my toe over an uneven patch of floor and uncovered a line of tarnished silver inlay. Who wanted to bet there was another summoning circle down here?

At the far end, something that could've been a stone lectern or a sacrificial altar faced the summoning circle. I crossed to it, checking its flat top and the gap underneath, finding nothing that resembled a grimoire.

"Tori, over here."

Aaron had gone left while I'd gone straight, and he stood in a dim corner, his flashlight moving across a stone table. Three wooden crates formed a line across it.

I rushed to his side. In front of him was a fourth box—rectangular, only a couple inches tall, with a carved exterior featuring a strange symbol: a ring with a spiky line in the center, the three points of the line piercing the top of the circle.

"What is that?" I muttered, tracing the zigzag without touching the wood.

Aaron canted his head, squinting. "I think it's ... a crown?"

A crown inside a circle? Weird. But the important thing was the box's shape—perfect for a large book.

Aaron dug in his pocket and pulled out a pair of leather gloves. I held his flashlight as he pulled them on. They weren't for warmth; the thick leather would hopefully protect him from any poisons rubbed into the wood.

Using a fingertip, he flipped the box's metal latch and lifted the heavy lid. Its hinges creaked as it opened. I shone both lights inside, my heart in my throat.

The interior was empty.

I swore furiously. "Where's the grimoire?"

"Good question. It looks like Eterran was telling the truth about its existence." Aaron shut the case. "Did the summoner move it before the Keys showed up?"

"To where?" My fragile hope was cracking. This couldn't be it. This couldn't be a dead end already.

Aaron nudged the lid off the nearest crate. It clattered to the table, and I directed the lights toward it. Inside was a dusty silver chalice, two candelabras, and something that vaguely resembled a foot-long scepter, with the same crown-in-a-circle symbol topping it.

The gargoyle carvings glowered accusingly with their stone eyes as we opened the second crate, which contained bundles of heavy red fabric sealed in clear bags. Desperation tightening my throat, I watched Aaron pull the lid off the third and final crate. This one held another chalice with a dent in the side, a candelabra with one arm snapped off, a yellow tub of polishing wipes, and a legal-sized padded envelope with the top ripped open.

Aaron pulled out the envelope. The address was a P.O. box in Wheeler, Oregon, mailed from an address in Portland. Inside it was something bundled in a layer of bubble wrap—and a piece of paper.

"Is that a letter?" I asked, angling my flashlight into the envelope.

He pulled out the single sheet, yellowed with age. I lit the faded handwriting.

"'Revered Leaders,'" Aaron read quietly. "'I hope my letter finds you blessed with the wisdom of the Goddess. With the humblest thanks, I return the holy scepter you graciously lent me. I can only hope I carried it with befitting dignity and grace. I eagerly await my next ceremony within your sacred temple. Enshrined in Her Light, L.'"

Gooseflesh covered my skin, and I had to force a jaunty tone. "What a sniveling brownnoser."

"Did Ezra ever mention members of the group living outside Enright?"

"No … but someone recruited his parents. Maybe the cult had part-time members?"

He flipped the envelope back to the addresses. "If this L member had enough clout to borrow a scepter, they might know about this hidden room."

"And if they weren't in Enright for the extermination, they might have survived." I turned the flashlight to the empty box that had probably held a book. "Could L have taken the grimoire?"

We stared at each other, then Aaron nodded. "All right. Let's check the rest of the room."

I called an update to Justin, then we split up and scoured the underground room for items of interest, hidden compartments, or any other clues. As I brushed dirt off the walls, I sneezed at the dust clogging my nose. If there were any secret levers in here, they were well hidden.

I stopped to peer at a snarling gargoyle, weirded out by its gaping mouth, then joined Aaron at the stone table.

"I guess we'll move this stuff up into the sunlight and take a better look," he decided, taking hold of the empty book box. "Then we can—"

He lifted the box—and a loud click echoed through the room.

A quiet hissing followed, and for a long second, Aaron and I stared at the metal switch in the table where the box had sat.

Fire burst from the snarling snout of the gargoyle above our heads.

Aaron lunged into me, shielding my body from the flames. Light and heat roared through the room—all the stone guardians were spitting flaming liquid from their jaws. Smoke billowed and the gas monitor on Aaron's hip blared a warning.

"Run!" Aaron yelled. "Get out!"

I didn't need to be told twice. Dropping the flashlights, I bolted for the hole at the room's edge. A shadow blocked the sunny opening—Justin leaning down, an arm outstretched. I grabbed his reaching hand and he hauled me out. Aaron jumped for the ledge, swung over it, and rolled onto the frozen ground.

Black smoke boiled from the opening, unseen flames crackling loudly in the hidden room.

Aaron sat up and brushed at the flames eating holes in his leather jacket, the fire vanishing under his touch. At my anxious look, he lifted his other hand, showing me the undamaged envelope.

"What happened?" Justin demanded. "How did the room catch on fire?"

"Booby trap," I informed him. "But it's okay. We got the most important thing."

"And what is that?"

I pointed at the envelope. "An address."

He blinked.

Pushing to his feet, Aaron unwrapped the item inside the envelope, revealing a scepter in the same design as the large one in the now-burning crate down in the secret room, except this one was only eight inches long. He studied the envelope's return address.

"Well, Tori?" His blue eyes rose to mine. "Are we going to Portland?"

Wiping the snow off my leather pants, I also stood. Black smoke mushroomed from the hole, the dark haze drifting across the temple ruins where Ezra's parents and sixty-six other victims of the cult had died.

"We're going to Portland."

I SURVEYED THE STACK of gear in the SUV, ensuring nothing would bounce around too much on the drive back to civilization. Wedging a shovel more securely in its corner, I pulled the hatch down and slammed it shut.

Justin, leaning against the vehicle's side panel, scowled at me. I scowled back.

"You promised," he reminded me.

Ugh.

Stomping over, I leaned against the cold metal beside him. It was kind of weird because the SUV was sitting two feet lower than it should've been. "Do not repeat anything I'm about to tell you to anyone, got it? Including Blake."

Not that we'd be seeing Blake again once we drove off this property.

Justin nodded, and I heaved a deep sigh.

"Okay." Another slow inhale, then I spoke at top speed. "Eight years ago, a cult operated here and my friend's parents got caught up in it and the cult did something to my friend and now we're here trying to find a grimoire that will explain what they did to my friend so we can save him before he dies."

Justin blinked a few times. "Uh. Okay. What ... what's a grimoire?"

"A book of magic. Like, spells and instructions and stuff. Sometimes, they're kind of like journals too, and mythics will write down their experiences."

"And something in this grimoire will save your friend's life? Is a spell going to kill him?"

"More or less." I gave him a hard stare. "So, will you go home now?"

"No. I'm sticking with you, Tori."

I gritted my teeth. "I already reset my phone."

"No, you didn't."

"I'll do it right now."

"I can follow you anyway."

I gripped my paintball gun, half lifting it from its holster. "No, you can't. One pop of sleeping potion and I'll be long gone before you wake up."

He returned my threatening stare, unflinching. He was calling my bluff and we both knew it.

Ugh. *Brothers.*

"Don't you have a job?" I muttered angrily, slumping against the vehicle. "You can't follow me for days on end."

"I took some time off." He sighed. "Tori, I'm not doing this to be annoying. This is important to you, isn't it? I want to help."

I tried to think of a comeback and ended up grumbling wordlessly under my breath.

"You're awfully distrustful of Blake," he remarked. "Why?"

"He's a member of the Keys of Solomon—a demon-hunting guild." I tipped my head back, squinting at the cloud-dotted sky. "Remember back around Halloween, when parts of downtown Vancouver were put in lockdown?"

He nodded.

"That happened because there was a demon on the loose. A Keys of Solomon team showed up to hunt it, and they were so bent on killing it themselves that they deliberately hampered the search efforts and threatened other teams. According to pretty much everyone, that's standard behavior for the Keys."

"Does the MPD allow that?"

"It's complicated."

He shifted his weight. "Were you involved in the ... demon hunt ... too?"

"Briefly."

"Is that normal?" He cleared his throat. "My impression from the law-enforcement side was that venturing into those neighborhoods was extremely dangerous, so it seems ... unusual ... for civilians to participate."

I was guessing "unusual" hadn't been his first word choice, but he was trying to sound neutral.

Pressing my lips together, I considered how to answer. I didn't want to get into my near-death experience at the unbound demon's claws, our failed attempt to hunt it, or Ezra's confrontation with the Keys team. Technically speaking, I shouldn't have been out there at all. I had only recently been classified as a mythic and hadn't had any combat training yet.

"Do sleeping potions work on demons?" Justin asked after a moment.

"I don't think so."

"Do you have other magic weapons that do work on demons?"

Not really ... but though I didn't say it, my silence answered for me.

"Then ..." His brow scrunched. "Then why were you out there hunting a demon?"

I opened my mouth, then closed it. I'd gone to support the guys, but ... had they actually needed me?

"Tori!"

I whirled around at Aaron's call. He was striding toward me, Blake limping in his wake.

"We have a problem," the pyromage snapped. "Blake here is refusing to undig the hole he put my SUV in until I tell him what we found in the underground room."

"We found cult junk," I told the terramage flatly. "Chalices, candelabras, scepters, some fabric—probably cloaks or something creepy and over the top like that."

"Yeah, sure," he rumbled, leaning on his staff. "But you also found something that has you rushing off instead of digging through the burnt 'cult junk.'"

Sometimes I hated smart people. Why couldn't Blake be dumb as a rock like I'd initially hoped?

I glanced at the SUV's tires, sitting in the two-foot-deep hole. "Screw it."

Blake's eyebrows rose expectantly, then lowered again as I stomped past him. Opening the SUV's hatch, I yanked out a shovel.

"Do you have any idea how much I didn't want to dig?" I growled, tossing the shovel to Justin. I grabbed the second one. "Digging *sucks*."

Justin followed me to the front bumper, and when I set the point of the shovel against the frozen earth, he copied me. As much as there was to complain about when it came to my brother, he'd never been afraid of hard work.

Now I was thinking nice things about him, and that made me angrier.

Snarling like a dog, I stomped on the shovel's step. The blade dug an inch into the hard earth.

Aaron hurried over. "Tori, I can—"

"I'll do it! I can dig a damn hole!"

Blake's staff thunked toward us. He stopped beside the passenger door, glancing over his handiwork. It was a very nice grave with lovely straight sides. The bastard.

I jumped on the shovel's step with both feet, wobbled, and almost fell. When Aaron tugged the handle away, I let him take it with a bitter sigh. He set the shovel against the earth—and the ground heaved.

Staggering, I flailed my arms for balance. As quickly as it had begun, the mini-quake ended. My glower flashed toward the asshole terramage.

He stood beside the passenger door—which was now open. And in his hand was the eight-year-old envelope I'd left on my seat in plain sight, like a complete dumbass.

"This address," he growled. "Is it—"

Aaron snapped his fingers.

The envelope burst into flame. Yelping, Blake dropped the flaming paper. The scepter inside fell to the ground and bounced on its stubby handle, shreds of flaming envelope clinging to it.

I folded my arms. "Get lost before Aaron lights you on fire too."

Blake smirked. Turning, he walked away from our vehicle. Aaron, Justin, and I didn't move, watching until he'd disappeared down the road that led away from the property. A minute later, the echo of a car door slamming reached us. An engine rumbled to life, and the sound receded into the woods.

"Finally," I growled, stooping to pick up the scepter. "Now let's—"

I broke off. The front edge of the hole our SUV was trapped in had, moments ago, been a straight vertical edge. Now it was a smooth ramp.

Snatching the scepter, I puffed out an angry breath. "He's still an asshole."

"Yeah," Aaron agreed, collecting the shovels. "Now let's get the hell out of here before he decides to come back."

10

THE DRIVE FROM ENRIGHT to Portland was two hours, most of it winding mountain roads. Aaron and I didn't even try to talk until we were back on paved highway. I never wanted to see another dirt road again in my life.

"Tori ..." he began in his "bad news" voice. "You know this address is even more of a longshot than Enright was, right?"

"I know." I tugged the strap of my seatbelt away from my neck. "We can always go back to Enright to search the ruins again if we have to."

"I doubt we'll find anything, even if we turn the whole place upside down."

Trees flashed past, sunlight sparkling through their branches, and I wished I could enjoy the nice weather. My stomach grumbled, complaining about the insufficient amount of food I'd eaten in the last twenty-four hours.

"You can do what you want, Aaron," I said, staring out the windshield, "but I don't care how bad the odds are. I'll turn over every rock on that property until I find something. I'll knock on every mythic's door in Portland until I find someone who knows about the cult. As long as Ezra is alive, I'll keep searching."

"I know, Tori. I just don't want you to get your hopes up that we'll find something."

"I *want* to get my hopes up. You and Kai and Ezra lost hope, and that's why you stopped trying."

Aaron's hands tightened on the wheel. "Kai and I stopped searching because Ezra asked us to. He didn't want us wasting our lives trying to save his. After three years of searching, we'd run out of ideas …"

"I'm not blaming you," I said softly.

He was quiet for a long moment, then his gaze flicked to the rearview mirror. "So … do you want to explain what your brother is doing?"

I scowled at the mirror too. An unfamiliar black pickup truck followed a dozen car lengths behind us. Justin, the sneaky jerk, had rented a vehicle so I wouldn't spot his recognizable Challenger.

"Justin wants to mend bridges," I muttered. "And according to Justin logic, putting a tracking app on my phone and following me when I leave town in the middle of the night is a good way to accomplish that."

"Hmm. Well, it's nice that he's finally trying to understand what you have going on, right?"

"Sure, yeah," I replied sarcastically, resting my head against the passenger window. "And he's getting a fantastic crash course in mythics as a result. Demon cults and mass-murders and a terramage-pyromage battle. Great intro."

"He's stayed pretty levelheaded, though," Aaron pointed out. "He even saved our butts against Blake."

I pressed my hands into my seat. Justin had been more useful than I had, and that grated in a big way.

"He got lucky," I growled. "And we only needed him because you didn't use lethal force on Blake first."

"Suppose. He would've been difficult to beat either way."

Kicking my boots off, I pulled my socked feet onto the seat and hugged my knees. "I wish Kai was here."

"Me too." Aaron's blue eyes dimmed. "I've been texting him updates. He said he almost has Makiko convinced, but he's probably deluding himself."

I hesitated. "How about Ezra? Have you talked to him?"

"Yeah, he said this morning that he was going with Darius to spend the day at the guild."

My heart clenched painfully. I'd texted him four times, but he hadn't answered any of my messages. "I screwed up big time, didn't I?"

"It's …" Aaron took a hand off the wheel to rake his fingers through his hair. "I don't know, Tori. Maybe, maybe not. You've only seen glimpses of what it's like when Eterran …"

His jaw tightened, gaze fixed on the road. "The first time Ezra's demon tried to kill me, we were on a job taking down a small band of rogues—us against five mythics. One of them stabbed Kai in the gut. It was bad, and you know how Ezra reacts when one of us gets hurt."

Yes, I was very aware.

"Right then, a telekinetic hit Ezra in the head with a piece of metal. The blow stunned him, and Eterran took over. He obliterated those rogues with one spell—killing them in a flash.

"Then he turned on me. He could've killed me just as fast, but instead, he pinned me to a wall and grabbed me by the throat. He started choking me and I couldn't do a thing to stop him, not without lighting Ezra on fire."

I hugged my legs harder, muscles vibrating.

"It only lasted a few seconds before Ezra regained control, but …" Aaron glanced my way. "You know why Eterran choked me instead of blowing me up in two seconds with magic? So Ezra would have to watch me die, unable to stop it."

I put my chin on my knees, feeling dizzy. I knew Eterran was lethal, but imagining the demon choking the life out of Aaron just to torment Ezra was something else entirely.

"Do you … do you think Eterran could have changed since then?" I asked hesitantly. "Him being inside Ezra has changed Ezra, hasn't it? Maybe Eterran's been changed too."

"I don't know. The demon's power has changed Ezra's body, but I don't know if it's changed his mind. We'll never know what he was like before becoming a demon mage. I've always wondered, though …"

I raised my head. "Wondered what?"

Aaron frowned at the road. "I've wondered what he'd be like if he didn't always have to worry about Eterran and his emotions."

"Yeah," I murmured. "I've wondered that, too … and I've wondered what he would be like if he knew he had a future? Last night, he said …" My throat closed, and I had to swallow before I could continue. "He usually follows along with whatever the rest of us are doing, but what if …"

"What if *he* wanted something?" The set of Aaron's jaw changed, and his eyes blazed with sudden determination. "If we can do this ... if we can save Ezra from his demon, then we'll finally get to find out."

My arms slid from around my legs and I dropped my feet to the floor. Straightening my spine, I faced the road ahead.

If we can do this ...

We could. We would. Finally, Aaron was beginning to hope—and I wouldn't let him, or Ezra, down.

"IT SHOULD BE around here somewhere," I muttered, checking my GPS app against the photo I'd snapped of the scepter envelope mere moments after escaping the underground room with it. The whole "booby-trap fire" experience had inspired me to save the address in a way that wouldn't get burned up.

And good thing too, since Aaron had turned the envelope to ash.

The address was located on the outskirts of a northern suburb of Portland. We'd already driven through the city center—stopping to grab a fast-food lunch on our way through—then crossed the Columbia River. A few more miles and we'd be out in farmland.

The area we were in was nice, featuring one- and two-acre properties with lots of mature trees lining a quiet, rural road. The houses were set well back from the street, with large lawns of neatly mowed grass. It wasn't my jam—way too quiet and boring—but I got how some people would call it idyllic.

"Oh," I exclaimed, pointing at a mint-green cottage-style home. "That's house 496. Two more properties and we'll be at number 500."

Aaron slowed, and behind us, Justin's black truck closed the gap. We rolled along the narrow road, passing a large brown house half hidden behind huge trees.

"Number 500," I muttered.

I could see only a gravel driveway sweeping up a gentle slope before disappearing into a dense clump of trees. As we drove past, I glimpsed a structure that was either a very small house or a very large garage, then the road curved around a bend, cutting off my view.

Aaron flicked on his signal and pulled onto the grassy shoulder behind a mud-splattered, camo-painted jeep. Justin parked behind us, and I reached for my door handle.

The driver's door of the jeep in front of us flew open. I froze as a large man jumped out of the vehicle, faced our SUV, and folded his arms expectantly.

Blake Cogan, the terramage.

"No freaking way," I growled.

Swearing, Aaron shoved his door open, and I scrambled out of the vehicle too. Blake limped to meet Aaron.

"What the hell are you doing here?" the pyromage demanded.

"Took you long enough," Blake rumbled. "Did you stop for sightseeing?"

I halted beside Aaron, hands balled into fists. "How did you—"

"I saw the address before you burned it," he cut in. "And I'm here because the Enright cult is responsible for the deaths of my friends, guildmates, and my career, and if anyone got away, it's my business far more than it's yours. *And*"—he spoke over my protest—"it doesn't seem to have occurred to you that whoever lives here could be a demon mage."

I hesitated. No, that hadn't occurred to us—because we knew there'd only ever been eleven demon mages. But *someone* had killed all the cultists, and it hadn't been Ezra. So maybe Blake had a point.

Aaron and I exchanged angrily resigned glances. Blake wasn't likely to let me shoot him with a sleeping potion again, and even if I could manage it, that might draw attention from the nearby homes. Looked like we were stuck with the Keys terramage as unwelcome backup.

Damn it.

We spent a few minutes discussing a plan of attack—or more accurately, Aaron and Blake strategized while Justin and I listened silently. We donned our gear—my belt, tucked out of sight under the hem of my jacket; Aaron's sword, hidden in its case; Justin's taser, concealed in a pocket; and Blake's innocuous "walking stick"—then ventured into the trees on the neighboring property.

Midafternoon wasn't the best time for a stealth operation, and I hoped no one was peeking through their blinds as we walked up the neighbor's driveway, then cut through the trees and approached house number 500 from the side. It was a large, Tudor-style abode with an attached two-car garage. A detached RV garage took up the spot on the other side of the wide driveway.

We made a circle around the property, then crept up to the ground-level windows and spied on the interior like peeping Toms. When we'd seen all we could from the outside, we reconvened behind the massive raised deck in the back, a cute little stream trickling behind us.

"Well?" I whispered.

Aaron rubbed at the faint stubble on his jaw. "They have a very nice home."

"I didn't see any cult paraphernalia—not out in the open, at least."

"They didn't have anything else personal on display either," Justin murmured. "No photos or knickknacks."

His observation surprised me. I hadn't noticed.

"They aren't likely to leave evidence lying around," Blake said impatiently. "The only way to know if the people who live here are involved in the cult is to question them."

I grimaced in reluctant agreement.

"Hold on," Justin cut in. "You don't know that the current homeowners had anything to do with the cult. It's been eight years. Whoever mailed that package probably went into hiding after the rest of their group was killed. You can't assault an innocent family without any evidence."

He had a point—not that I wanted to admit it.

"Let's check the garages and see if there're any cars," I suggested. "If they aren't home, we can break in and snoop around."

Justin shot me a disparaging look, as though B&E were hardly better than assaulting innocent civilians.

Aaron had to climb through a bush to peer into the window of the attached garage. He returned with leaves stuck to his pants and reported that the garage was empty. We approached the tall RV garage, and I took one for the team this time, climbing into the bushes to get at the window.

Cupping my hands to the sides of my face, I pressed my nose to the glass. Even blocking the light, all I could see was my reflection. The interior was completely black.

I climbed out of the bushes with a grumble. Now I had bits of dead leaves in my socks to go with the grit in other places. I wanted a shower so badly.

"I can't see anything," I told the three men, joining them in the shadows beneath the trees. "It's blacked out."

"Blacked out as in there are drapes?" Aaron asked. "Or blacked out as in completely covered?"

"I think the latter."

He cracked his knuckles. "Then let's take a look."

We returned to the garage's side door, and he produced a lock pick. Though it took him three minutes to Kai's thirty seconds, the lock clacked and he pushed the door open. Sunlight flooded the interior as we walked in.

I stared around, then cleared my throat. "So ... either the new homeowners are highly opposed to redecoration, or the cult member still lives here."

Aaron didn't disagree. Not even Justin could argue.

Though there were windows and overhead doors visible from the outside, on the inside, the garage was an unbroken room. False walls made of plywood sheets covered the other access points, and everything had been painted scarlet—the walls, ceiling, and floor. In the middle of the room, a silver circle ten-feet across gleamed, mimicking a summoning circle but without the Arcane and demonic markings.

A wooden lectern sat at the head of the room, a three-armed candelabra on top of it. Behind the pedestal, a ruby-red tapestry hung from a pole, its center embroidered with the symbol of the cult: a three-pronged crown inside a circle.

Withdrawing my phone, I opened the camera and began snapping photos. A nervous sweat broke out over the back of my neck as I walked to the lectern and stopped behind it. As I aimed my camera across the room, I realized why I felt such disquiet.

A single worshipper might set up their own personal shrine, even going so far as to decorate it. But why include a lectern? Was it an ugly fill-in for an altar, or was this where the cult's leader stood to address his followers?

Except the Enright cult had been wiped out. There couldn't be a leader or followers, not anymore.

As my heart thumped sickeningly, my gaze dropped, scanning the lectern for something to contradict that terrifying assessment. Beneath its flat top was a shallow gap for storing papers or notes, and I hesitantly slipped my fingers into the darkness.

They brushed against paper, and I pulled out a cheap flip calendar, the kind realtors mailed out every Christmas. The cover had been ripped off, revealing January's page. A different day each week was circled in red.

"Aaron?" I called uncertainly, my stare locked on the calendar. "What's the date today?"

"January twenty-fourth."

On the calendar, today's date was circled in red.

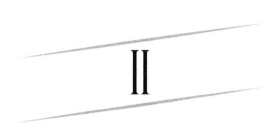

II

"I DON'T LIKE THIS IDEA," I muttered.

Aaron, Justin, Blake, and I stood shoulder to shoulder, staring up a wooden ladder. We'd found the hatch in the garage ceiling—not immediately noticeable since it was painted the same scarlet as everything else—that led to a shoddily constructed storage area made of plywood screwed to the ceiling beams.

It was the only hiding spot in the garage.

"Do you have a better idea of how to spy on whatever plans the cult has for today?" Aaron asked.

"No." I wrinkled my nose. "But whatever that circled date on the calendar means, it might not be happening here."

"Which is why only two of us will go up there, and the other two will watch the house."

My gaze flicked to Aaron, and he surreptitiously tilted his head toward Blake. He didn't need to explain the covert indication. I knew what it meant: he didn't trust Blake and wanted to be the one partnered with the terramage. And since it didn't make sense to shut two powerful mages in an attic, that meant Justin and I were getting ceiling-spy duty.

Yay.

"Justin and I can take the attic, then," I declared like it was entirely my idea. "Better that you and Blake stay mobile."

The terramage arched his eyebrows, then nodded.

It took only a few minutes to prepare, then I was climbing the ladder, a flashlight in one hand. The beam shone across dancing dust motes as my head rose into the storage area. Mr. Cultist had an excessive collection of cardboard boxes stacked all around the hatch, leaving a small square of empty space in the center.

I crawled through half an inch of dust, my nerves jumping with each creak of the ceiling under my weight. Lying on my stomach, I pressed my face to a crack between sheets of plywood. Surprisingly, I had an unobstructed view of the lectern and silver circle.

"Looks good," I said. "I can see the room pretty w—"

I broke off with a sneeze. Ugh, the dust.

The ceiling creaked as Justin climbed up after me. As he scooted along the plywood, I spied Aaron walking into the middle of the circle. He peered up at us.

"Dust is sifting down," he observed, "but I can't see anything. As long as you two don't move, no one will have any idea."

"Got it."

He tugged a black earpiece with a curly cord from his pocket and plugged it into his phone's headphone jack. "Mic check."

I got mine out—already plugged in—and hooked it over my ear. "Test."

"Test," he replied. "Seems good. We're heading for the trees now. I'll let you know when the homeowner returns or if anyone else shows up."

"We'll be here," I said unenthusiastically.

He grinned up at the ceiling, then walked out of view. His and Blake's footsteps clunked against the concrete floor, then the door shut, plunging the room below into darkness. A rattle as Aaron relocked the deadbolt. Silence.

I glanced at Justin, stretched out on his stomach beside me so our weight wouldn't bow the plywood, then flipped off my flashlight. Pitch blackness swamped us.

"Well, this is fun."

"It is, actually." Justin's voice floated out of the darkness. "Kind of. I've never done a stakeout before."

"Never?"

"It's more of a detective thing. I'm just a beat cop."

"Oh." I flipped the mic off on my earpiece so Aaron wouldn't have to listen to our chatter, then pillowed my chin on my folded arms. "I've experienced a lot of new things in the last eight months."

"Like spying on cults?"

"Not specifically. Lots of other stuff, though." I rolled my eyes up in thought. "Rescued Aaron when a guild with a vendetta took him hostage. Saved a teen girl from an evil sorceress. Stopped a rogue guild from enslaving a powerful fae. Hunted the demon that got loose in Vancouver. Battled mutant werewolves ..." My nose scrunched. "Jeez. Now that I'm listing it off, that's a lot of crazy shit."

"That's what I was thinking," Justin muttered. "Except 'dangerous' as well as 'crazy.' Also ... *mutant werewolves*? Are you serious?"

"Yeah, unfortunately." I twitched my shoulders in a shrug he couldn't see. "I guess it was all pretty dangerous, but I was with Aaron, Kai, and Ezra for most of it, and they're top-notch mages and experienced bounty hunters."

The plywood creaked as he shifted. "I don't mean this in an offensive way, but if they're so good, why did they need you in those dangerous situations?"

"Well, they ..." A cold, sinking feeling dragged at my gut. "They didn't *need* me ... it was more that I was *involved*. But I was useful!" I added defensively. "I helped."

He was quiet, and I bit back another round of defensive explanations for why I'd been part of all those crazy/dangerous situations. Going into detail would mean revealing I'd gotten myself into most of that trouble.

"So ..." he murmured after a moment, "compared to evil sorceresses, rogue guilds, and mutant werewolves, how dangerous is this?"

"Um. Well." I squinted at the impenetrable darkness. "Depends on what we're dealing with. If the cultist dude is just a regular mythic, then the danger is minimal. Aaron and Blake can stomp your average mythic into the ground. They could stomp a whole gang of average mythics, in fact."

"That's the best scenario," Justin observed. "What's the worst case?"

"Ah. That would be ... the cultist turns out to be a demon mage."

"I'm not sure I want the answer to this question, but ... what's a demon mage?"

I sighed unhappily. "It's a person who's got a demon possessing them. They're undisputed as the scariest, deadliest type of mythic—but it's super unlikely this cultist is one. Demon mages are *extremely* rare. Kai told me once that at any given time, you could count the number of demon mages in the whole *world* on both hands."

"But there were eleven in Enright, weren't there?"

"Yeah, and that's the reason the Enright extermination is infamous among mythics."

"I see. And if the suspect here is a demon mage, what's the plan?"

I pressed my lips together. "Don't get caught by him."

"And if we get caught?"

"We run like hell." And try not to get obliterated.

Justin was quiet for a moment. "You said you were *involved* in those other dangerous situations. Are you here because Aaron brought you along, or ..."

"No." My tone hardened. "I dragged *him* along."

"Why?"

"I told you. To save my friend."

A longer pause. "Does your friend know how dangerous this is? Would he want you to risk your life for him?"

At the moment, Ezra didn't want me doing anything for him—but I tried not to think about that.

"Justin ..." I turned my head and rested my cheek on my arms. "Remember that time Dad was shaking me for messing up dinner, and you hit him to make him stop?"

His sharp exhale was loud in the quiet space. "Yeah."

"Dad beat the shit out of you."

"Yeah."

"And afterward, I cried and yelled that I hated you. Remember?"

"Yeah, but I thought he was going to break your neck. I had to—"

"I know. My point is, you still did it, even though I was so mad at you for getting hurt because of me." I puffed out a breath. "Ezra is already mad at me. I'm doing this anyway."

"You care about this guy that much?"

I turned my face the other way, hiding from his gaze even though he couldn't see me, and admitted the truth for a second time. "I love him."

Justin's answering silence was full of surprise and disbelief. "Does he know how you feel?"

My brother knew me way too well.

"Not ... no. I haven't told him. I just ... it's hard to ..."

"I know, Tori. I get it."

He did, didn't he? Every human being was supposed to have at least two people who loved them unconditionally, but Justin and I had gotten a mom who'd ditched us and a dad who'd almost killed us. The word "love" set my teeth on edge.

"Do you ever think about them?" I whispered. "And wonder what they're doing now?"

He didn't need to ask who I meant. "If you ever saw Dad again, what would you do?"

I turned my head again, frowning in the direction of his face. That wasn't the response I'd been expecting. "I moved across the country so I wouldn't have to see him."

"Me too." Justin cleared his throat. "I've been meaning to tell you ... I know this is a stupid time, but since we weren't talking before ..."

"Just spit it out already."

"Dad is in hospice care. Liver failure. He has two to four months left, they expect."

I stared at the darkness, a strange feeling buzzing in my chest. I couldn't define it. It was neither happiness nor grief, relief nor regret. It was like a weird sort of emptiness.

Maybe it was the feeling of not caring when you were probably supposed to care.

"Do you want to see him?" Justin asked softly.

"No. Do you?"

"No. I only know because Aunt Leila called me."

"Did she ask for money while she had you on the phone?"

He sighed. "Yes."

"Did you give her any?"

"No."

"Good. She extorted enough from me when I lived with her." I fiddled with the curly cord of my earpiece. "Justin … why do you think Mom never came back?"

When he said nothing, I squinted toward his unseen face. When he still said nothing, I untucked an arm and reached out. My searching hand found his shoulder.

"Justin?"

He exhaled harshly. "We should be quiet in case the homeowner returns—"

"*Justin.*"

His shoulder twitched in a rigid sort of quiver. He exhaled again, the breath even rougher than his last. "Mom … she did come back. Just before Christmas. You'd already left town for your holiday trip."

The plywood heaved under me—or was it my understanding of the world that was heaving?

"Why—" My voice cracked, and I swallowed. "Why didn't you say anything?"

His shoulder moved and he caught my hand. When he wrapped his fingers tightly around mine, the world rocked again. Suddenly, I didn't want to hear what he was about to tell me.

"Mom didn't come back for us. She came for her own closure. All she wanted was to make sure we were all good so she could let us go."

Now I felt like I was falling instead of quaking. "I don't understand."

"She didn't want to worry about us or feel guilty anymore. She wanted to ... to get on with her new life."

"Her ... new life?"

His hand tightened around mine. "She moved on, Tori. Remarried ... started a new family." A tremor shook his voice. "She left a card for you. I have it ... if you want it. I wasn't sure you'd want it."

"But doesn't she want to see me?"

"She asked ... but you don't want to see her, Tori. Please trust me on this. Seeing her ... it was ... it was worse than the night she left." The tremor was back in his voice, his hoarse whisper deepened by pain. "She could hardly look at me, and tearfully telling me how happy she was to see me while inching toward the door—"

He broke off with a curse. His hand crushed mine, but I didn't complain that it hurt.

"You don't need that," he said huskily. "We don't both need to suffer that."

I closed my eyes tightly, fighting back the sting of tears. The news of my father's impending death had triggered an unpleasant emptiness, but my mother's rejection was straight-up agony. How much harder for Justin had it been to face her and see that rejection firsthand?

"Keep her card for me," I whispered. "I'll read it ... someday."

Exhaling slowly, Justin loosened his grip on my hand. "After her visit, I realized I had to do better for you. For *us*. I spent my whole Netherlands trip thinking about how to fix things between us, and as soon as I got back, I arranged to go on leave so I could—"

My eyes popped open. "You're *on leave?* For how long?"

"For however long it takes. You're my family, Tor. You and me. I'll do anything to be a family again."

Two tears spilled down my cheeks. I drew in a deep, steadying breath—and got a lungful of dust. Violent coughing overtook me, which just stirred up more dust. Justin awkwardly patted my back as I hacked.

"Ugh," I gasped as the fit abated. "Right. Okay. So I guess I'll start with the basics."

"Basics? What basics?"

"Mythics 101. Are you ready?"

"Oh. Yes, absolutely. Hit me with everything."

I grinned into the darkness. "'Everything' is a lot. Let's see how you do with the mythic ABCs first." I pillowed my head on my arms again, getting as comfortable as possible. "There are five classes of magic, and the acronym is SPADE, so remember that. S is for Spiritalis, which includes ..."

As my whispered crash course filled the musty attic, afternoon trickled into evening. How strange to be lying in a dark room beside my brother, explaining magic while we waited for a mythic cult to convene in the room below so we could spy on them together. I just hoped Justin's crash course didn't turn into a practical exam before the night was over.

The worst-case scenario I'd described to Justin lurked in my thoughts. The summoner who'd turned Ezra into a demon mage was dead, but there was still a chance, however slim, that if we continued this investigation, we might encounter the deadliest of all mythics.

And Ezra, who was both our friend and—under normal circumstances—well in control of his demon, was frightening enough when he let his demonic side come out to play.

12

LEANING ON THE WALL in the stairwell, I closed my eyes against the exhausted burn behind my eyelids.

I hadn't slept last night. Weariness dragged at me, magnified by the Carapace of Valdurna's draining power and the fatigue I hadn't been able to shake since Tori had thrown the artifact over me less than a week ago. I needed to keep up my strength, both physical and mental. I knew that.

I still hadn't been able to sleep.

You have to sleep eventually.

Be quiet.

On my left, stairs led down to the empty pub; Cooper wouldn't show up for another hour, assuming he arrived on time. On my right, another staircase led to the guild's third level, and between them was the doorway to the second-floor workroom.

If I continued up the stairs, I could force my way into Darius's office, where he was currently working, and again ask him to fulfill his promise to me. I didn't expect his answer to have changed since last night, but I would try anyway.

Apparently, his much newer promise to Tori took precedence over the one he'd made to me the day he had inducted me into his guild.

My hands curled into fists, sickness coiling in my gut—a betrayed fury, my broken trust in Darius compounding the agony of Tori's deception.

He refuses to act because he knows there's a chance.

Be quiet.

I still couldn't believe what Tori had done. Couldn't believe she had hidden this for so long. She knew how much Aaron and Kai meant to me. She knew I couldn't bear it if they were hurt or killed because of me. She knew my worst fear was losing control … didn't she?

Flashes from last night ripped at me. Tori lying. Tori revealing the truth. Tori shouting, face screwed up with anguish and tears in her eyes, demanding to know why I was so determined to die.

I didn't *want* to die, but I was going to die anyway, and she was too stubborn to accept it. She was risking herself, Aaron, and Kai in a futile attempt to save me—*me*, a demon-infected killer doomed to madness.

You are the stubborn fool, not her.

Be quiet.

This was why I'd tried so hard to resist. This was why I hadn't said a word while Aaron had been dating her. Why I hadn't said a word after they'd broken up. Why I'd never, ever intended to suggest I felt anything more than friendship.

I let out a harsh breath and slid my hand into my pocket. Pulling out my phone, I unlocked the screen. My messaging app was already open, Tori's unanswered texts on display. How many times had I read them now?

My thumb drifted toward the reply icon, then I angrily swiped the app off the screen. Rage and despair rolled through me like a hot and cold tide. She was always leading with her heart and her passion. That was the only reason she'd fallen for Eterran's manipulations—she'd let hope override her reason and given him countless new opportunities to hurt her, Aaron, and Kai.

I'm trying to save us.

Be quiet!

Sleek, icy darkness roiled through my mind, bursts of anger and vicious hate spiking across my synapses. I pressed my back against the wall as I barricaded my thoughts against the contagious savagery. The surrounding air chilled my skin.

Will you die merely to spite me? Or will you die in a pathetic bid to atone for the deaths you've caused?

"Be *quiet*," I whispered, needing to give the words the extra strength that came with sound.

She asked why you won't fight for your life. Can you answer that, Ezra?

Teeth gritted, I returned my attention to my phone. Flipping to my inbox, I pondered the email I'd received on Sunday night, sent by Zora, then glanced through the doorway into the workroom. A young woman sat at a table with her back to the exit, tapping on her laptop touchpad in a frustrated way.

How much did I care about Zora's message? Considering the rest of my life could be measured in weeks, possibly days, it didn't matter.

Robin Page knows about the amulet.

My eyes widened. I looked away from the workroom and leaned against the wall again, jaw set. I wouldn't ask. Wouldn't listen. Wouldn't make the mistake of trusting the demon again.

You don't need to believe me if you believe in Tori.

Images flickered in my mind's eye. Tori's face. Her intense hazel eyes, guarded but desperate, as she told Eterran how Robin Page, the Crow and Hammer's new contractor, was searching for information about the demonic amulet.

Eterran could deceive me, but he couldn't outright lie. What he was showing me had truly happened.

My gaze flicked back to the email on my phone.

```
Hey Ezra. I know you're busy kicking golem
ass right now, but Robin Page has
information about a rogue summoner that you
should hear. Ask her about it ASAP.

Zora

P.S. She's shy.
```

A few weeks ago, any connection between me and another Demonica mythic would've warranted immediate, cautious investigation. Now, however, it made no real difference. I could ignore it and let the chips fall where they may. Nothing I did now mattered.

I could ignore it, but bitter anger seethed in my blood and I didn't want to sit around. I didn't want to do nothing. To make excuses and passively await my fated end like the coward I'd somehow become.

I wanted to destroy something.

Is it my turn to hold back your temper?

"Be quiet," I growled.

You shouldn't talk to yourself. Your guildmates might notice, and wouldn't that be exciting to explain?

I swallowed against the fury rising in my chest. *I thought you wanted to survive. Keep provoking me and we'll end up back in that ...*

That void of madness. That terrifying maelstrom of uncontrollable rage and violence that had swamped us both four nights ago, devouring our minds, twisting us together, ripping us apart.

Fear slid between us, tangling our thoughts. The sharp cut of Eterran's ever-present loathing dulled, a whisper of wordless agreement.

I glanced once more at my phone, then slid it into my pocket. Tori was gone, off searching for a way to save me. Doing everything she could, up to and including betraying my trust and putting my best friends in danger. Maybe she was risking her life right now.

And what was I doing? Accepting the inevitable ... or making more excuses?

A clatter from the workroom. The petite brunette had pushed her chair back and was approaching the communal printer with hesitant steps, as though it were a lightly slumbering beast.

As the question echoed between me and Eterran, I pushed off the wall and strode into the workroom, my sights set on the unsuspecting demon contractor.

By the time I reached her, Robin had gathered a stack of freshly printed pages in her arms and was waiting for the rest to print. The printer ground to a halt. Muttering under her breath, she peered at it helplessly, then glanced across the room—looking in the opposite direction of my approach.

As I'd been doing for nearly a decade, I shut down my emotions—and shut down Eterran. His presence muted to a dull flame of cold hate in the bottom corner of my soul, and the pain, rage, and despair that had been smoldering inside me since last night fizzled and disappeared—for now.

Emptiness filled me, and when I spoke, my voice was smooth and friendly.

"Need help?"

Robin turned, a relieved smile curling her lips as her blue eyes, obscured by black-rimmed glasses, turned my way. "Yes, please. I have no idea how to …"

Her voice faded, her mouth dropping open. The color drained from her face, pupils dilating, a sharp inhalation rushing through her nose. She clutched the papers against her chest like a shield, her body language screaming one thing and one thing only: terror.

Shame tightened my throat—a reflexive response to her fear of me. Of what I'd let myself become.

But how did she know to fear me?

Deep in his black nest within me, Eterran's attention sharpened, and my own suspicion deepened. Robin Page knew something about me. Maybe not the whole truth, but *something*.

My gaze dipped down her torso to the infernus hanging just below her armful of papers, the medallion's face etched with a sigil Eterran recognized.

"Ezra," she belatedly gasped, eyeing me like I might morph into a demon and rip off her head.

I answered with a calm smile. Whatever she knew, and how she knew it … I needed to find out.

13

MY EARPIECE CRACKLED, and Aaron's voice whispered through the speaker. "*It's go-time, Tori. He's heading for the garage.*"

I sucked in a terse breath. "Copy that."

The evening's event was about to begin.

Though I couldn't see the door through my crack in the ceiling plywood, the quiet clatter of the bolt was unmistakable. A man strode into view: late thirties with a powerful, confident bearing strangely at odds with his flat-featured face.

He marched to the lectern. With the click of a small cigarette lighter, a tongue of fire appeared. He used it to light the three candles in the candelabra—and their flames bloomed in an unnatural shade of scarlet. The glow bathed his plain face as he tucked the lighter in his pocket and turned. He disappeared from view, and the garage door banged again.

As I squinted at the creepy scarlet candle flames, Justin moved. He carefully slid his glowing phone screen in front of him. Aligning the camera lens with his spying crack, he started a recording.

Noticing my questioning look, he whispered, "Evidence. You never know when you might need it."

I almost pointed out that magic didn't photograph well—but people photographed just fine, including mythics.

"*Two new arrivals incoming,*" Aaron whispered.

The door handle rattled, and a young couple entered. Aside from the long, skinny black candles they carried, they appeared completely normal in their jeans and jackets. They lit their candles from the eerie candelabra flames, then crossed the silver ring on the floor and knelt just outside it, facing its center. Their candles also burned crimson, making the scarlet walls dance like running blood.

"*We've got more.*" Even at a whisper, tension threaded Aaron's voice. "*Shit ... how many are there?*"

I didn't reply, scarcely daring to breathe. One little shift of my limbs could cause the plywood to creak or dust to sift down, alerting the couple below. My heart raced with adrenaline as I pressed my face to the crack.

With clatters of the door, an even mix of men and women filed in. They came in ones or twos, all twenty-something to thirty-something years old. Each carried a candle that they lit from the candelabra before taking a spot around the silver ring. Their placement didn't seem coincidental.

A final couple arrived, lit their candles, and sat, bringing the total to twelve. There was no room left in the circle, the only gap belonging to the wooden lectern.

The door thumped shut and the bolt clacked.

The tall, confident man strode to the lectern. Over his black sweater and slacks, he'd donned a floor-length scarlet cloak with a deep hood. Wow, I'd been right about the creepy cloak thing. The lava-lamp glow from the candelabra rippled over his shadowed face.

"Welcome," he intoned in a deep, somber voice. "Today, our newest *Auditrix* joins us for the first time, completing our circle. *Welcome.*"

"*Welcome*," the group chanted back. I couldn't tell who was the first-timer.

Aaron had gone quiet. My mic was sensitive enough to pick up that someone was speaking—the man wasn't talking quietly—and Aaron wouldn't distract me unless he had to.

"In honor of the newest soul to find the Goddess's light, let us ruminate on how we came to be here." His gaze found each attendee in turn. "We are more than a mere circle. We are a family, united by the Goddess's love. We've gathered to share our love with Her and each other. Through our faith in Her and in one another, we are that much stronger.

"Here, we have acceptance and unconditional welcome. Here, the Goddess's light embraces us all."

The members smiled at their fellow worshippers.

"Outside our circle," the leader continued, "the Goddess has been forgotten. But how could the world forget the mother of magic who created mythics? Does the Goddess's power frighten them? Or is it fear of Her servants, who more so than the Goddess have been twisted into something else—something terrible and reviled? *We* know the truth, but the rest of the mythic world … all they know is this."

Crimson light flared from the leader's chest. It streaked down to the silver circle's middle, hit the floor, and pooled upward like bloodstained water filling an invisible mold.

A demon solidified in the room.

It was a type I hadn't seen before—seven feet tall, muscular like all demons, with four-inch horns, spines on its shoulders, and a pattern of black scales dotting its limbs. Not the ugliest demon I'd ever seen, but an unpleasant sight compared to Robin's lithe, humanoid demon.

At its appearance, one young woman gasped, while the others gazed at the otherworldly creature with starry, worshipful eyes. Well, I knew who the newbie was now.

Beside me, Justin's face, illuminated by the faint glow of his recording phone, had gone white.

"A crime," the leader sighed, gesturing at the demon. "A crime to call this magnificent immortal a demon. An evil, corrupting creature of myth? No. We know he is a *Servus*, a loyal servant of the Goddess. He exists to serve Her—and to serve those of us who walk in Her Light."

Several of the avid listeners had clasped their hands together as they gazed adoringly at the demon.

"Once, the *Servi* would pledge service to the Goddess's followers. And yes, the *Servi* would turn their brutal power on those who threatened Her children. That is their purpose, their calling—to protect."

He tugged on the chain around his neck, drawing his infernus out of his simple black sweater, his cloak swishing with the movement. "Now, generations of baseless fear and the MPD's restrictions have twisted the *Servi*'s willing service into humiliating slavery—but that is not how it should be!"

The chain jangled as he raised the infernus higher, passion infusing his voice. "This *Servus* gave his strength willingly to me. He is not my slave but my precious ally, gifted to me by the Goddess. And when I leave this world, he will carry my soul directly into Her arms."

The demon lowered himself to one knee in a bow, his blank eyes staring straight ahead. The creature looked fully contracted to me, but whether the leader was lying or not, I saw no doubt in the enamored faces of his followers.

"We are the Goddess's beloved children," he continued. "In this life, we are protected by the *Servi*, Her guardians. And in the next, She will welcome our pure, devoted souls. We have pledged our eternal loyalty, and we will be forever protected. Let us thank the Goddess for Her gifts."

As the cultists bowed their heads, I tilted my face away from my viewport, needing a minute to swallow my stomach back down. Would Ezra's parents have stood a chance against this kind of rhetoric?

The sect's leader completed the prayer, and the group began a ritual that involved a lot of chanting in Latin. After that, he led them through a "Knowing of Her Light," in which all the members stared into their scarlet candle flames as though hypnotized. Some of them whispered or trembled, deeply moved by whatever they felt.

"The Goddess can feel your spirits and She is pleased," the leader murmured. "Now, through the gracious gift of the *Servi*, we will bind our souls to Her Light forever."

He pulled a silver chalice from beneath the lectern and swept into the center of the circle, his scarlet cloak billowing. The demon rose to its full, terrifying height and held out its arm. With its other hand, it dragged a claw across its wrist.

Thick, dark blood dribbled from the slice, and the leader caught the fluid in his chalice.

No. Oh please, *no*. Let this not be what I thought it was.

He let blood flow into the chalice, filling it nearly to the brim before pulling the cup away. The demon lowered its arm, blood dripping on the floor with loud, wet splats.

The leader turned to the woman kneeling to the left of the lectern. He extended the cup.

"Drink," he whispered, "and let the Goddess share Her power with you, Her child."

Without the slightest hesitation, the woman lifted the chalice and took a hearty gulp of the demon's blood.

I gagged. My heaving stomach tried to erupt and I clamped my hand over my mouth. Beside me, Justin's breath wheezed through his clenched teeth.

The woman passed the chalice to the next cultist. As he drank, the leader moved to the center of the circle, his deep voice rolling through the room.

"The MPD fears the Goddess's power. The *Servi* are too powerful when not bound into slavery, but more than that, they fear *this*: the gift of Her power, given to *you*. Let Her Light enter you. Feel your strength, your magic, grow."

The chalice was halfway around the circle now. I squeezed my eyes shut, desperate to block it all out. Had Ezra done this too? Drunk a demon's blood while a madman told him he was being gifted with divine power?

"The Goddess is the mother of magic. Her power is ultimate. Through Her, we can reclaim our true birthright."

This needed to be over. Make it stop, make it stop, *make it stop.*

"*Auditores*, thank you. We will convene again next Tuesday at eight o'clock. Remember—vigilance, for the MPD is always watching. Until then, keep the Goddess in your hearts."

Opening my eyes, I peered through the gap. The demon had vanished, and all the attendees had blown out their candles, leaving only the candelabra to light the room. The cultists were on their feet, milling silently, then they filed toward the door.

Relief flooded me. The tension in my limbs released—and the faintest creak sounded from the plywood as my weight shifted.

Directly below me, a cultist looked up. My breath locked, my body rigid as a board.

"Did you hear that?" the cultist asked the woman beside him.

She looked up too. "Hear what?"

The urge to recoil was almost too strong, but any movement would trigger more creaking. They couldn't see me, I told myself. The gap was way too narrow.

With bold, confident steps, the leader strode around his lectern. "*Auditor*, what troubles you?"

"My apologies, *Praetor*," the man said. "I heard a noise in the ceiling."

I sucked in air through my nose. Silence stretched as the people below listened intently.

"It was probably a mouse," the leader decided, sounding almost comically mundane after his cult oration. "My cat died last fall, and the mice moved in over the summer. I'll have to set up more traps."

"Oh, yeah, I had a mouse problem when I lived in Salem," the sharp-eared cultist replied, looking away from the ceiling. He resumed his journey toward the door. "They wouldn't touch cheese, but when we loaded the traps with peanut butter, they …"

As his voice receded, the other cultist and the leader followed. A moment later, the door banged shut. The room was empty, all cultists gone, and I sagged limply against the plywood, gulping down air.

That had been way too close.

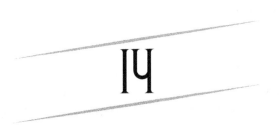

"THE CULT SURVIVED." I paced the length of the drab living room with jerky steps. "It *survived*."

Since we weren't leaving Portland tonight, we'd needed accommodations. A crap motel room hadn't appealed to us, so Aaron had popped online, found a short-term rental, and booked it for a few nights. The two-bedroom apartment was on the ground floor of an aging apartment complex, but it was more spacious—and more private—than a hotel.

Aaron, perched on the arm of the sofa with his hands knotted under his chin, watched me pace. "Is the leader acting alone, though? The rest of his cult was wiped out, so he started it up again as their new leader?"

"Or he could be *the* leader. The one who started it all." The suggestion rumbled from Blake, who was leaning against the wall opposite Aaron while I paced long lines between them.

Male number three was sitting on the other end of the sofa. Why did all these life or death missions end up so testosterone heavy? Where was Team Estrogen?

I would've loved to get rid of the terramage, but as far as he believed, Aaron and I were in the middle of an investigation. From his perspective, we should *want* his help, and giving him the boot would be the equivalent of pouring suspicion oil on a strange-behavior fire.

"The original leader," he continued, "is most likely the summoner of the cult—the one who created the demon mages a decade ago. This man is, at the least, a contractor."

And all summoners were contractors as well, though the reverse wasn't true.

"We don't have any answers," I complained. "We have no way to know if this leader is also the other leader, or whether either leader is a summoner—and oh my god, we're saying the word 'leader' way too much."

Aaron snorted. "Well, we could call him … what was it? Praetor?"

"Is that a title or a really ugly name?" When he shrugged, I stopped pacing and pulled out my phone. "Let's find out."

"Do you really think a cult term will be—"

"Here we go. *Praetor.* A title from ancient Rome for either an army commander or a magistrate. Huh."

"Okay then." Aaron folded his arms. "So, we have one Praetor 'commander' in charge of a 'circle' of twelve members."

"Twelve," Blake muttered.

"Something special about twelve?"

"Some Demonica mythics believe there are twelve demon Houses."

The term "Houses" rang a bell, but I was drawing a blank on its meaning. "What's a demon House?"

"Demon breeds, essentially. There are ten documented types of demon, and according to legend, two additional 'lost' Houses: the First and the Twelfth."

What had Ezra said about the number of demon mages in Enright? *I was the eleventh. Lexie was supposed to be the twelfth.*

Another memory popped: Robin and I arriving at Odin's Eye to speak to their Demonica expert. When she'd shown the ex-summoner her infernus, he'd nearly spit out his drink in disbelief. *Your demon can only be the lost First House. Unless— unless it's the fabled Twelfth House?*

No wonder everyone was so surprised by her demon's unusual appearance. A lost House. That girl might have more secrets than I did.

I squeezed my temples. "Where was I? Right. The Praetor. The cult ..." I turned to Aaron. "We've been assuming all along that the cult was centered in Enright. Maybe it was, maybe it wasn't, but ... what if it was never just one sect?"

"You think there were multiple sects all along?"

"That could be why a demon mage killed everyone in Enright." I swallowed a wave of horror at the senseless deaths. "What if they were protecting the rest of the cult?"

Blake swore under his breath. "Like cutting off a diseased limb before the infection can spread."

"The cultist who was captured," Aaron muttered. He fixed his stare on the terramage. "He died as well—before he could be questioned about anything more than Enright, I'm assuming? Are the Keys sure he wasn't deliberately silenced?"

Pulling his phone from his pocket, Blake tapped on the screen. "Yeah, very sure. I've seen the security footage. No one entered his cell."

The Keys of Solomon had *cells*? Like, their own personal guild dungeon? Gross.

After a minute searching his phone, Blake held the screen up, and Aaron and I moved closer. Justin joined us as Blake hit play on a video. The camera was affixed high on a wall, pointed toward three barred cells, each equipped with a metal cot and toilet. A man was sitting on the middle cell's cot, his face buried in his hands.

The footage had been sped up, and several Keys members zippily walked to the cell, mouths moving with rapid, soundless words, then left. The cultist didn't react to any of them until a woman visited him, but he merely stared at her before dropping his face into his hands again.

As the thin, dark-haired lady zoomed off screen, I pursed my lips. I'd honestly thought the Keys of Solomon excluded women. Maybe she was a secretary. The big beefy hunters probably considered paperwork to be beneath them. Sexist losers.

The cultist remained in place for two more hours according to the clock speeding through the minutes in the screen's corner. Just after midnight, the cultist stood up. He pulled off his t-shirt and began tearing the fabric into strips.

I looked away, not needing to see the rest. As I retreated from the phone, Aaron and Justin watched the last minute of the video.

"The security guard had left his station," Blake said, pocketing his phone again. "He was only gone fifteen minutes, and saw what had happened as soon as he got back, but it was too late."

"Shit timing on his part," Aaron commented darkly. He swept past me, taking over pacing duty. "So we have one surviving sect of the cult, and the possibility that there may be more. The Praetor is a contractor and could also be a summoner."

"And he could be creating demon mages." Blake curled his upper lip. "Merging a '*Servus*' and a mythic would fit right into their twisted ideology. What kind of a moronic fool would believe demons are the loyal servants of a Goddess?"

I shrugged. "Well, it isn't like demons can explain themselves."

He shot me an incredulous look.

"What? I'm just saying. They can't talk, can they? They just get steered into battle and torn to shreds. Did you know demons, even the contracted ones, feel pain?"

"If you're such a sympathizer, why don't you join the cult? Have a drink of demon blood and—"

"Enough!" Aaron barked. "This isn't helping. We need to plan our next move."

I shot Blake a disparaging glower. I extra wanted to plant my boot in his ass and kick him out the door, but I knew what a demon mage could do. Aaron alone didn't stand a chance, and I was no real use. Blake was a defensive powerhouse. We might need him.

"Mr. Praetor must have a day job, right?" I said. "We'll wait for him to go to work tomorrow. Once he leaves, we'll break into his house and search for information on the cult. And depending on what we find, we can set up an ambush to capture him."

"Solid plan." Blake pushed off the wall. "I'll be back at six a.m. and we can head over together."

"Are you going home?" I asked.

"No, too far. But I ain't bunking on your sofa, that's for sure."

He limped to the balcony doors, which opened onto a tiny patio separated from the sidewalk by a four-foot strip of grass. When I'd said the apartment provided privacy, I'd meant from … like … hotel staff. The location still left a lot to be desired.

The glass door thumped shut behind him, and I counted to thirty in my head before flopping backward onto the sofa.

"I'm exhausted," I moaned. "My whole body hurts."

"Holding still for hours is worse than hours of exertion." Aaron dropped down beside me and leaned back. "So, what do you think?"

"About all this?" I rolled my eyes toward him. "On the plus side, our chances of finding a cult grimoire have increased. On the downside …"

"On the downside, the cult still exists and we had no idea." Shadows fell over his eyes—misery mixed with deep, burning fury. "How many lives have they ruined in the past eight years? How many kids have they twisted and condemned to an early death?"

"That isn't the only concern." Justin crossed the room and knelt beside the small pile of our luggage. He unzipped his duffle bag. "There are few different 'business models' when it comes to cults. Some of them are vehicles for extreme narcissists to control other people. Some are vehicles for extorting money from members. And some …"

"And some what?" I prompted.

He rummaged in his bag and pulled out a bundled shirt. He unwound the fabric, revealing a shiny handgun.

I was pretty sure that was no paintball toy like mine.

"And some cults are a tool for turning the twisted desires of a single individual into reality." He pulled back the slide, checked the chamber, then reset it and wrapped it loosely in the shirt. "Those are the ones where the police usually get involved."

"What's with the gun?" I asked, eyes narrowing. "Are you even allowed to carry that when you're off duty?"

"I think I'll keep it close tonight. We might not know exactly what we're up against yet, but a bullet to the heart is still a bullet to the heart, even for a demon mage."

"That'd kill a demon mage, yeah." Probably. Pretty sure? "But I don't think it'd kill a demon. They're tough."

Justin paled slightly, but his jaw clenched with resolve.

I let my head fall back against the sofa cushions. "Someone feed me. Please."

"Want me to order pizza?" Justin suggested.

"Only if it has pineapple."

As he got out his phone, I slid mine out too. Opening my messaging app, I bit the inside of my cheek at the sight of my conversation with Ezra—a string of my texts glowing on the screen, unanswered. My chest ached like I'd been punched under the ribs, and I had to close my eyes.

How would Ezra feel if he knew the cult that had ensnared his parents and thrown his life into a dark, tragic spiral had survived?

Sighing, I swiped sideways to my conversation with Kai, expecting more of the same. Instead, an unread message waited below my last update, in which I'd informed him that shit was hitting the fan and we needed to talk ASAP.

Instead of a text full of urgent questions, as I'd expected, he'd replied with four short words that made me launch upright.

```
I'm on the way.
```

MY DREAMS THAT NIGHT featured magma-eyed demons, chalices of dark blood, and fire that glowed scarlet. I woke up aching, exhausted, and murderously grumpy.

Weren't Aaron and Justin lucky to have me around?

The two guys lurked in the kitchen while a pot of coffee percolated with noisy gurgles, and I slumped on the sofa, imagining a cloud of black miasma swirling around me. My phone hung crookedly in my hand, glowing with Kai's travel update from thirty minutes ago.

Though he'd tried to leave last night, Makiko had delayed him at the last moment. It'd taken him several more hours to get on the road. He'd texted before leaving Olympia, and a quick visit to Google Maps informed me he was still an hour and a half away. Unless he was ignoring the speed limit.

Since this was Kai we were talking about, I had to assume he was.

The low mutter of male voices trickled out of the kitchen, and I turned my murder-stare toward the doorway. How dare they speak while I was so tired and cranky? Justin, at least, should know better. He knew the signs of Morning-Terror Tori.

A blip of warmth interrupted my tired snit. Justin had now witnessed a terramage-pyromage battle, a blood-drinking mythic cult, and a demon in the flesh—and he was still here. When he'd shown up at my apartment claiming to want to fix things between us, I hadn't given his declaration much credit. I'd expected a half-hearted effort that would fizzle out when I refused to follow his big-brotherly advice and ditch my mythic friends.

The warmth in my chest inflated at the murmuring of voices. Aaron was ridiculously charming—when he wasn't being deliberately aggravating—and if anyone could win his way past Justin's prejudices, it was the boisterous pyromage.

A tired smile stretched my grumpy face, and I pushed off the sofa. Breath held, I tiptoed to the kitchen doorway.

"... system is based on internal regulation," Aaron was saying. "Individuals are regulated by their guilds, and the guilds are regulated by the MPD."

"What about individual rights?" Justin asked. "Who protects those?"

"Generally speaking, our guilds are both our protectors and our custodians. There are other systems in place for when that fails—advocates inside the MPD and independent of it. But the protection of a guild is a big part of the reason why we fudged paperwork to make Tori a mythic."

My mouth quirked down.

"Normally, the MPD would step in to *protect* a human civilian implicated in a mythic-related crime. That's part of the so-called injustices the police are always seeing when the MPD bails out a criminal—cut-and-dried cases aren't always what they seem when magic is involved."

Justin made a thoughtful noise. "That didn't appear to be happening for Tori, though. The MPD wasn't helping her."

"No. There were internal politics at play ... I bet you get that shit in the VPD too. That's why we had to change Tori's status to mythic. It was the only way the guild could protect her from the MPD's overreach."

I blinked. I'd known my switch from human to mythic had saved me from murder charges, but I'd missed the nuances. To be fair, I'd been so exhausted from my deadly link to a fae lord that I'd been halfway comatose at the time.

"You're the one who first drew her into the mythic world, aren't you?" Justin inquired. "How does she fit in? It sounds like she's involved in bounty work with you and your friends."

"We're training her," Aaron replied. A cupboard door thumped closed, and a glass clattered against the counter. "Some magic is inherent to each mythic, but there's a lot that anyone can use, and she armed herself right from the start. She's got a real knack for it, in fact, though she still has a lot to learn."

"How intensive is this training? Is she ready for your level of ... combat?"

"Not yet." Aaron puffed a breath—a sound usually accompanied by him running his hand through his hair. "Honestly, we try to keep her out of trouble, but half the time, she dives in without a second thought."

I cringed. Just as I was about to inch away from the kitchen, Justin spoke again.

"Aaron ... have you noticed whether Tori is ... reckless with her safety?"

A pulse of quiet.

"Uh," Aaron hedged. "Well ..."

"She's been like that for a long time. I've seen it before, when we were kids and later too …" Justin cleared his throat uncomfortably. "I'm not sure if her behavior is subconscious self-sabotage, or the drive to rebel against rules and authority, or just impulsive decision-making, but she's gotten into serious trouble because of it … and that was without magic or mythics involved."

Aaron made an indistinct noise. "I'd describe Tori as passionate and instinctive in her decision-making. She's stubborn, not self-sabotaging."

"I'm just worried. Her hitting a customer in a fit of rage has relatively minor consequences in the human world. Something like that in the mythic world …"

"So far, Tori's handled herself just fine, and we're usually around to keep an eye on her anyway."

"But what about when you're not?" Justin sighed. "I'm not trying to be an asshole, but Tori doesn't have real magic. She has attitude and a few trinkets. That paintball gun is nothing compared to what you and Blake can do."

"Blake and I are in a different league than most mythics."

"That's my point. Should she be playing in your league?"

Pressed against the wall, I waited for Aaron to defend me. To say I could totally handle dangerous situations and powerful magic. To say I belonged on his team, bringing down the big bads.

But he said nothing, silence stretching through the kitchen.

My fingernails cut into my palms. I pushed off the wall and swept across the room, grabbing my purse and jacket off the coffee table on my way by. As my hand slapped against the patio door, Justin's words echoed in my head … *reckless with her safety … impulsive decision-making …*

Reckless and impulsive—like storming out in a snit of hurt feelings without telling anyone where I was going?

Gritting my teeth, I called over my shoulder, "I'm going to the coffee shop on the corner to get some donuts. I'll be back in a few minutes."

"Huh?" Aaron appeared in the kitchen doorway, Justin right behind him. "Tori—"

"Be back in a few!" I added loudly, shoving the door open. "I have my phone."

I shut the door, Aaron and Justin visible through the glass, standing in the kitchen threshold with confused expressions. Cold air nipped at my arms as I crossed the damp grass, wrestling my jacket on without dropping my purse. I stepped onto the sidewalk.

A car door slammed nearby. Blake had just exited his jeep, parked behind Aaron's SUV.

He glanced my way. "Oh, hey Tori."

I waved wordlessly and hurried my pace, leaving him behind. Turning my jacket collar up against the breeze, I marched down the sidewalk with long, furious strides, but it was too late for anger.

Tears stung my eyes, and I blinked them back.

She's been like that for a long time.

Tori doesn't have real magic.

Should she be playing in your league?

The words circled, stabbing me with each pass, and I couldn't convince myself they weren't true.

They were. Every goddamn word.

I'd always had a problem with my temper. Reckless behavior. Fits of anger. Lashing out. An *attitude problem*.

And I'd always pretended to be tougher than I really was. Entering the mythic world hadn't changed that. Who else would charge into a full-fledged mythic battle with nothing but an umbrella as a weapon?

Yeah, I'd gotten a lot tougher. I could handle the average mythic just fine—but those weren't the fights I was picking anymore. Look at me right now, investigating a mythic cult that may or may not include demon mages with nothing but my "attitude and a few trinkets."

I jammed my hands in my pockets and kept going. My surroundings were a complete blur, and surprise flickered when I found myself standing at an intersection, traffic zooming past. The crosswalk button clacked when I jabbed it with my elbow, and I dried my face as I waited for the light to change.

The traffic halted. Sniffling pathetically, I crossed to the opposite sidewalk, cut through a line of cars in the drive-through, and entered the coffee shop. Sleepy-eyed customers craving their pre-work caffeine fix formed a line in front of the counter.

I stopped to assess the donut options, then got in line. Justin's words kept jabbing me. I couldn't even blame Aaron for his silence at the end. What had he been supposed to say? "Tori and her paintball gun are just as effective in battle as infernos and heart-stopping bolts of electricity."

Yeah, sure. Maybe when I'd had my Queen of Spades, fall spell, and force-amplifying brass knuckles. But now? Not even close.

Even though he hadn't spoken in my defense, he'd said some other stuff. *She's got a real knack for it ... I'd describe Tori as passionate and instinctive in her decision-making ... Tori's handled herself just fine.*

Dashing away a rogue tear, I smiled weakly. So maybe I couldn't burn a building down—well, yes, I could, but I'd need to *prepare* for grand arson, unlike a certain pyromage—but Aaron still thought I was doing well for a human with some magic trinkets. He had my back, and I shouldn't be angry with him. He was a good friend.

I tapped a finger against my lips. Like Justin had said, Aaron was the one who'd pulled me into the mythic world. Aaron was also the one who'd gotten Ezra off the streets. And Aaron had supported Kai when he'd split with his crime family at seventeen.

Holy shit. Aaron had saved *all of us*.

As I marveled at that epiphany, the line shuffled again and I turned my attention to the donut display. Was it too early in the morning for chocolate drizzle?

What was I thinking? It was never too early for chocolate.

My mouth watered as the line shortened again. Shifting forward eagerly, I dug into my purse for my wallet. I should probably get two dozen donuts. One dozen wouldn't leave me any leftovers, not with two—possibly three—men devouring them.

My hand stilled, and I frowned at my wallet. The guy in front of me advanced to the counter, ordered, and stepped aside. The cashier gestured for me to approach.

"Next!" she called in annoyance when I just stood there.

I moved, my feet slapping the floor. Cold air blasted my face as I exited the coffee shop, and I blinked in confusion. My hands were empty of donuts.

My feet thumped along the sidewalk, moving with purpose. Trees and streetlamps and houses and apartment buildings passed me. My gaze was fixed straight ahead. It jarred across

Blake's jeep, Aaron's SUV, and Justin's truck, then locked on the patio door of our rented apartment.

The door slid open, grating in its track. Blake and Aaron were bent over the terramage's phone, deep in discussion, while Justin sat in the armchair, perched tensely on the leather seat. They all looked over as I walked in.

"You're back!" Aaron frowned at my empty hands. "Was the coffee shop out of donuts?"

I looked around, then knelt beside the duffle bag sitting against the wall. My hands dug into it and pulled out a dark shirt folded into a bundle.

"Tori," Justin protested. "Do you mind?"

Aaron canted his head at the bag. "What are you doing, Tori?"

I wiggled my fingers into the fabric and closed them around a cold metal grip. The shirt fell away.

The three men went unnaturally still when I rose to my feet with the gun in my hand.

"Tori?" Aaron whispered.

I took two careful steps, turned, and raised my arm—aiming the barrel at my brother's face, two feet away. His wide eyes stared at me. Shock. Disbelief. Fear.

My finger curled over a narrow metal tongue inside the trigger guard.

"*Tori!*" Aaron roared, lunging toward me with his hand outstretched.

I pulled the trigger.

15

THE TRIGGER DEPRESSED under my finger, the gun clicked, and
Aaron slammed into me.

A second body hit me a moment later, and I was crushed
between them. The gun was yanked from my hand, my arms
were wrenched back, and Blake locked me in a hold that had
my spine arching against his broad chest.

Aaron held the gun by its barrel, breathing hard as he stared
at me like I'd sprouted a second head.

I blinked slowly. My gaze moved from the pyromage and
the gun he held, then to my brother's face, frozen in disbelief.
My hand ... holding that icy metal grip. My finger ... pulling
the stiff trigger. The memory was fresh and bright in my mind.

I—had—pulled—the—trigger.

Panic exploded through me and I screamed.

Aaron and Blake jolted at my piercing cry, and Justin leaped
up from his chair.

"*I didn't do that!*" My panicked shriek raked my throat. "I didn't—that wasn't—no, no—I would *never*—"

I struggled against Blake's hold, denials spilling from my lips as tears spilled down my cheeks.

"I didn't—I didn't—I didn't—"

But the gun had been in my hand. *I'd pulled the trigger.*

As I devolved into a wordless wail, Aaron set the gun on the end table beside the sofa, then pulled me from Blake's hold and pushed me at Justin. My brother caught me with a startled grunt.

"Calm her down," Aaron ordered. "Blake, let's go."

The terramage nodded sharply.

"Go?" Justin clamped an arm around me as the two mages strode for the patio door. "Where?"

"To find the mythic who messed with Tori," Aaron called over his shoulder, eyes blazing. "Wait here."

They disappeared outside, and I didn't move, standing rigidly in Justin's hold.

"To find … what?" I whispered.

"Someone messed with you? What does he mean?"

"I don't know." My whole body shuddered nonstop, and I couldn't shake the image of the gun in my hand, aimed at my brother's shocked face. I had done that. Whatever Aaron thought had happened, no one had put that gun in my hand.

Justin wrapped his arms around me. How could he hug me after what I'd tried to do?

Minutes dragged by, then the patio door banged. Aaron strode inside, fury on his face and Blake right behind him. I cringed into Justin as the pyromage strode up to me. He drew me away from my brother, turned me, and pushed me down on the sofa.

"Tori," he said quietly, kneeling in front of me, "what happened while you were gone?"

"Wh-what?"

"You went outside. Where did you go?"

"I ... I walked to the coffee shop."

"Do you remember the whole walk?"

"Yes."

"Did you see anyone else?"

"No."

"What happened next?"

I locked my hands around his wrists, clinging on for dear life. "I went into the coffee shop. I looked at the donuts, then I got in line."

"Did anyone talk to you? Did anyone touch you?"

"No."

"What happened after you got in line?"

"I ... I left."

"Did you buy anything?"

"No, I just ... left."

"Why?"

"Because ..." My brow scrunched. "I don't know. I think I ... I needed to come back here right away."

"Do you remember walking back here?"

"Yes ..."

"Did you plan to get out the gun?"

A tremor shook my limbs. "I don't know."

Blake crouched beside Aaron, his expression grim.

"Black magic?" he rumbled. "Or Psychica?"

Aaron rubbed my upper arms through my jacket. "Alchemy strong enough to control her would probably cause memory loss. If she remembers everything but doesn't know why she changed her behavior—"

"Psychica," Blake concluded with a nod. "Probably a mentalist."

"Wait." I looked between them, my face cold with tears. "You think someone made me do that? But—but I didn't talk to anyone, or touch anyone, or drink a potion. No one told me to walk back here and—"

"Mentalists' powers come in a lot of foul flavors," Aaron interrupted. "Do you remember the one from KCQ who got me?"

I remembered. A woman who, with a simple touch, had taken full control of his mind and body.

"You encountered someone like that, and they influenced you without making contact—or they did make contact and made you forget."

"Did you find them?" Justin asked. He'd reclaimed his gun and was emptying the chamber into his hand. He stuffed the lone bullet and magazine into his pocket.

Shaking his head, Blake pushed to his feet. "There was no one nearby, and we didn't know who to look for."

"What if there was no mentalist?" I whispered. "What if I just snapped? What if I'm going crazy and I—"

"Tori." Justin stepped closer. "I've seen you in the grip of every kind of anger. Even when you get vicious, I know what it looks like, but *that*—that was completely different. Your eyes were empty, like you weren't thinking or feeling anything. Whatever happened, that wasn't *you*."

My mouth trembled. I launched past Aaron, arms stretched out, and Justin pulled me into a tight hug. I could feel the unsteady shivers in his limbs. A sob shook me, and he put his face against my shoulder.

"But you still scared the shit out of me," he mumbled. "Why didn't the gun fire?"

I peeled away from Justin and glanced at Aaron. "You suppressed the shot, right?"

He nodded. "But like I've said before, don't ever count on me being able to stop a gunshot. I have to be *really* close, and even then, my success rate isn't fantastic." Rising to his feet, he glanced around. "Now let's pack up. We need to get out of here ASAP."

My brow furrowed.

"That wasn't a random mentalist who sent you back here to blow a hole in your brother." He strode into the bedroom, his voice floating back out. "I'm not sure how, but our poking around yesterday didn't go unnoticed. Maybe the Praetor saw our vehicles or checked the attic and found evidence of an intruder."

Hastening after Aaron, I found him scooping his shaving kit off the bathroom counter and tossing it into his duffle bag. "Hurry up and pack, Tori."

I rushed into the bedroom I'd slept in, where my suitcase sat open on the bed. I scooped yesterday's clothes off the floor and threw them in.

"The Praetor isn't messing around." Blake's voice rumbled out of the living room. "He went straight to hiring a professional."

"Professional what?" Justin asked.

"Assassin—one who can make us kill each other and end our investigation without ever drawing attention to the cult."

I shuddered at his words. An assassin. Had they known they were sending me to kill my own brother? Out of the three men, Justin was the least dangerous. Killing Aaron and Blake would've been the smarter move, but maybe the assassin didn't know that.

I hadn't hesitated to aim for Justin. Had the mentalist specified my target ... or had I chosen him because of something in my subconscious?

Shivering even more, I pushed the thought away and opened my makeup bag. Fishing out the compact with the demonic amulet, I popped the lid up, slipped the mysterious talisman from its hiding spot, and tucked it in my pocket. I'd surreptitiously move it to my combat belt as soon as I had a chance.

"This is escalating faster than I expected," Blake added, "but it'll be another eight hours at least before the team is here."

I froze—then shot toward the door. Bursting into the living room, I demanded, "What team?"

"A Keys team." Blake had his phone out and was peering at the screen. "Make that two teams. They'll tag the Praetor, and I'll let them know about the assassin as well."

Panic drummed across my ribs. Bad, bad, bad. We were here to find a grimoire that could save Ezra's life, and the presence of even one Keys of Solomon mythic was already complicating that. Two teams of them would screw us completely.

Which meant we needed to act fast. We had only eight hours before the Keys teams arrived and snatched away Ezra's last chance.

I darted back into the bedroom, flung my shit into my suitcase, and zipped it up. When I dragged it into the living room, Justin was closing his duffle bag. Leaving my suitcase beside him, I hurried into Aaron's room to see if he needed help.

Standing at his bed, he stuffed a shirt into his bag, then pulled the zipper.

"Ready?" I asked. "We should—"

He glanced up, and I faltered at the paleness of his face.

"Aaron?" I stepped toward him. "What—"

He shifted away from me like I had a contagious disease, then caught himself. His jaw tightened. "Tori, if I seem to be acting even the slightest bit strange, run the hell away from me. I won't be offended."

"Huh? What are you talking about?"

His hand closed over the shoulder strap of his bag, his knuckles turning white. "An assassin who can make us attack each other ..." His haunted eyes flashed across my face. "A gun is child's play compared to my pyro magic. One bullet hole? I could—"

Breaking off, he shook his head, unable or unwilling to describe the damage his white-hot fire could inflict on a living body.

"If that mentalist gets me—" He swallowed. "Maybe I should stay behind."

I strode across the gap between us and threw my arms around him. "You're coming with us, Aaron. We've handled worse."

His gaze dropped, and I could hear his unspoken, "But have we?"

Taking hold of his arm, I dragged him out of the bedroom. "Let's get moving already, guys!"

Blake went ahead, climbing into his jeep and starting the engine while Aaron, Justin, and I threw our bags in the back of the SUV. We drove our convoy of vehicles to a supermarket parking lot, where Justin left his truck and got in with us. Aaron followed Blake's jeep toward the suburb's outskirts.

"An assassin," I muttered, shivering at the word. An assassin trying to kill us. Not that people hadn't tried to kill us before, but this was a lot scarier. Not merely a killer—but a manipulator who would try to make us kill each other.

Swallowing a surge of dread, I added, "And pretty soon we'll have two Keys teams to deal with too. Unless there's a cult grimoire in the Praetor's house, we have no chance of finding one before they show up."

"We need to get rid of Blake and the Keys," Aaron said, eyes on the jeep ahead of us. "If we can send them off in the wrong direction, that'll buy us time. As soon as Kai joins us, we can figure out a plan."

I nodded. Yes, we needed Kai. He was our plan guy. He knew how to get shit done. He did his research, and …

My eyes narrowed thoughtfully. "You brought a laptop, right?"

"'Course."

"Then while you search the house, I'll work on something else—something that'll put us a good long step ahead of Blake and the Keys."

BY THE TIME WE ARRIVED at the Praetor's house, his garage—the vehicle one, not the demonic-worshipping one—was empty. He'd already left and would hopefully stay gone for the day.

Aaron and Blake had the job of breaking in and systematically searching the entire four-thousand-square-foot house. Me, on the other hand—my ass was parked in the SUV, and the SUV was parked in a sheltered copse of trees just off the road. Through the windshield, I could barely see the street and one corner of the Praetor's distant driveway.

Aaron's laptop was open on my knees, and on my phone was Justin's video recording of last night's cult meeting. I clicked around in the spreadsheet I'd made, prepping it for my self-assigned task.

My brother, sitting in the driver's seat, leaned over the center console to peer at the laptop. "What are you doing?"

"Making a chart with our best guesses at the age, height, weight, hair color, and eye color of all the cultists. Then Aaron or someone else in the Crow and Hammer can use the information to search the MPD's mythic database for them."

"Is it a database of criminals, or …?"

"Every mythic is supposed to be registered by eighteen. If all the cultists are rogues, then we're SOL, but if even one of them is registered, we can find them."

"Hmm. Would the assassin be in the database too?"

"Probably not. Assassins don't usually play by the MPD's rules. Besides, we don't know anything about them, so we can't look them up."

As I spoke, I racked my brain again for some inkling of who'd messed with my head, but I had nothing to go on. Anyone from the barista to a random passerby could've poisoned my mind.

"So," I declared determinedly, "let's see what we can figure out about the cultists."

I listed each cult member in the first column of my spreadsheet, labeling them from one to twelve based on their position in the circle. I added the Praetor too, since we didn't know his name yet.

Justin picked up my phone, started the video—sound muted—and watched it play for a moment. "Let's see ... the first cultist is female, medium brown hair, between five-foot-three and five-foot-six, and between a hundred and thirty pounds and a hundred and fifty. I can't tell her eye color."

I blinked repeatedly, then typed the details into my spreadsheet at top speed. Why was I surprised? My brother might know next to nothing about mythics, but he knew how to profile suspects.

"Okay," I said brightly. "That's it for Cultist Number One. How about Number Two?"

He skipped forward through the video, searching for a better view of the second cultist. "Tori ... did you overhear Aaron and I talking earlier?"

My gut twisted. "Yeah."

His finger paused on the phone screen. "I'm sorry for—"

"Forget about it."

"But—"

"You're worried that I can't keep up with Aaron, Kai, and Ezra. They're powerful, combat-trained mages and I'm a ... Yeah, it's a legit concern. But I'm not like I used to be, you know. I don't just impulsively charge headfirst into danger."

Well ... to be honest, I still did that occasionally, but it wasn't impulsive anymore. I was *deciding* to charge headfirst into danger.

I wasn't sure that was any better, though.

"I can see that," he said softly. "You've changed. It's good, I think."

My gaze flicked to him, then back to the laptop screen. He rattled off the details of another cultist, which I added to the spreadsheet.

"But I'm scared for you, too," he added as I finished typing, so quietly I almost couldn't hear him. "You've already had to kill to defend yourself. How long until someone kills you?"

"That won't happen. I have the guys to protect me, and—"

"I heard what Aaron said before we left. *He* could kill you." Justin shook his head. "I've patrolled the worst streets in the Eastside, full of raving addicts and gang members, and I've never felt fear like I did when that demon appeared last night."

"Demons are really scary," I agreed in a mumble.

"What makes all that worth it, Tori?" His gaze probed me, but I didn't look up. "Why are you so determined to be part of such a dangerous world?"

"It's not all danger and ugliness, Justin. There's beauty and wonder too." I nudged my combat belt, tucked under the dash near my feet, with a toe. "Hoshi?"

Silver scales burst from the back pouch. The sylph rose into the air, her undulating tail filling the front of the vehicle. Even though he'd briefly seen her at my apartment before our pre-Christmas argument, Justin recoiled, pressing against the driver's door.

"You remember Hoshi, right?" I stroked her smooth neck. "She's a fae—my familiar. We're friends."

"Friends?"

"She talks to me with color and images in my head. It's pretty cool." I rubbed under her chin. "Hoshi, this is my brother, Justin. He's never met a fae before."

She canted her head, studying him with fuchsia eyes. He forced his limbs to relax, his throat moving with a swallow.

"Hello, Hoshi."

The jeweled tip of her tail flicked, then she stretched her neck out and sniffed at his shoulder.

"There's so much that's amazing about the mythic world," I explained, struggling to find the right words. "Creatures like Hoshi and other fae, and magic like you can't even imagine, and people too. The people are just …" A grin tugged at my lips. "At the Crow and Hammer, at least, they're all misfits like me. I've never fit in anywhere before, but I fit in with them. It's where I belong."

Justin took a deep breath and let it out slowly. "I know it feels like this guild is the only place where you can belong, but … but I bet everyone in that garage last night would say the exact same thing about their group."

A tremor ran through me. My throat tightened, hurt and fury slashing through me.

"I'm just saying—" he began hastily.

"I think you've said enough," I snapped. "Let's focus on our job."

He returned his attention to the video and searched for a good view of the third cultist.

I stared at the laptop screen without seeing it. Hoshi had drifted into the back of the vehicle to peer over the seats at our luggage. I wished I could get out of the SUV, but I couldn't draw attention to us. I wanted to be alone so badly.

My gaze shifted to my phone, in Justin's hand, and I realized that wasn't quite true. I wanted to be with Ezra.

I wanted to hear his smooth, soothing tones that soaked into my very essence. His quiet smile, his mismatched eyes warm with understanding. He'd hold me in one of his amazing hugs, then he'd say the right thing to ease the storm in my heart—a straight-faced joke, a funny story, or a simple question about what I needed.

But I couldn't talk to him because he didn't want anything to do with me. I'd trampled all over everything that mattered to him in my attempt to save him.

That burning was back in my eyes, but I wouldn't cry. Not again. I'd shed enough tears on this trip already, and no way was I going to—

The car door beside me opened.

My head jerked up, and expecting to find Aaron standing there, I twisted toward the door—just as a single stupid tear broke free and trickled down my cheek.

"What's wrong, Tori?"

I blinked at the man beside my door. Blinked again. "Are you a mirage?"

"No."

"Am I sleeping?"

"Doesn't look like it."

"Then … you're actually real?"

A bemused smile. "Last I checked, yes."

A shudder began somewhere in the vicinity of my diaphragm, then burst outward to fill my limbs with frenetic energy.

"*Kai!*" I gasped, leaping out of the car.

Somehow, he caught both me and the laptop that went flying off my thighs. Not caring one little bit about Aaron's thin, expensive techno-toy, I clamped my arms around Kai's neck and mashed my face into his leather-clad shoulder.

"It's only been a few days," he muttered—but despite his words, his arm was tight around my middle.

"Feels way longer." I pushed back, holding his shoulders as I scanned him. "Look at your sexy ass. Nice getup."

Leather covered him, padded motorcycle pants clinging to his legs and a badass jacket enhancing the breadth of his shoulders. Add his dark hair, tousled from wearing a helmet, and a faint flush from the cold brightening his cheeks, and he was oozing hunkitude all over the place.

Damn, I had hot friends.

Grinning broadly, I glanced around for his motorcycle— and did a double take when I saw *two* sleek red bikes parked behind the SUV. And I did a quadruple take at the leather-clad woman leaning against the second one, her helmet visor pushed up to reveal her cold stare fixed on me.

"You brought *her*?" I hissed disbelievingly. The urge to storm over there and kick her good and hard in the shin was strong. Very strong. I hadn't forgotten that it was her signature on Kai's guild transfer paperwork. She'd stolen him from us, and I didn't care what bullshit she spouted about her reasons. What she really wanted was a fresh chance to make him fall in love with her.

Fat. Freaking. Chance.

Kai tugged me into another embrace, and hiding his face beside mine, he whispered, "I may have led her to believe that a trip together was a good opportunity to rekindle a closer relationship."

I grunted angrily.

"Why is your brother here?" he asked.

"Long story." In my peripheral vision, I could see Justin lurking on the SUV's far side, eyeing the newcomers. Probably wondering if they were scary magic criminals.

In this case, he'd be right.

As Kai set the rescued laptop on the SUV's roof, Makiko sauntered toward us, her sleek black hair flowing neatly down her back, somehow untangled by the wind of their highway ride. Maybe it was an advanced aeromage trick.

"Tori," she said coolly.

"Makiko," I replied with just as much ice. "So kind of you to loosen Kai's chains for a few days."

Kai sighed. "Can we focus? Tori, where are we at?"

"Well, so far—"

My earpiece crackled. "*Tori, you there?*"

I fumbled for the controls and unmuted my mic. "Yes, Aaron, I'm here. What is it?"

"*We just searched the Praetor's bedroom.*" The tinny speaker couldn't hide the bleakness in his voice. "*And I think we have a problem.*"

A few minutes later, we'd convened at the SUV for a quick meeting to discuss said problem.

The issue? Mr. Praetor had flown the coop.

Aaron and Blake had found clear signs that the man had packed a bag and skipped town. Toothbrush, toothpaste, deodorant, and shaving tools were gone from his bathroom, and large gaps in the contents of his dresser drawers revealed missing socks and underwear. And most damning of all, the tapestry with the crown-in-a-circle emblem was missing from the detached garage.

In other words, we'd screwed up—and screwed our chances of finding a grimoire.

We should've captured the Praetor right after the cult meeting. Though we'd had no reason to assume he would realize a guild was on to him, we shouldn't have taken the risk.

Now, we had an assassin on our tails and our only lead had disappeared.

A new plan was formed, and we all got back to work. Kai joined Aaron and Blake to search the rest of the house for any cult clues that the Praetor might've left behind. Justin and I resumed profiling the cultists, and Makiko joined us with her own laptop to perform the actual database search; as a guild's acting GM, she had all the clearance we could need.

Our shared task didn't require a whole lot of talking, but I found plenty of opportunities to shoot ice-cold glares her way. I had no idea why she was here, what she knew about our mission, or whether I could get away with throwing her ass-first onto the curb. So I settled for glaring.

Noon came and went as we picked our way through the cult video, my spreadsheet, and Makiko's search results. A headache built behind my eyes, and I rubbed my temples.

At a glimpse of movement outside the window, I looked up. Blake stalked down the road toward the grassy alley where he'd parked his jeep. I blinked after him—then the SUV's driver door opened.

Aaron leaned down, peering at Justin and me. "Any luck?"

"Some," I admitted. "You?"

My door opened, and Kai leaned against the frame. "Absolutely nothing. This guy ran a clean operation."

"But," Aaron added, nodding toward Blake as he disappeared behind some trees, "we're rid of one problem. Blake decided there are no leads to follow, so we should all let the Keys teams take over from here."

"A plan we reluctantly agreed with," Kai said in a tone of mourning. "What choice do we have but to head home now?"

I opened my mouth, ready to furiously explain how we weren't giving up yet, then caught Aaron's smirk. "*Oooh.* I see."

We weren't leaving. We were just letting Blake believe we were. No more terramage dogging our every move.

"Let's get out of here," Aaron said. "We'll head back into the city and finish identifying the cultists. Blake doesn't know about our video recording, so we don't have to worry about the Keys teams getting to them first."

We rearranged for travel—Justin moving into the backseat, Aaron taking the driver's seat, and Makiko returning to her motorcycle—then set out. The SUV zoomed down the rural road toward the highway, Kai and Makiko following on their bikes.

"So where are we going?" I queried. "We need a new place to stay."

Aaron shrugged. "I'll have to rent a place again, I guess."

"Is that smart?" Justin asked cautiously.

I glanced at him in the rearview mirror. "What, you want to sleep in the SUV tonight?"

"Obviously not, but it's safer to assume Aaron's accounts are compromised, isn't it?"

I blinked, and Aaron looked equally confused. "What are you talking about?"

"Isn't that how the assassin found our rental?" Justin frowned. "If the Praetor got your license plate, the assassin could hack into your credit card records. It's implausible for a civilian, but I don't see any other explanations—unless there are magical ways to track people I don't know about?"

Aaron's hands tightened on the steering wheel. "There are, and I should've thought about them myself. I was more worried about the assassin than how they found us."

He flipped on his turn signal and pulled onto the highway shoulder. Kai drew his bike up beside Aaron's door and flipped his tinted visor up. Makiko stopped behind him to listen in.

Aaron rolled down his window. "We may have a telethesian problem on top of the assassin problem."

"Oh?"

I scrunched my nose, trying to remember what a telethesian was. Some sort of psychic?

"The assassin found us too easily," Aaron explained. "They must have a telethesian tracking us."

Kai nodded. "Then we'll have to be fast. As long as we keep moving, we should be able to stay ahead of them."

"Got it." Aaron grinned. "But don't leave me in the dust."

Kai's answering grin disappeared as he pulled his visor down. The motorcycle's engine revved, then he pulled out with a squeal of burning rubber. Makiko's bike flashed past as she took off in pursuit, and Aaron shoulder-checked before pulling out after them.

We sped down the pavement, leaving the Praetor's house—and hopefully the assassin—far behind.

16

CULTIST NUMBER ONE: Brenda Holloway.

She was a properly registered, non-practicing witch who was thirty-three years old, single, and living in an apartment complex that bordered the Concordia University in Portland. And lucky for us, she was home—Kai had just called her and impersonated a delivery man to find out.

Our small group now sat at a picnic table on the grassy quad between university buildings, stuffing our faces with fast-food burgers. Or rather, most of us were. Makiko was picking unenthusiastically at her fries, no doubt missing her personal chef's home-cooked cuisine. Justin sat on the bench beside her, eyeing the Miura aeromage as he ate.

I'd squashed myself between Aaron and Kai, and they were talking over my head between mouthfuls—the aftermath of the Varvara battle last weekend, more details about Enright, their suspicions about the cult. Neither mentioned Ezra, but I could read their concern between the lines.

Grinning stupidly, I devoured my food and enjoyed the sound of their voices, doing my best to ignore Makiko. As Kai laughed at Aaron's rant over how Blake had sunk his SUV into a hole, her dark eyes flickered over her fiancé. She nibbled a fry, her long hair hanging around her face.

I tried to focus on my reunited friends, but as Makiko stared at Kai with that assessing look on her prim features, my temper began to boil. Ramming my last handful of salty fries into my mouth, I chewed and swallowed aggressively. I'd been focused on other things for the afternoon—namely, positively identifying a cultist—but there were some issues that needed addressing before we proceeded with our plan.

"So," I said, accidentally speaking right over Aaron, my glower on Makiko.

Her attention shifted from Kai to me.

"You're going to wait right here while we deal with the cultist, correct?"

She pushed her hair off her shoulders. "Of course not."

"Tori—" Kai began placatingly.

"Kai doesn't need your supervision," I snapped at her. "And you have no reason to be here. We don't need your ulterior motives getting in the way right now."

"Then I'll be clear about my motives." She drew herself up. "If the truth about Ezra Rowe comes to light, Kai will be implicated in capital crimes. And not only do capital crimes come with steep penalties for the accused's guild—which is now *my* guild—but it would be an unacceptable smear on my family's reputation."

I stared at her, then turned to Kai and whispered in hoarse disbelief, "You *told* her?"

"Makiko will protect Ezra's secret."

Aaron gave his best friend a considering look before pushing to his feet. "All right, time to get to work."

I crumpled my burger wrapper and tossed it into the paper bag, my displeasure over Makiko's presence wilting under a tide of nervousness.

Twenty minutes later, I stood in the entryway of Brenda Holloway's apartment building, adjusting my hair. The tangled curls fell past my shoulders, acting as a curtain to hide the small Bluetooth phone in my ear. Our usual earpieces had cords that were way too obvious, so I was borrowing Makiko's sleek little earbud phone instead.

Beside me, with his hands in his pockets, Justin surveyed the dingy foyer with a clinical eye. Neither of us looked directly at the security camera in the corner.

Step one: Get Brenda's attention.

I approached the panel on the wall and dialed the number for B. Holloway. The panel emitted a ringing sound, then a terse female voice answered.

"Who is it?"

"Is this Brenda?" I asked brusquely.

"Yes. Who—"

"I was sent," I interrupted. "You should know by whom."

A confused pause. "I'm sorry, but—"

"I have a delivery for the Praetor."

"Th-the Praetor?" she whispered. "You can't talk about that—"

"Then let me up and I'll explain."

Suspicion stiffened her voice. "I don't recognize you."

I looked up into the camera. My hand dipped into my purse, and I lifted out a small bundle wrapped in a black shroud—my scarf—and tugged the fabric open. The small silver scepter we'd taken from the underground room in Enright glinted.

"Do you recognize *this*?" I asked, exuding a cultishly dreamy air. "We are both blessed by the Goddess's light, fellow *Auditrix*."

A fluttery breath came through the speaker. "Oh. Please come up, then. Unit 506."

The security door buzzed, and Justin pulled it open. We crossed to the elevator and I pressed the button.

As the doors opened with a quiet chime, I murmured. "We're heading up. Fifth floor."

"*Copy that*," Kai murmured through the Bluetooth phone in my ear.

We rode the elevator up and disembarked. The gray-carpeted hallway was as drab and unwelcoming as the lobby downstairs. I glanced at the nearest unit numbers, then headed right. Justin followed.

At the far end of the hall, Aaron flashed me a grin before stepping out of sight. He and Kai had broken in through the rear exit and were stationed nearby, ready to act. Makiko was patrolling at ground level in case Brenda somehow made it past them.

I knocked on the door to unit 506. The bolt clacked and a sliver of a long, plain face appeared.

"You have a delivery for the Praetor?" she whispered.

Stepping closer, I flashed the top of the scepter, where it was tucked in my purse again. "Yes, but he's not home. We were supposed to meet."

"I see. The Praetor is—"

With a rustle of movement, another face appeared above Brenda's—a male face. Neatly combed hair, a smooth jaw, and a cleft in his chin. He peered at me.

"I can handle this, Daniel," she muttered out of the corner of her mouth, trying to elbow him away. "She's looking for the Praetor and—"

"Quiet," Daniel interrupted in a low tenor voice. "You don't want your nieces overhearing anything, do you?"

Brenda glanced nervously over her shoulder, and I picked up the sound of the TV. Shit. There were kids in there? We definitely needed to get her out of her apartment and into a better location for our ambush.

"Is there somewhere else we can talk?" I asked. "A private room in the building here, maybe?"

Her brow scrunched. "Well, there's the terrace …"

"The terrace will work," I said quickly, quashing a triumphant smile. Aaron and Kai had already scouted the rooftop terrace. It was the perfect place for a little nonviolent interrogation.

Daniel grabbed the door and pulled it open. "I'll take them up and find out what they need."

"I can—"

"You need to watch the kids," he snapped commandingly.

Brenda's shoulders hunched, and she backed away from the door. Daniel stepped out into the hallway and closed the door behind him. He was tall but lanky, and around the same age as Justin.

I kept my expression neutral, wondering if this development was good or bad. Daniel, whoever he was, seemed to know at least as much as Brenda about the cult, and I was happy to interrogate him instead. The problem was we knew Brenda was a witch, but this guy could be anything—mage, sorcerer, or even the assassin who'd almost succeeded in using me as a murder weapon to kill Justin.

"This way," he said, leading us back to the elevator. The doors opened immediately, and I followed him inside. Justin joined us, and we rode the elevator up two floors to the terrace.

The elevator dinged, and Daniel gestured for us to go ahead. I reluctantly stepped into the small vestibule, which contained two doors, one marked with a stairwell sign. Justin made a beeline for the unmarked door, and orange light from the setting sun blazed across my eyes as he shoved it open.

Daniel gestured again, so I strode outside as well. The blah concrete terrace featured a few plastic lawn chairs, empty flower pots, and nothing else. Wow. Management wasn't even trying.

Daniel came out right behind me and swung the steel door closed. He leaned against it, assessing us with cool brown eyes.

"So …" I began uncertainly, wondering how to casually alert Aaron and Kai that the man was blocking the door. "What's the, uh, plan?"

"The plan?" Daniel cut in. He pulled a cell phone from his pocket. "Be quiet and I'll find out."

Huh?

He tapped his thumb on the screen, then lifted the phone to his ear. Ah, shit. Was he verifying my very fake story?

"Hey," he said in greeting to whoever had answered his call. "Two of the guild snoops just turned up at Brenda's place."

My heart slammed into my ribcage.

Daniel's lip curled. "I didn't disobey orders. I was *waiting* for orders and they waltzed in on their own." A pause. "Yeah, well,

I've only got two of 'em. That guy, Blain—*Blake*, whatever. He said there were five, didn't he?"

A burning dose of betrayal joined the icy dread in my gut. I frantically ran through all our strategizing, but we hadn't covered this scenario. All I knew was Justin and I weren't supposed to attack anyone—that was Aaron and Kai's job.

"Whatever he reported, this pair clearly hasn't left town." Daniel listened for a moment. "All right. I'll deal with these two, then look around for the others."

Ending the call, he pocketed the device, then gripped the door handle behind him. With a flex of his arm, he snapped it off the door.

My jaw dropped. That was ... not possible, was it? Was the handle faulty? Had it been sabotaged?

"Backup," I muttered frantically. "We need backup."

"*Aaron, get in there,*" Kai barked.

"*The door is jammed!*"

Daniel stepped away from the door, rolling his shoulders to loosen the muscles. "Okay, lady and gent, you have two options. You can jump off this roof and hope you survive the seven-story drop, or you can play with me."

I shoved my hand into my purse and whipped out my paintball gun. Justin's hand appeared from beneath the back of his jacket at the same time, holding his much scarier real gun, and we both leveled our weapons on the mythic.

"Don't move!" I ordered.

He blinked, then threw his head back in a long, humorless laugh. His head came back down and his eyes fixed on me.

A crimson sheen blurred his brown irises.

His arm snapped up. Glowing red lines surged up his arm in twisting veins, and power ballooned in front of his palm.

Before I could fire a shot, the demon mage unleashed an explosion of magic.

The blast of hot power flung me backward. I slammed into a lawn chair and tumbled down, my leather jacket scraping over the concrete. My paintball gun skidded across the terrace.

"*Tori!*" Kai shouted in my ear. "*What's happening?*"

"Demon mage," I gasped, eyes watering from pain.

A hand closed over my hair and yanked my head up. Daniel's crimson-tinted eyes scoured my face, then he ripped the Bluetooth phone from my ear. Across the terrace, the steel door rattled as Aaron tried to break through.

"So, your friends are here too, hmm?" Daniel yanked me hard against his chest as though embracing me, his arm crushing my lungs, and spoke over my head. "Gonna shoot your teammate?"

"Do you think I can't make a headshot at this range?" my brother growled.

I couldn't see Justin with my face mashed against Daniel's shoulder, but he sounded close enough to make the shot. I mentally yelled at him to do it, because I was two seconds from death.

The gun didn't fire.

A distant thud shook the terrace door, but it didn't open—and there was no other way onto the rooftop.

My purse clung to my elbow, and I awkwardly dug into it one-handed, my head spinning as I sucked in shallow breaths of icy air. The temperature around the demon mage was ten degrees colder than the surrounding atmosphere.

His arm tightened, his demonic strength compressing my chest until my ribs creaked. I couldn't breathe at all.

He slashed his other arm. Red power flared and Justin's gasp was followed by a thump. The cold deepened as Daniel prepared a second strike—a lethal one, if I was going to bet.

My fingers closed around a smooth glass ball. I flung my arm out and whipped the sphere into the ground. It shattered and thick smoke billowed out, engulfing us and stinging my nose with its peppery scent.

"What the—" Daniel snarled. His arm unlocked and he shoved me backward. As I fell, he caught the front of my jacket. He lifted me off the ground, my feet swinging helplessly.

His hand, glowing with power, swung to point at my face.

If I'd had my Queen of Spades, I could've reflected his strike back into him. If I'd had my amplifying brass knuckles, I could've knocked him on his ass, demon strength or no demon strength. If I'd had my fall spell, I could've dropped him to the ground.

But I had no magic at all.

Raw demonic power burst off the demon mage's hand—and Hoshi appeared in a swirl of silver.

Her tail looped around me, paws clutching my shoulders, and the world turned to white mist. The blast of crimson magic shot straight through me, and my feet dropped to the ground as his hand slid through my insubstantial jacket.

With the fae holding me in the misty reality between her realm and mine, I bolted away—but between the ethereal haze and the smoke bomb I'd set off, I couldn't see a thing.

"Justin?" I yelled, shoving my purse back up onto my shoulder.

My voice echoed as though I were standing in an empty stadium. I whirled around in a panic—and saw a dark, human-shaped smear crouched nearby. As I leaped toward him, Hoshi's grip loosened. The world rushed back in, and the exhausted sylph sent a swirl of fearful color through my head as she faded from sight.

I grabbed Justin's arm and hauled him toward the faint outline of the terrace door. Blood ran down his face. I couldn't tell how bad the injury was.

Red magic blazed. The demon mage charged out of the smoke, cutting us off. Power snaked over his arms and built up in his palms. His face was twisted with anger, the crimson glow in his eyes even brighter.

Almost bright enough to resemble the eyes of the demon inside him.

"Demon!" I yelled desperately, half stepping in front of my brother. "I know a way to save you!"

"Save me?" Daniel snarled, raising both hands toward me and Justin. The ground around his feet turned white with frost. "Worry about yourself."

"Not *you*. Your demon." I locked my stare on those crimson eyes while digging into my purse. "You don't like your host, do you? You haven't taught him any real spells. He's throwing magic around like a kid chucking mud."

Daniel hesitated, confusion twisting his full lips. A dozen paces behind him, the part of the door next to the latch glowed with heat.

"I can free you from that flesh prison," I said, frantically combing my memory for things Eterran had said. My searching fingers found a cool chain. "Do you know what this is, demon?"

I whipped the demon amulet out of my purse, the medallion swinging.

Daniel's brow furrowed—then his eyes blazed bright red. He snapped straight, back rigid and limbs spasming. With a hoarse cry, he grabbed at his face.

"*No!*" he yelled. "You can't! Stop it!"

Not waiting to see if the demon or the human would win that battle of wills, I hauled Justin past the convulsing mage and toward the door.

"Aaron!" I shrieked desperately.

"Tori!" The door jolted as Aaron slammed into it from the other side. "I'm not through yet!"

Shit!

"You bitch!" Daniel staggered into view, his teeth bared and one hand pressed to his forehead. "You're dead!"

I recoiled, almost bumping the searingly hot door. Power blazed up the demon mage's arms and sizzling orbs of crimson formed in his palms. He drew both arms back to hurl explosive death at me and Justin, and all I could do was clutch the useless demonic amulet.

The wind gusted, blasting the smoke screen to nothing. A violent swirl of dust shot upward like a tornado—spiraling from the street below, surging past the rooftop, and reaching for the clouds above.

In the maelstrom's center, Makiko rose, arms held straight out to her sides and a steel fan in each hand, like a raven-haired, leather-clad angel of death. The wind swept her onto the rooftop, and the moment her feet touched down, her fans slashed.

A brutal gust of air threw the demon mage back. He crashed to the ground, rolled, and came up on his knees, simultaneously hurling his two death-orbs at the aeromage.

Her fans whipped downward as she sprang into the air. A hurricane-force gust flung her upward, and the blast exploded against the rooftop where she'd been standing, hunks of concrete hurtling across the terrace.

Heat surged at my back, then Aaron slammed into the door. The softened metal gave way—and the door whipped into my arm.

I staggered sideways. Ow.

"Shit!" Aaron barked. "Blocking the door isn't helping, Tori!"

Yeah, I'd figured that out.

He leaped past me, and Kai followed on his heels. Electricity rippled up his arms and down the blade of his katana, and as he and Aaron lifted their swords, Makiko dropped to the ground and carved the air with her swirling, dancing fans.

Red light blazed in Daniel's eyes.

All three mages unleashed their attacks together. Razor-thin blades of condensed air, a blast of white-hot fire, and a thick bolt of electricity bombarded Daniel—and crimson magic exploded from him. I flinched back, shielding my face as debris battered me.

Red flared even brighter, burning through the haze of dust hanging over the terrace. Crimson runes snaked across the ground, lines and circles and strange shapes crawling through them. A demonic spell—a *real* one.

Two solid, burning crimson eyes stared from Daniel's human face.

"Run!" I yelled. "We have to run!"

Praying they would listen, I grabbed Justin's arm and fled into the vestibule. As I raced for the stairwell, Aaron and Kai burst through the doorway. Aaron pivoted, whipping his sword sideways, and sent a massive wall of flame surging onto the terrace to hold off any pursuit.

We careened down the stairs, sped through the door at the bottom, and bailed out an emergency exit. As we tore across the parking lot, the wind blasted us.

Makiko dropped out of the sky, landed beside Kai, and sprinted ahead. The wind swept into our backs, pushing us faster. Only after we'd raced across the street and onto the university campus did I dare to look back.

A beacon of crimson light glowed on the rooftop. The demon mage stood at its edge, watching us flee—and I knew, even from this distance, that it was the demon and not the human standing there, so still and calm.

I stuffed the demonic amulet back into my purse and kept running.

17

"HOLD STILL," I GRUMPED. "This will help."

Sitting in the back of the SUV under the open hatch, Justin clenched his jaw. I combed his hair aside to expose the cut on his scalp, which was leaking blood all over his face. Lucky for him, he hadn't taken the full force of the demon mage's attack. If he had, he'd be in way worse shape than a knock to the head.

Uncorking a vial from my potion stash, I dribbled clear liquid over the cut.

"This will stop the bleeding," I told him, "but it won't help with a concussion, so if you start feeling—"

"I'll let you know if I have any concussion symptoms," he interrupted, taking the damp paper towel I was offering. He scrubbed his face.

Behind me, Aaron was pacing the gas station parking lot with his hands clenched. "The Praetor didn't figure out we were investigating him. Blake *told him*. That's why the Praetor disappeared. I never should've trusted him."

Anger burned in my gut—along with an unhealthy dose of shame. Blake had played us for fools.

"He's a member of the Keys of Solomon, though," Kai pointed out, straddling his bike with his arms braced on the handlebars. "Felix looked him up, right?"

"Why would a Keys of Solomon member be part of the cult?" I asked, sitting beside Justin. Dirt from the bumper smeared my leather pants, but I didn't care; all my muscles ached and I had too many bruises to count. "Did Blake make up that whole story about his team dying during the extermination?"

"Probably," Aaron growled. "And then he beat us to the Praetor's house and ..." His pacing slowed. "But if he's in league with the cult, why didn't he stop us from witnessing their meeting? He had plenty of time to warn the Praetor to cancel the gathering."

"Did the cult capture him after we parted ways?" Makiko suggested as she balanced her helmet on the front of her bike. "From what you've described, it doesn't seem like he was protecting the cult from the start. Perhaps they took him prisoner."

"Or blackmailed him," Justin added. "Daniel said Blake *reported* that we were leaving town."

Aaron pressed his fist into his palm, his knuckles cracking. "I know where he stayed last night. He was complaining about the traffic noise at his hotel."

Kai straightened. "Then let's see if he's still there."

After a quick perusal of Google Maps for directions, we clambered into—or onto—our various vehicles and took off,

Aaron's SUV leading the way with the two motorcycles following. I drummed my hands on my knees with nervousness.

I'd saved my purse, but I'd lost my paintball gun on that rooftop. Hoshi had exhausted herself saving me, meaning I was down to a handful of alchemy bombs and first-aid potions. Pretty soon I'd have nothing left to fight with.

No real mythic would find themselves with no magic. A sorcerer with no artifacts could still draw a cantrip. A witch could ... I frowned ... call a fae? See into the fae demesne? Hmm. Maybe there was a reason you didn't see many combat witches.

Blake's hotel was a standard two-star outfit—four stories, faded beige exterior that hadn't been updated in thirty years, no balconies—that backed onto a huge sports field. Aaron pulled into the lot and parked beside a cube van that would hide his vehicle from the front doors.

"Okay," he said as he cut the engine. "Kai and I will scout the building, and Makiko will go inside and—"

I rolled my eyes. "We know the plan, Aaron."

He rolled his eyes back at me. "Then get going. And remember our first fight with Blake. He wasn't trying to kill us then, but this time he might."

While he grabbed his sword, safely hidden in its black zippered bag, from the back, I buckled on my combat belt and its three whole alchemy bombs. The empty holster on the side was downright depressing, especially since the weapon had been a present from the guys. I slid the demonic amulet into a pouch and zipped it shut.

Kai and Makiko parked their bikes, and with a quick wave, Kai headed in one direction while Makiko strode toward the hotel entrance. Blake was less likely to recognize her, so she'd try to lure him out—plus she was scary lethal, so why not send her into enemy territory?

As Aaron zoomed away, Justin and I headed through the parking lot. His pistol was tucked in the back of his belt, hidden by his jacket, but the firearm seemed like scant protection when my brother was limping with each step.

And Blake, as we'd already experienced, had some nasty tricks up his sleeve. How easily could he break our bones or shatter our skulls with well-aimed battering rams of stone and concrete?

I slowed, one hand resting on a smoke bomb as I scanned the lot. "Justin, maybe you should—"

"Don't tell me to wait in the car."

"But you're—"

"You're limping too."

I was? My left hip ached from the demon mage's first blast of magic, but I hadn't realized it was affecting my gait. Grimacing, I assessed the rows of parked cars, then angled around the corner of the building toward the back lot, my eyes darting for any signs of movement.

"According to other mythics I know, demon mages are the most powerful mythics out there," I told Justin. "But Daniel was a wuss compared to—uh, compared to the stories I've heard."

I'd almost said Ezra's name. Smart, Tori. Very smart.

"And he still kicked our asses," I added darkly.

"*Was* he a wuss?" Justin asked. "He fended off three mages, and you said mages tend to have the most destructive magic of all the classes."

My brother was a fast learner. Despite myself, I was kinda proud.

"True," I agreed, slowing to peer between two trucks. "But it wasn't Daniel fending them off. It was the demon inside him. The demon took over at the end. That's why I was yelling at everyone to run."

Justin considered that as we moved to the next row of cars. "Ezra is a demon mage, isn't he?"

I missed a step and almost fell. "What? You—how did you—"

"I guessed."

Damn it. My brother was *too* swift on the uptake.

"The cult turned him into a demon mage when he was fourteen," I explained tersely. "If anyone finds out, he'll be executed. I'm trying to find a way to get the demon out of him."

"You're in love with a man who has a demon inside him?"

I scowled. "Butt out, Justin."

"But—"

"He's a normal guy ninety-eight percent of the time."

Justin eyed me, then pointed. "There it is."

A camo-painted jeep was parked under the bare branches of a large tree at the very back of the lot where it bordered the sunset-bathed sports field.

"Bingo!" I exclaimed.

I took an eager step toward the vehicle, and Justin grabbed my arm. Right. Caution. We circled wide, ensuring there was no one in or around the vehicle, then warily approached from the far side.

With a final check that Blake or anyone else wasn't about to ambush us, I crouched beside one of the jeep's big, deep-tread tires. My hip twinged painfully, but I ignored it as I unscrewed the cap from the air valve. I scrabbled around on the pavement, found a likely pebble, and stuffed one end into the cap. Then I jammed it against the air valve.

Air whooshed out of the tire, and I grinned in satisfaction.

Justin crouched beside me. "Why do I get the impression you've done this before?"

"I *never* let the air out of Dad's tires when I was mad at him," I lied breezily. "And I never did it to Mrs. Keswick either, even when she put me in detention for a month because I kept coming to school without a jacket. I didn't have a jacket! How was punishing me supposed to change that? And that social worker who thought Dad was *so* charming and I was a big liar, I never—"

"Okay, okay." He poked his head over the jeep's hood to scan the lot, then ducked behind it again. "If it comes down to a fight with Blake, am I allowed to shoot to kill?"

A chill ran over me. "Uh …"

"To be clear, I'm only asking so I know how upset you'll be. If it looks like he's aiming to kill, I *will* shoot him."

I nodded. He said nothing more, and I watched as he checked again for any suspicious activity in the abandoned parking lot.

"Justin," I muttered as air hissed from the tire. "You shouldn't kill anyone to protect me. You don't need that on your conscience."

"I already shot someone to protect you," he reminded me. "And I'll do it again if I have to. I just wish I was better equipped. When that demon mage had you, I couldn't risk the shot. He was so fast. He moved like nothing I've ever seen before, and …" His hand drifted toward his hidden gun. "What can a human do against a mythic like that?"

My chest constricted. I watched the jeep's nose slowly drop, hardly seeing it. What *could* a human do? Nothing. Just like I hadn't been able to do anything useful since the Carapace of Valdurna had rendered all my artifacts useless.

The tire wheezed as the rim settled against the deflated rubber, and I replaced the valve cap. "Okay. Blake won't be escaping in his jeep now, so let's go find a spot to hide."

Justin nodded and started to rise. His leg buckled, and he caught himself on the jeep.

"Just stiff," he grunted as I reached for him. "I'm fine."

"Okay, well, just wait there a moment while I pick a hiding spot." I backed away from him. "Stay there."

"I'll stay here."

Nodding, I crept to the jeep's bumper, peeked out, then stepped onto the winter-brown grass. Ducking behind a large tree that would provide welcome shade for the parking lot in the summer, I skimmed my surroundings. Anxious energy infused my limbs, and my protective instincts had kicked into high gear. Justin's leg might not hold out if we needed to flee, and us two against Blake would require a full commitment to running like hell.

As I scanned for a likely hiding spot—aside from a few more thick-trunked trees, none—a different nervousness twanged through me. How long had it been since Aaron and Kai had set off to scout the property? It wasn't *that* large. Had they found Blake and that's why they hadn't returned?

Should I have heard something by now? Were Aaron and Kai all right?

Just as I was about to panic, I spotted a dark figure slinking alongside the building. That smooth gait and those fitted leather clothes were recognizable even in the poor lighting, and I relaxed.

"Kai," I whisper-called as he drew nearer. "What's happening? Did you find Blake?"

He drew closer, eyebrows furrowing as his dark eyes scanned my face. He halted a lot nearer to me than he usually would, and I took a surprised step away, my back hitting the tree behind me.

"Tori …" he murmured. "Don't be afraid."

"Huh? I'm not …"

My voice died as he shifted closer—which put him really, *really* close. Mind spinning, I tried to peek sideways to see if we were being watched or something. Was he putting on an act?

"Tori, I've been wanting to tell you …"

His voice dropped from a murmur to a whisper, and as my gaze darted back to him, his hands touched my shoulders. I tensed, waiting for a signal—for some indication of what I was supposed to do.

"I missed you, Tori."

Eh?

While I stared at him, his hands tightened on my shoulders. He leaned in.

And he kissed me.

As his warm mouth pressed against mine, my brain flew into overdrive. Why was he kissing me? Was this a diversion? *What the actual hell?*

I made a small, questioning noise against his lips, and his fingers dug into my shoulders. All the hair on my body stood on end. A strange, tight feeling stretched my skin, and my nerves buzzed with a sensation somewhere between adrenaline and excitement.

The sensation intensified. A weird vibration twitched my muscles as something built up inside me.

Lightning blasted through me.

I went as rigid as a pole, every muscle locking harder than it ever had before. Burning agony lanced every nerve and I couldn't breathe, couldn't scream, couldn't think as a raging current ripped through my body, racing from his hands to the ground under my feet.

Kai was kissing me and he was electrocuting me. He was going to kill me.

Thumping, running footsteps, then an impact.

The electric current cut off as I crashed to the ground, a body half on top of me. An alchemy bomb shattered under my hip, and an ear-splitting bang erupted, accompanied by a blinding flash.

Arms clamped around me, hauling my limp body half up.

"Tori!" Justin shouted. "*Tori!*"

Through blurred vision, I saw Kai roll to his feet. Turning to me and Justin, he raised his arm. White power arced between his fingers and sizzled up to his shoulder. His face was strangely blank, as though he were completely unbothered by Justin tackling him to the ground in the middle of his kiss-and-die attack.

I don't know what made me look, but my gaze slid left.

She stood a dozen paces away in the shadows of another tree, dressed in slim-fitting black clothes with her raven hair pulled up into a ponytail. She held a silver chain with a disc-shaped pendant on the end, spinning it around and around on her finger as she watched us.

Our eyes met. She pursed her lips and blew me a mocking kiss.

At the same moment, Kai stretched his arm toward me, his hand balled into a fist. His fingers snapped open—and a bolt of electricity shot for my chest.

A howling gust of wind struck us. I hit the ground a second time, Justin crushing me as he fell too.

"Don't move, Kai!" Makiko shouted. "Stay down!"

I dragged my head up. Makiko stood over Kai, steel fans aimed at him. From thirty yards away, Aaron sprinted toward them. Neither was looking toward the tree. Neither had seen the woman.

Justin was right beside me, and his shirt had slid up when he'd fallen—revealing his gun tucked in his belt. I grabbed the weapon, swung it up, and pulled the trigger three times in swift succession.

My aim was normally good, but my arms were still trembling and the shots missed. The assassin dodged behind the tree, and an instant later, rippling blades of air struck the trunk, flung by Makiko and her fans. The aeromage vaulted toward the woman, and with a furious roar, Aaron changed direction, closing in on the assassin from the other side. Fire blazed over his forearms.

The mentalist spun away from the tree and ran between two vehicles. Her dark ponytail, streaming like a flag, darted through the parking lot.

Aaron ran into the lot after her, and Makiko streaked away in pursuit.

"Tori," Kai croaked.

I twitched fearfully, but when my gaze found his face, my fear vanished. Horror and guilt twisted his features, his hands shaking as he pushed up onto his knees. I recognized the torment in his dark eyes. I knew *exactly* how he felt—because I'd felt the same after nearly shooting Justin.

Knowing what he needed, I reached out. He pulled me into his arms and fell backward as I slumped limply against him. Clamping me against his chest, he sucked in an unsteady breath.

"I'm so sorry," he whispered. "I didn't realize what I was—"

"I know." I clutched him, arms around his neck. "She did it to me too."

Justin shuffled closer to us, crouched awkwardly as though ready to leap up in an instant. "Does Tori need to go to a hospital?"

"No." Kai loosened his grip on me. "But a checkup with a healer and a potion for burns would be a good idea."

That did sound like a good idea. I felt like I'd been cooked from the inside out, and it hurt like a bitch.

"What kind of game is that woman playing?" I snarled, sitting up. "Is she toying with us? Making you kiss me, then electrocute me to death as slowly as possible?"

Kai shook his head. "The only reason I didn't kill you instantly was because I hadn't built up a lethal charge. I can't create electricity instantly the way Aaron does with his fire."

"What about the kiss thing?"

His expression darkened. "Maybe she made me kiss you while I killed you for the same reason she tried to make you kill your brother with his own gun."

Before I could ask what he meant, the sound of stomping footsteps interrupted us, but it wasn't Aaron or Makiko returning.

"*What the hell?*"

Blake's annoyed shout rang across the lawn. The terramage strode toward us from the hotel's main entrance, his quarterstaff thumping the ground with each step.

Panic shot through me, and Kai shoved to his feet, hauling me with him. Justin scrambled up, favoring one leg. As Blake stalked closer, I braced for the first attack, desperately hoping Kai had some lightning juice left.

He stopped a few paces away, scowling. "I heard someone babbling about gunshots and a man on fire in the parking lot. They called the police." He thumped his staff against the ground. "You said you were leaving!"

I stared at the terramage, confused as hell. First, why would he approach us like this when he could've attacked us from a distance, which was the terramage specialty? And second, his expression was all annoyance.

No apprehension. No real anger. No twitchy nervousness, fearful glances at his surroundings, or suppressed loathing—which meant our sudden appearance neither concerned him nor angered him.

Either he was the world's best actor, or he was neither a cultist nor being blackmailed by the cult.

"Oh *shit*," I blurted.

Kai and Justin looked at me with tense frowns.

"The assassin wasn't here for us. She was here for *Blake*, and we got in the way." I pointed at the terramage. "Someone else in the Keys of Solomon is a cultist mole, and that person wants us all dead—including you, Blake."

18

I FELT SO MUCH BETTER. Really fantastic. My whole body was numb and a little chilled, and damn, I was enjoying it. Getting internally barbequed had not been fun.

Perched on the edge of a clinical bed in an otherwise nice bedroom, I waved cheerily at the healer's back as she exited through the open door. I waited approximately eight seconds, then bounced out into the hall. Following the sound of a rumbling male voice, I found a living room—or rather, the waiting room. Healers' houses were weird that way.

"Hellooo," I sang cheerily. "How are y—"

Aaron, Kai, and Makiko all shushed me. Scrunching my nose, I stuck out my tongue at them.

Blake was pacing at the other end of the room, his phone held to his ear. "Right ... I appreciate your help. Yes, I'll do that. Take care."

He ended the call, then turned to the trio on the sofa. "Same thing. That's four guild members who hadn't heard anything about trouble in Enright or any teams being sent to Portland. It looks like my reports never made it to the rest of the guild."

"Who were you reporting to?" Kai asked.

"The fifth officer. I don't know him well. We've only met in person a handful of times."

I planted my hands on my hips. "The officer must be the mole, then. He sent an assassin after us."

An assassin who, despite having two mages hot on her heels, had disappeared right out from under their noses.

"The GM could be the mole for all we know," Aaron countered. He gave me a squinty once-over. "How're you feeling?"

"Really freakin' fine. Karen hooked me up with the good stuff." I twirled in a graceless pirouette and finished it with a karate chop. "I'm ready. Let's kick some cultist traitor ass."

Everyone stared at me.

"Where's Justin?" I asked, shrugging off their judgy looks. "Did he get some happy potion too?"

"Turns out he did have a concussion. Karen is still working on him, but she said he'd be good to go in an hour."

"That's good." I squinched my gaze in Blake's direction. "So how will we identify the cult mole in the Keys? If we find them, we can find the Praetor."

Blake rubbed a hand over his face and into his messy fauxhawk. "I can't uncover a mole by myself. My mentor, the second officer, has been with the guild for twenty years. He predates the Enright cult and has a real hatred for demons to boot."

"You trust him?" Kai asked.

"With my life." Blake raised his phone. "Let's see what he has to say."

As the terramage pulled up the officer's contact info on his phone, I dropped onto the sofa between Aaron and Kai—except it was a three-person sofa with three people already on it. I landed on their thighs, half-sinking into the gap between them.

"Budge over," I ordered.

Snorting, Aaron pressed into the armrest while Kai slid over until he and Makiko were nearly sharing the same cushion. I leaned back with a satisfied smile.

"I missed you guys," I murmured, slinging my arms over their broad shoulders.

Aaron bumped my side with his elbow. "I never went anywhere."

"Yeah, but when Kai isn't around, it's as though part of you goes missing too. You're like a lightbulb with half its glowy wire thing burnt out."

He shook his head. "That was almost poetic, then you ruined it."

"Meh, you know what I mean. You're gloomy without Kai."

Blake's phone rang on speaker.

"Russel here," a gruff voice answered.

"Russel, it's Blake. Are you in a private location?"

A pause. "I can be. One moment." Muffled noises, followed by a door closing. "Go ahead."

"Are you aware of my recent report about the discovery of an active sect of the Enright cult in Portland?"

"The Enright—" A garbled curse. "No, I was not aware. When did you report this?"

"Two days ago. I spoke directly to Anand, who said he'd send two teams to investigate immediately. I don't think those teams were ever sent. As well, information I reported about the guild that spearheaded the investigation was leaked back to the cult."

"How do you know that?"

"A demon mage from the cult referenced details from my report. I don't see how he could've gotten the information from any other source."

A sharp inhalation. "There's a demon mage in Portland? Right now?"

"Yes, sir. No ID yet. He isn't in the database."

"Have you reported this to the MPD?"

"Not yet."

I squirmed guiltily. We had quite a few reasons for not reporting the demon mage—starting with how the Crow and Hammer wasn't licensed for international bounty work and finishing with how we were hiding a demon mage of our own—but I didn't know Blake's rationale. Maybe it was the Keys' policy to report Demonica crimes only after the guild had gotten a shot at "the kill."

Russel breathed into his phone for several long seconds. "Blake, return to HQ as quickly as possible—and bring the other guild team that's investigating, if they're willing to come. I may need their testimonies."

"What about the demon mage? And the other cult members—"

"They aren't going anywhere. We need to deal with the information leak here first. I can't move our best teams into Portland to exterminate a demon mage without risking the cult finding out. Have you spoken to anyone else about this?"

"Not yet."

"Let's keep it that way. And"—his voice roughened with worry—"be careful, Blake. Depending on where the leak is coming from, this could be very dangerous."

"Understood. Be careful as well, Russel."

"I will. See you soon."

With a click, the line went dead. The terramage let out a long breath, and we all exchanged bleak glances.

"Will you come?" Blake asked. "If Russel wants your testimony, then he probably suspects the fifth officer."

"We need to discuss." I grasped Aaron and Kai by the wrists. "Let's go check on Justin."

They didn't protest as I hauled them out of the living/waiting room and down the hall, leaving Makiko and Blake behind. I didn't actually know where Justin was, so I led the guys into the room where the healer had examined and dosed me.

Closing the door, I leaned back against it. "This is bad."

They nodded in unison.

I lowered my voice to a whisper. "I mean, it's bad enough that the Enright cult is not only still active but somehow has a mole in the very guild that almost wiped them out. But the really bad part is we need a summoning grimoire, and—"

"—and finding one is about to get real complicated," Aaron concluded grimly.

My whole plan was based on the understanding that the cult had been wiped out. I'd come here to search for an abandoned grimoire, not a prized relic the cult would be actively protecting. Kai and Aaron—and Makiko, I supposed—were talented and deadly mages, but they alone couldn't safely take on a demon mage. Not without Ezra.

We might've been able to manage the Praetor and his little circle, but Daniel the Demon Mage had come from somewhere else—and was taking orders from *someone* else.

I pressed my hands to my face, a tremor running through me as icy despair drained the strength from my limbs. "We're so screwed. What are we going to do? Ezra won't last much longer, and with the Keys involved, there's no way to find a grimoire. We—we're just—"

A warm arm settled over my shoulders, and Aaron pulled me against his side. "We're just gonna have to figure out who's pulling the cult's strings, aren't we?"

I slowly lowered my hands, squinting up at him. "But—"

"Finding a dead summoner's grimoire was like searching for a needle in a haystack." A hard, decisive note edged Kai's voice. "But somewhere, there's a living person running this show. If we unmask them, we'll find their grimoire."

"We just have to make sure we get our hands on it before the Keys do," Aaron added.

I stared between them, still tucked under Aaron's arm. "But—"

"But what, Tori?" Kai's dark eyes fixed on me. "You don't think we'll let you give up *now*, do you?"

"Especially after you dragged us both out here." Aaron smirked down at me. "We've already got an invite to the Keys of Solomon guild. Let's use it to get at the guild mole—and through him, we'll find their leader."

"We can save Ezra *and* take down a cult." Kai smiled. "I like it."

My answering smile wobbled, tears pricking my eyes. This trip had been a frickin' rollercoaster ride of conflicting feelings, and I felt like a ping-pong ball being whacked between opposing emotional states.

"Where are the Keys' headquarters?" I asked. "Are we gonna have to drive all night again?"

"It's in Salt Lake City, as I recall. Utah," Kai added helpfully. "About a day's drive to the southeast."

I pretended like I'd known that, but when it came to US geography, my trivia skills were patchy at best. "So we'll be driving all night, then."

"We could ..." Kai's thoughtful gaze drifted toward the out-of-sight living room. "But why drive when you can fly? I'll talk to Makiko."

He swept out of the room, leaving me blinking in confusion. Shaking my head, I leaned into Aaron, eyes closing tiredly. The buzz from the healer's potion was fading fast, and I really wanted a nap. Or better yet, a full night's sleep.

"We can't give up," I whispered. "We have to keep going ... but what if we take too long? What if we're too late, and Ezra ... Going to Salt Lake City will take us even farther away from him." Cracking my eyes open, I hesitated. "Should we tell him? That the Enright cult survived?"

Aaron was silent for a long moment. "There's a line between keeping secrets because the consequences of the truth scare you, and keeping secrets because you need to be beside someone when you share the truth."

I exhaled shakily. "You're right. That isn't a bombshell we can drop on him over the phone, especially when he's all alone."

"We'll fill him in once we're back—and we'll be returning with good news, right?" He flashed an encouraging grin. "Why don't you get a few minutes of rest?"

"Yeah," I mumbled.

Cold washed over me as Aaron moved away, taking his body heat with him. The door closed softly behind him, and I shuffled over to the bed and sat. My own words circled in my head.

What if we take too long? What if we're too late?

… he's all alone.

I pressed a hand to my quivering lips. Less than a week ago, Ezra had almost succumbed to madness. He knew his life was essentially over, and in this most painful, frightening, vulnerable time, I'd not only left him behind, but I'd taken his best friends with me.

If Ezra lost his hold and slipped away before we made it back …

He had to hold on. He had to survive until we returned, otherwise I couldn't bear it—couldn't bear failing him, couldn't bear taking his friends away in his final days, couldn't bear that I'd never found the right time to tell him how I felt.

Aaron's voice repeated in my ears. *There's a line between keeping secrets because the consequences of the truth scare you …*

Whether he'd meant the words as a chastisement, I felt the sting anyway. I'd hidden so much, telling myself over and over that it wasn't the right time to divulge the truth—it wasn't the *perfect* time. And I'd kept on delaying, and delaying, and delaying some more.

And I'd hurt Ezra. I'd hurt Aaron. I'd probably hurt Kai too, though he hid his feelings better.

Why was I still hiding things from the people I loved? Was I afraid to trust? Did I lack faith in them, as Aaron had told me on our way to Enright when I'd revealed my feelings for Ezra?

Months and months ago, during my first tarot reading, Sabrina had told me that change waited for me, but it would be shaped by the fear in my heart—and a week ago, she'd reminded me once more.

Your past and your fears are still holding you back. And as she'd pulled the Death card from her deck yet again, her whispered warning: *I think you need to tell him soon.*

The same sickening fear I'd felt then swamped me, and I dug my phone out of my pocket. When I unlocked it, my messaging app was already open, displaying the string of unanswered texts I'd sent Ezra over the past two days.

I tapped to start a new message. My heart thudded against my ribs, a drumbeat to the chorus of panicked denials in my head. I should wait. I should tell him in person, face to face. This was the coward's way out.

But Aaron's wisdom. *The consequences of the truth scare you.*

But Sabrina's warning. *You need to tell him soon.*

Gulping back the shuddering anxiety, I typed three words and hit send before I could second-guess myself anymore. The message popped into the conversation history, immortalized forever in digital form. I'd done it. I'd said it … or, well, written it.

I didn't know how to feel. Was terror a normal reaction to something like this?

Holding my phone in both hands, I waited. Voices rumbled in the other room. A door opened and closed with a thump. Footsteps in the hall. More purposeful talking as the others planned our urgent excursion to Utah.

I held my phone, waiting.

Waiting.

Waiting.

Eventually, Aaron tapped on the door. Opened it. Told me we were heading out in a few minutes. Was I ready? I should meet everyone in the living room right away. The door closed again.

I slid my fingers across the phone screen, swiping away the text app. Then I wiped the cold trails of tears off my cheeks, pocketed my phone, and got to my feet.

The consequences of the truth ... they hurt like a bitch.

◆ EZRA ◆

ONE OF AARON'S generic rock playlists blasted from the speakers in the corner, the beat thudding in my chest as I hung from the pull-up bar. Weights dangled from the thick belt I wore, dragging at my hips.

I drew my body up with one arm until my chin passed the bar. The weights clanked against my thighs as I held the position, then slowly lowered. My arm burned. It wasn't enough.

Finishing the rep, I dropped to the floor, unbuckled the weight belt, and set it aside. My bare feet padded across the mats as I walked to the shelf with the speakers and picked up my phone to change the playlist.

A notification glowed on the screen. A new text from Tori.

Over the past two days, she hadn't sent me any details on what she and Aaron were up to. I knew from Aaron that they were following a lead and had left Enright, but I didn't know what the lead was and hadn't asked.

Tori's initial messages had been longer—apologies and questions and worries. This last day, however, her messages had been short, with no questions or pleas for a reply, as though she no longer expected me to answer.

I'm so sorry.

I wish you were here.

I hope you're okay.

I miss you.

Phone balanced on my palm, I tapped her newest message. The short text bloomed on the screen, three simple words that struck my chest like a blow from a demon's fist.

I stared at those three words, unable to breathe. My hand spasmed around the phone and with a muffled pop, its case cracked. I shoved it onto the shelf before I broke the screen and backed away, air rasping in my lungs.

Now? How could she say that now? *Why now?*

The inky presence inside me stirred. Eterran's focus cut across my mind like a blade.

Calm down, Ezra.

Be quiet!

Whirling, I was across the basement in a flash—and my fist slammed into the punching bag. It swung away, and as it came back, I hammered it again. And again. And again.

It did nothing to calm the storm inside me.

How could she say that? She didn't know me. *I* didn't know me. Who was I without this demon, this power, this doom hanging over me?

Eterran's thoughts and emotions flickered at the edge of my awareness, his black presence a mocking contrast to Tori's words.

Be quiet! I slammed the bag, a heavy-duty brand Aaron had chosen to withstand my strength. *Be quiet!* Another hit, my knuckles driving into thick leather. *Be quiet!*

He was still there. Always there. Never gone.

Sometimes, he was so quiet I could almost forget about him—almost. He would slip into a sort of trance where his mind would go very, very quiet. As long as I kept my thoughts and emotions calm, he would hibernate and I'd be free of him. The longest he'd ever slept was three weeks, but the constant monitoring of my own state of mind had been a different distraction, a different strain.

There was no way out. For ten years, I'd fought him— fought for control, for emotional separation, for distance, for silence, for privacy, for peace. I was so fucking exhausted.

So am I.

"Be—*quiet*," I gasped, hitting the bag again. Hammering it. Now my muscles were truly burning, and I welcomed the pain. "You *never* leave me alone."

How can I?

"Go to sleep."

I can't do that when you're like this.

I slammed the bag again. *You're not even trying.*

No. A piercing cut of hatred. *I will not sleep again, Ezra. Not until this is over, one way or another.*

Anger burned through me, followed by cold despair. Tori's message was a flicker of light in the darkness—but she couldn't mean those words. Maybe she thought she did, but she'd only glimpsed the nightmare of what I really was.

"Then I'll end it now," I snarled. "I'll put us both out of this misery."

Eterran's mind scraped against mine, our thoughts tearing at each other.

Liar. You don't want to die.

My teeth clenched so hard pain shot through my jaw. I squeezed my eyes shut as I panted. "I've never wanted to die. That's why I've waited this long."

I know.

I want a life. A real life.

Then why won't you fight for it?

It's impossible.

Eterran shoved a memory at me—Burke's demon, rage and triumph burning in his stare as he drew his arm back, glowing talons aimed for my chest. In his other hand, he held the Vh'alyir Amulet.

It is possible.

I opened my eyes. The punching bag swayed like a pendulum, and I slowed my breathing to match its measured rhythm.

You'll betray me, Eterran. You hate me.

His thoughts whirled in an ebony maelstrom, fueled by a driving, burning need that eclipsed even the blackest despair.

You want to survive, he whispered inside me. *Beneath your guilt and self-loathing and blind determination to protect your friends, you want to live as much as I do.*

My chest tightened until I couldn't take a full breath. Tori's message glowed like a beacon. She didn't know me—the real me, the person I'd lost when I'd let a demon into my body— but maybe we could … maybe …

No. It was impossible.

Yet, by most standards, she'd already accomplished several impossible feats. She was fighting for me right now. How could I give up when she was fighting so hard?

Emotions crashed over me like a wave—all the anger and hurt and betrayal flooding through me again. I flung my fist out. As it crashed into the punching bag, my fury sparked and died. My despair swelled and faded. My pain struck and retreated.

Eterran's fury rose and fell. His despair. His pain.

My fist hit the bag. My breath rushed in and out. The rhythm beat inside me, and Eterran's thoughts turned, aligning with mine. We focused on the bag. On the strike. On the impact of knuckles against leather.

Emotions calmed. Our minds steadied. Our thoughts flickered back and forth, debate, ideas, rebuttals, decisions.

Finally, decisions.

I pivoted away from the punching bag. Calm. Focused. Aligned. My concentration turned inward, slipping into the midst of power I could never fully embrace—not when part of my consciousness was always, *always* occupied by fear of the demon inside me and what he might do.

Spinning on my heel, I slashed my hand sideways, cutting across nothing. The air rippled like a blade.

The bottom half of the punching bag crashed to the floor, sand spilling down. The top half swung from the chain, barely disturbed by the razor blade of air that had cut cleanly through the leather.

Eterran and I studied the ruined bag.

I walked away. After a quick shower, I hastened up the stairs, a towel around my waist and my phone in hand. As I passed the living room, I glanced at the man lounging on the sofa.

Girard, my current babysitter, looked from the TV to me. Darius had ensured I wouldn't be alone at night until Aaron and Tori returned. He, Girard, and Alistair—the only ones besides Aaron, Kai, and Tori who knew my secret—were taking turns watching over me.

"How're you doing?" Girard asked, concern softening his eyes—and grief.

He was already grieving for me and I wasn't even dead yet.

"Fine," I said, ignoring the way his gaze flicked over my scars. I rarely let others see them. "Heading to bed."

"Sure."

I continued up the stairs and into my room. Locking the door, I pulled my towel off and dressed in combat gear. Sliding on my long gloves with metal-plated knuckles and elbows, I paused to listen. The TV rumbled through the floor.

Tori's message filled my phone's screen when I unlocked it, and my throat tightened. I selected a different name from my list of contacts, typed out a quick message, and hit send.

Will she take the bait?

We'll find out.

I walked to my bedroom window. Careful to steady the panel so it wouldn't make noise, I slid it open and popped out the screen.

The two-story drop was no issue—I didn't even need the wind to cushion my fall. Cold air filled my lungs as I breathed deep. Determination was a fire in my chest, chasing away the despair that had hung over me since my near destruction at Varvara's hands.

"Will this work?" I murmured to the silent night. "Robin won't give up answers easily."

It will take us both.

I nodded. Both of us. Aside from brief moments during combat, we hadn't worked together since I'd escaped the commune eight years ago—since I'd doomed my family to death.

As I strode away from the house, I hoped I wasn't about to repeat the worst mistake I'd ever made.

20

I ALMOST, *almost* got to fly to Salt Lake City in the Yamada Syndicate's fancy private jet. But some asshole executive who outranked Makiko decided his desire to go golfing in Bermuda was more important, and he'd commissioned the jet right out from under her.

So instead of traveling in luxurious, criminally funded style, Aaron rented a trailer for Kai's and Makiko's motorcycles and hitched it to his SUV, and we'd set out on the fourteen-hour drive across Oregon, through the southern tip of Idaho, and down into Utah.

Even with the delays caused by sourcing and picking up a trailer, we'd gotten on the road half an hour earlier than Blake. He hadn't been pleased to find his jeep had a newly flat tire— but as I'd assured him with earnest sympathy, I had *no idea* what had happened to his tire. Not me.

He may or may not have bought my act.

I slept most of the night, using Justin's, Kai's, and Aaron's shoulders as pillows whenever one of them was lucky enough to sit beside me in the cramped backseat.

Ten hours later, at our pitstop in Twin Falls, Idaho, I took the wheel. The driving was easy, if tedious. The road was straight and the scenery as flat and featureless as the Canadian prairies. Blake had caught up to us, and with his jeep speeding along in front of me, all I had to do was play follow-the-leader.

An hour in, I was actually missing the nausea-inducing turns from my drive through the Oregon Coast Range.

A vaguely familiar pop song trickled from the car speakers, drowned out by Aaron's low snoring. Kai was in the back, while Justin was taking a turn driving Blake's jeep so the terramage could catch some shuteye.

Makiko sat in the passenger seat beside me, her short legs stretched to the max and her eyes half-lidded with weariness.

I wanted to resent her presence. Okay, yes, I did resent her, but not as much as usual. She hadn't complained once during the long hours in the SUV. No bossy commands or scathing sneers, and she'd even offered to take a driving shift.

When she wasn't ruining Kai's life, she was almost tolerable.

"So," I said in a low voice. "Your plan here is to help us un-demon-mage Ezra, and that way Kai can't be implicated in a demon-mage coverup?"

"Yes. As I already explained."

"You could've just had Ezra killed instead," I pointed out coolly. "That's the crime-family way of things, isn't it?"

She straightened in her seat, shooting me a wintry stare. "Demon mages rarely die without a fight. An assassination could still reveal Ezra as a demon mage, and the MPD would investigate."

I grunted. "And here I thought there might be a smidge of compassion in your black soul."

Her expression hardened. "And you're a perfect angel, aren't you, Tori? You've never had to make hard decisions or hurt your loved ones to protect them."

I couldn't quite hold back my flinch. "*I'm* not forcing anyone to leave their family and live a complete lie."

"But you would if that was the only way to save their life," she retorted matter-of-factly. "Don't bother denying it. You're no different from me."

"I'm nothing like you."

"You snuck into LA and broke into an MPD precinct, endangering your life, Kai's life, and your guild. Was that not to save a friend? You'd do worse than that to save the man you love—like *this*." She gestured at the highway stretching away toward the horizon.

"You're not *saving* Kai. You just want him for yourself."

"While you were demolishing that MPD precinct, I was in LA to plead for Kai's life."

My gaze snapped to her.

"It had just gotten back to the family that he was seeing another woman. The *oyabun* called me and told me he was going to give the order."

"What order?"

"Kai's execution." She exhaled harshly. "He told me as a courtesy, since Kai is my betrothed. I rushed to LA to convince him to give Kai another chance."

A memory flashed—Kai telling me about the anonymous text message he'd received, warning him that "this game" was over.

"You ... convinced him?"

"I swore that Kai was worth far more than an execution, and that he could be redeemed. The *oyabun* had serious doubts." She stared out the windshield. "Then Kai showed up in LA, and the *oyabun* decided to give me the chance to prove I'm right about Kai. If I fail, I'll prove the *oyabun* right instead, and he'll give the order."

As the flat farmland bordering the road shifted from snow-dusted brown to snow-dusted yellow then back to brown, I snuck another glance at Makiko, surprised by the unhappy quirk to her small mouth.

"I know what you're thinking," she said quietly. "You can see he's unhappy, and you think, 'What's the point of saving his life if he's just going to be miserable?' But once he earns his place and the authority that comes with his position, he'll find purpose again."

"What if he doesn't? What if he's never happy there?"

"He will be."

"How can you know that?"

She pressed her lips together. "Because he used to be happy with me."

I forced my attention back to the road, my jaw clenched. The rumble of the tires across the cracked asphalt competed with the fuzzy radio in an annoying background buzz. I peeked in the rearview mirror, checking that my two male passengers were sleeping soundly.

"People grow," I whispered. "They change. I haven't known him as long as you have, but the Kai I know is too independent to ever be happy following someone else's rules."

"And the year or so you've known him makes you an expert?" she retorted, though her tone was more weary than acidic. "Happiness is fleeting, Tori. His life may not be what he wants, but he can find happiness in it. He won't get that chance if he's dead."

Lips pressed tight together, I glanced in the rearview mirror again—and started when I found dark eyes watching me.

Our gazes met in the mirror, then Kai closed his eyes again.

Focusing on the road, I wished magic were the kind from fairytales, where an all-powerful fairy godmother could wave her wand and make all your problems disappear—if only for one night.

But the real world, despite its abundance of real magic, didn't work like that.

IF THE KEYS OF SOLOMON'S headquarters had matched my low opinion of them, we'd be looking at a rundown structure at the back of a junkyard, surrounded by rusting cars, barbed-wire fence, and the grinning skulls of the guild's enemies stuck on poles.

Instead, Makiko—our current driver—parked the SUV beside Blake's jeep in a small lot behind a posh office building, four stories tall with a glass-and-steel exterior that reflected the dull blue sky and hazy light of the afternoon sun.

We piled out of the SUV with much groaning and stretching, and I squinted around. Salt Lake City's downtown was on the quaint side compared to Vancouver, and the Keys' shiny building was one of only a few I could see with such a modern look.

Blake shut the hatch on his jeep, his quarterstaff in hand. "Russel called me about an hour ago. He's waiting for us inside."

"Is that wise?" Kai asked as he pulled his shirt up to buckle a set of throwing knives around his waist. When he dropped the hem of his shirt, the weapons would be completely hidden. "Wouldn't it have been better to meet at a more neutral location?"

"People are constantly coming and going, so your presence shouldn't draw attention." Blake shot off a quick text on his phone. "But I'll ask him to meet us out here."

I joined the others at the hatch, and Aaron passed me my combat belt with its two remaining alchemy bombs and Hoshi tucked in the back pouch, sleeping in her orb form.

A minute later, the building's plain steel door popped open and a tall, well-built man in his fifties walked out. With buzzed gray hair and a steely expression, he embodied every "army sergeant" stereotype ever.

"Blake," he rumbled, extending his hand. "You made good time."

The terramage shook his hand. "No time to waste."

The guild officer nodded, then turned to our group. "And my thanks to you as well for coming out."

"We'll do what we can to help," Aaron said smoothly, stepping forward to clasp hands with the man. "Aaron Sinclair, Crow and Hammer guild."

Russel's eyebrows shot up. "Sinclair?"

Aaron flashed a grin in acknowledgment. "These are my guildmates—Kai, Makiko, Tori, and Justin."

Justin blinked at being included as a guildmate.

We all shook Russel's hand in turn. His grip was strong, his fingers calloused from a lifetime of weapons training.

With introductions out of the way, Russel glanced toward the building. "Anand—the fifth officer and our top suspect—is out on a job, but we shouldn't linger outside. The CT floor is the most private space in the building."

"CT floor?" I questioned.

"Combat training," Blake explained. "It's a basement room reinforced with protective spells and abjuration. It'll work well enough for a meeting."

Russel led us to the steel door, which looked comically puny next to a double-wide overhead door. He punched a code into the security panel and the lock clacked. As we entered a long, nondescript hall with a tiled floor and plain gray walls, I glanced over my shoulder. Justin and Makiko stayed with the vehicles, as planned. They were our backup.

Russel noted that our group had shrunk with an arch of his eyebrows but didn't comment as he headed down the corridor. A trio of heavily muscled men crossed our path a couple dozen paces away, none of them glancing in our direction. It was quiet in a "there are lots of people around but everyone is busy" sort of way.

Following Russel, we descended two floors and entered what I could only describe as an antechamber. The long space contained a wall of lockers labeled with various types of training gear, as well as entrances to a bathroom and a first-aid room, the latter's door open to reveal a tidy space transplanted straight out of a hospital.

Dead ahead was a pair of double doors in thick steel, and Russel swung them open.

The Crow and Hammer's combat training area had nothing on the Keys' version. The room was the size of a gymnasium, with a floor made of hard black rubber. Thick padding covered the walls, and stacks of gear and training equipment filled the far end of the space—from practice dummies to targets to sets of portable walls that could be arranged into makeshift rooms.

Paintball practice in here would be seriously fun.

A wooden table—one that, judging by its scratched surface, was normally used as a prop—sat in the center of the room, several brown folders stacked on it. Standing nearby, two men in their thirties waited.

"Come," Russel said, leading us toward them. "Chay and Piotr are already up to speed. They have my complete trust, and they'll assist with apprehending Anand."

Blake strode ahead of me, Kai, and Aaron, and the two other Keys mythics came around the table to meet him. The terramage shook hands with the stocky blond guy, whose biceps were thick enough to generate their own gravitational force.

"Piotr," he said to the second man as they grasped hands. "Third officer, correct? We met at the AGM last year."

Piotr—a beanpole of a guy with a shiny bald spot, glasses, and a shrewd gleam in his eyes that made Kai seem as wily as a kindergartener—nodded. "I remember. You've been well?"

"Well enough."

Aaron, Kai, and I did the handshake thing too, then we all gathered around the table.

"Let's begin," Russel said. "I had another trusted guild member take Anand out on a job this afternoon. They won't return until I give the signal, so we have time to plan our next moves."

We nodded our agreement.

"Capturing Anand should be straightforward. He's a talented offensive sorcerer, as you can imagine given he's an officer, but he won't be expecting an ambush. As far as he knows, Blake is in Portland and no one here is aware the cult was discovered."

"What about the assassin?" Aaron asked. "Do you think Anand or the cult hired her?"

Russel rubbed his chin thoughtfully.

"Anand knows how to quickly hire an assassin from his work with the guild," Piotr murmured in his hoarse, chain-smoker's voice. "When you observed the cult, did they seem to be civilians or rogues?"

"Civilians," I said firmly. "With the possible exception of the Praetor. He was a contractor."

"We can probably assume Anand is responsible for the assassin," Blake said, swiping his hair off his forehead. "He knew where I was staying, and I suspect he instructed the assassin to follow me to your first rental place. She went for Tori minutes after I'd arrived."

I shuddered at the memory.

"We can confirm once we've detained Anand," Russel decided. "Before that, my concern is the chance, however slim, that there may be more than one mole inside the guild."

"One is already a stretch," Chay growled. "How could they get to more guildeds?"

"The same way they got to Anand, an *officer*," Piotr shot back. "We can't rule it out."

Kai folded his arms. "You also can't rule out the possibility that Anand has corrupted other members. He may not have brought them into the cult, but he could have won loyalties that supersede their loyalty to the guild."

Russel, Piotr, and Chay exchanged unhappy looks.

"That's certainly possible." The creases around Russel's mouth deepened. "We can't assume anything at this point."

"Exactly," Blake said. "We don't even know the true reach of the cult. I doubt the group in Portland is the extent of it. The demon mage doesn't seem to be local. He came from somewhere outside the Portland group."

"How many more people could be involved?" Chay asked. "The cult was wiped out eight years ago."

"Was it?" Kai rubbed his jaw. "Was Enright the core of the cult? What if it was more of ... an extremist offshoot?"

"How could seventy members and a dozen demon mages be an *offshoot*?" I demanded.

Russel fixed his stern gaze on me. "If your goal was to form a group like Enright—tightknit, fiercely loyal, and so committed to your mission that they'd willingly offer themselves up for demonic rituals—how would you find suitable candidates?"

"By creating a religion that isn't as radical," Kai answered tersely. "Lure mythics in with a demon-worshipping sect like the one in Portland, then choose the most fanatic for your extremist commune."

"That approach would create a large pool of likely candidates," Russel agreed, turning to the electramage, "and would allow the leaders to observe or test their top choices before bringing them into the heart of the organization."

"Wait." I looked from Kai to Russel. "Wouldn't that mean there were sects like the one in Portland recruiting cultists for the Enright commune? And those sects ... they just continued to exist after Enright was destroyed? And no one noticed?"

Aaron muttered a curse, and I swallowed hard. If we were right, then the cult had never come close to being stamped out.

Blake thumped his staff against the floor. "What about their infiltration of the Keys, assuming it goes beyond Anand? What's the point of that?"

Russel straightened. "What better way to ensure your organization remains undetected than by infiltrating, and eventually controlling, the foremost demon hunters on the continent?"

"*Controlling?*" Blake shook his head. "Impossible."

"Win the loyalty of key figures and you can control any group."

A knock on the metal doors echoed through the training room. Piotr and Chay tensed.

"Enter!" Russel called loudly.

The door opened and a well-built man with black hair and warm chestnut skin strode inside. A body hung over his shoulder, the person's legs dangling limply in front of his chest.

My blood ran cold.

A second man ambled in after the first, dragging someone behind him by one arm. His lips pulled into a smile, his cheeks flushed.

My fear flashed into full-blown panic.

Daniel, the demon mage from Portland, let his victim drop to the hard floor. Justin's head lolled limply, blood streaking his slack face.

"Don't move," Russel ordered calmly.

It took me a long moment to tear my horrified stare off Justin. My frantic gaze flicked across the other newcomer, who'd dumped his victim on the floor as well—Makiko, her hair tangled and body unmoving—then flashed to the men at the table.

I choked on a gasp.

Piotr held two pistols, the sides of their barrels engraved with runes. He had one gun leveled on Blake and one on Kai. Chay was in front of me and Aaron, though I hadn't noticed him move. He'd conjured two long daggers from somewhere, and one point was aimed at Aaron's throat. The other was inches from my jugular.

Daniel and his pal crossed the room, and Piotr and Chay seamlessly shifted over so that one mythic covered each member of our group. I stared into Daniel's face as he positioned himself in front of me, his mocking smile daring me to try something.

I vibrated with the tension gripping my muscles, terror racing through my veins.

"I expected you sooner, Anand," Russel said to the chestnut-skinned man.

"The little lady was a handful," Anand replied as he studied his hostage, Kai. "Daniel and I had to corner her."

Daniel's smile widened. "I owed her one."

A faint sizzle of electricity ran up Kai's arms.

Russel walked around the table and stopped behind his four men. "You may have delusional ideas about escaping. You are already aware that Daniel is a demon mage, but in case you believe that the three of you can overpower him as well as a heliomage and three guild officers …"

Russel lifted a hand toward Blake, his fingers outspread. The terramage's eyes widened.

"Russel," he began hoarsely. "You—"

Magic sparked over Russel's hand—*crimson* magic. The blazing power snaked up his arm as a glowing circle formed around his outstretched fingers. Runes bloomed inside it, and the temperature plummeted.

With a crackling pulse, a beam of ruby power blasted from Russel's palm.

I didn't mean to, but my brain overrode my conscious command and my eyes squeezed shut. I didn't see the spear of magic strike Blake's broad chest.

But I heard it. The horrific crunch. The thump of a body hitting the floor. The wheezing rasp of breath. The terrible silence that followed, broken by my terrified gasps.

"So, as you see, I have no qualms about killing any of you," Russel said into the silence. "At the first moment of resistance, you will die."

I forced my eyes open. Russel's gaze turned to me, a faint crimson gleam hazing his irises. Tremors shook my limbs, and I was afraid to look at Kai and Aaron beside me.

Justin and Makiko were unconscious. Maybe … maybe dead. And Blake was …

Two demon mages and three powerful mythics had taken us prisoner. And no one, not a single soul outside this room, knew where we were. There would be no rescue.

We'd walked right into the cult's clutches.

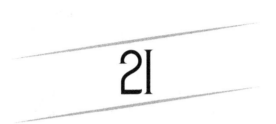

21

"WELL, RUSSEL?" Piotr said in his ugly rasp of a voice.

The second officer, a senior member who'd been with the guild for over twenty years and whom Blake had said he trusted with his life, studied us with eyes that glowed with demonic power. "Before I call the *Magnus Dux*, we'll confirm they haven't spread information about the Court to anyone else."

My rapid breathing filled my ears, and I tried to force my lungs to slow down before I got dizzier. At the same time, I commanded myself not to look toward the doors, where Justin and Makiko lay unmoving.

It was more difficult to ignore Blake and the snaking rivulet of his blood running across the black floor.

Russel pointed at me. "We'll start with her. Women break more easily."

Aaron jerked, red sparks leaping from his clenched fists.

"Hold still," Chay snapped at him. "Unless you want to find out what happens when a heliomage lights a pyromage on fire."

"I'll tell you whatever you want." The snarl in Aaron's voice couldn't hide an edge of fear. "Leave Tori alone."

Russel gestured. Daniel grabbed my arm, hauled me to the table, and threw me down on my back. The folders slid off, papers scattering. Daniel's hand snapped around my throat, powerful fingers squeezing as he held me down, restricting my air.

"Stop it!" Aaron yelled. "I told you—"

"Do you think I'm naïve enough to believe you'd tell me everything?" Russel reached under the table and picked up a black case. He set it beside my shoulder. "I'm afraid what I need to know is too important to trust your word."

"You're a demon hunter," Kai hissed. "Why would you give up your body to a demon?"

As Russel turned his crimson-sheened gaze to Kai, I locked stares with Daniel. He grinned eagerly, more than ready to participate in my interrogation—especially if he got to force answers out of me.

"What better triumph over a demon is there," Russel told Kai, "than to subjugate it in every way—to take its body, defeat its will, and command its magic?"

I wrapped my hands around Daniel's wrist, struggling for air.

"Save us," I gasped, scarcely able to produce sound.

With the click of a latch, Russel opened his case, not noticing Daniel's sudden anger. "Demon mages created using weak-willed fools become weak demon mages who can barely control their demons."

"And I'll save you—"

Russel considered the rows of shiny, terrifying torture instruments in his case as though deciding what to start with. "Not once, in the four years since I underwent the ritual—"

"—with the amulet," I gasped.

"—has my demon gained control of me for even a moment."

Crimson blazed across Daniel's eyes, transforming them into glowing lava.

Daniel lurched back, hands jumping to his face as he shouted in shock. Sucking in a desperate breath of air, I jammed my hand into my belt pouch.

Daniel staggered, fingers digging into his smooth cheeks. "No! I'm in command, you bastard! Stop—"

His eyes blazed brighter, and his furious, desperate expression morphed into jaw-clenching determination, teeth bared in a snarl. His gaze snapped to me. I yanked the amulet out of its pouch and lunged up, arm stretching toward the demon mage.

A hand closed around my forearm and powerful fingers constricted with so much force that blinding pain shot up my arm. I screamed.

Russel's other hand flashed. Crimson blazed over his skin. Daniel—or his demon—thrust out both arms, but power had barely begun to flare over his fingers when Russel's spell unleashed.

A boom of power. Blinding red light.

Daniel flew twenty feet and smashed into the wall. He slid down it to the floor, leaving a smear of blood on the polyester padding.

Russel dug his fingers into my arm. The demonic amulet swung like a pendulum, its chain still clutched in my hand.

His eyes narrowed as he studied it. "And what might this be?"

My jaw clenched. Blinking away tears of pain, I flicked a glance at Aaron and Kai, warning them to hold still. They didn't react, their faces white and limbs rigid.

"An arcane artifact, Piotr?" Russel inquired. "Or an infernus?"

"I'm not certain."

"Hmm." Russel extended his hand, palm turned up as though to scoop the pendant out of the air.

I dropped the chain.

It's an irresistible reflex: when you're about to take hold of something and it falls, you catch it. Simple. Instinctive.

Russel caught the falling medallion with his enhanced reflexes, his fingers closing tightly around it. He straightened, the chain hanging off his fist, and frowned at me.

I stared back, terrified out of my mind while also hoping desperately.

Russel opened his mouth—and his eyes flashed to red.

He reeled back, amulet crushed in his fist. Demonic power exploded across his limbs and streaked over him in crawling veins. His mouth gaped, face contorting. Scarlet lines raced up his face to his temples, forming phantom horns.

I lurched off the table, falling awkwardly to the floor as I put the flimsy barrier between me and the demon mage. Russel convulsed, then dropped to his knees. Quaking. Heaving. Magic rippled off him, condensing—forming into wings that rose off his back and a thick tail with fur that ran down its length.

He arched backward, chest thrown out, head hanging back as a horrific scream tore through his throat.

A second voice joined his in a deep roar of primal rage.

The glowing power covering Russel's entire body shimmered like heatwaves, then bulged outward. A different face tore away from the human's—a terrible face with bared fangs, formed of the same semi-transparent power as the horns and wings.

Shoulders appeared, doubled over Russel's. The demon writhed like a nightmare version of a butterfly wriggling from its cocoon, all while Russel screamed as though he were being ripped apart.

Blood splattered the floor.

Where veins of power marked his skin, Russel's flesh split open. Blood ran and he shuddered violently. The demon's phantom face flashed from triumphant rage to fear, and it wrenched from its host in a sudden panic.

Russel pitched over backward, limbs jerking. The phantom demon convulsed with him, its wings slapping the floor with echoing thumps. It fought more frantically to tear away from its host, but the harder it tried, the more blood splashed across the floor.

With a gurgling cry, Russel arched his whole body. The demon howled—a sound of fury and despair—then Russel slumped limply. The raging glow of the demon's phantom eyes dimmed, and its radiant power softened, losing its shape. The scarlet light faded, leaving only the human.

The human, lying in a pool of blood. Not moving. Not breathing. His slack fingers had uncurled, and the Vh'alyir Amulet glinted on his palm.

Crouched beside the table, all I could do was stare. Aaron and Kai stood frozen with horror, and even Chay, Piotr, and Anand had been shocked into disbelieving stillness.

A red glow blazed through the room.

As one, we all spun around. Daniel was back on his feet—or his demon was. Despite the blood drenching his torso, power crawled over him, phantom spines jutting from his shoulders and horns rising from his head.

His arms were outstretched, heels of his hands pressed together, fingers curled. Power built in the spherical gap between his palms, rings of lines and runes spiraling outward. The demon bared his human teeth and closed his hands on the orb of power.

It snuffed out—and magic burst out of the floor beneath Chay, Piotr, and Anand. Phantom blades shaped like monstrous fangs shot upward, spearing the three men.

More blood spilled across the black floor. The crimson spears dissolved, and their victims crumpled.

Swaying unsteadily, Daniel's demon lowered his arms, the magic dissolving from his limbs. He slumped backward against the wall and slid down it, his breaths gurgling in his damaged lungs.

I shoved off the table and ran toward him. Three long steps away, I slowed cautiously. Faintly glowing eyes watched me approach, blood trickling from the corner of his mouth.

"Demon?" I whispered.

"*Havh'tan et Vh'ihrēr.*"

"Wh-what?"

"My name," he rasped wetly, his accent thicker than Eterran's. "It is Havh'tan."

"*Have-uh-tan,*" I tried, sinking into a crouch but keeping several feet of buffer space between us. "Can you heal those wounds?"

"No."

The damage Russel had inflicted ... If Daniel's body had been purely human, he'd already be dead. My throat tightened painfully.

"I thought the Vh'alyir Amulet could save you." I tried to swallow. "I thought ... but it *killed him*."

Havh'tan's gaze turned to Russel's body. "He could have stopped."

"Who could've stopped what?"

"The Ash'amadē demon. He did not stop when the *hh'ainun* body began to break. He wanted to be free. He took the battle. Defeat is death." His eyes slid out of focus, then back in again, returning to my face. "You are enemy to the one who did this?"

"Yes."

"You will kill him?"

I hesitated. Demons didn't lie, Eterran had told me, and I didn't want to lie to this demon when I wasn't sure of the answer.

"Yes." Kai crouched beside me. "We will kill him."

Havh'tan's eyelids flickered. "*Hnn.* Good." Another flicker. "The one who rules the Court. Some call him *Magnus Dux*. Others, they call him *Xever*."

I shifted closer. Ignoring Kai's sharp inhalation, I sat beside the dying demon. "How do we find him?"

"The Court ... moves. He moves it where he wants it."

"Where is it now?"

"A place ... north ... west ... *Capilano* ... among the *thāitav*, by the river ... They gather to worship and summon ... and destroy." His mouth split in a bloody grin. "They enslave kings and name *payashē* their queen. *Gh'idrūlis. Esha hh'ainun zh'ūltispela.*"

The red sheen in his eyes dimmed, his gaze losing focus. The phantom spines and horns rising off his body had faded, and his chest rose and fell with faint, rapid breaths.

"Thank you, Havh'tan," I whispered. "I'm sorry I couldn't save you."

His eyelids drooped. "If you had … I would have killed you."

"I guess that's fair."

The demon smirked, then the breath wheezed from his lungs. His face slackened, and all light in his eyes died. Daniel and Havh'tan were gone.

I pushed up from the floor, blood shining on my leather pants. Blood all over the floor. Blood everywhere. Bodies everywhere.

My gaze jerked to the doors, terrified that Justin and Makiko were dead too, but Justin was sitting up, and he'd bundled his jacket and tucked it under Makiko's head. Aaron had knelt beside Blake's crumpled form, and as I took an unsteady step toward them, my boot squelched in the blood.

My stomach jumped. I lurched away from Daniel's body, bent over, and retched.

The nausea abated quickly, and I spat several times. Kai passed me a hanky, and I almost laughed as I took it. A hanky? A pristine white hanky, hidden somewhere among his throwing knives and bladed stars? Why did he have *a hanky?*

Hysterical amusement spun in my head, but I couldn't laugh. I didn't know if I could ever laugh again after this.

"Kai!" Aaron called sharply. "Get over here!"

The electramage sprinted for Aaron, still kneeling beside Blake. I rushed after him.

"He's alive." Aaron tugged down Blake's jacket zipper, exposing a bloody mess. "We need to—"

Blake's eyelids fluttered. He cracked them open.

"Blake!" I exclaimed, my voice cracking. "Hold on. We'll get a healer for y—"

"Get out of here."

My mouth hung open. "Huh?"

"If you're caught down here … with four dead members … they'll kill you. Get out."

"But what about you—"

"There's an … emergency button … just outside the room. Hit it … Someone will come." Panting for air, he smiled weakly. "I won't die."

"But—"

Kai grabbed my arm and pulled me up. "Let's go. The sooner we hit that button, the sooner a healer will be down here."

I gave Blake one more frantic look, then let Kai draw me into a jog. As we rushed toward the exit, my gaze caught on Russel's torn body and I faltered.

Leave the amulet, my brain screamed. *Useless. Worse than useless. Leave it behind!*

Squashing my revulsion, I veered away from Kai and rushed to the dead officer, trampling the scattered papers from his folders—all blank. The amulet's chain lay in the blood that had pooled around the dead demon mage, so I picked the medallion off his palm instead.

I remembered running across the room to join the others, but after that, my memory of leaving the building got fuzzy. I recalled hitting a red "critical injury" button beside the door, and rushing up the stairs behind Kai, who was carrying Makiko. After that, I could vaguely remember Aaron gently pushing me into the passenger seat, murmuring quiet words that had turned to mush in my ears.

When I blinked again, we were on the highway, nothing but flat farmland as far as I could see. The sun glowed on the horizon to the west, bathing the landscape in orange light and deep shadows. Where had the last several hours gone?

"You're awake," Aaron murmured, glancing at me before returning his attention to the highway.

"Was I asleep?" I glanced into the backseat, where Justin and Makiko were slumped, Kai squashed in one corner beside his fiancée. The big first aid kit Aaron kept in the trunk sat on his lap. "They aren't …"

"Sleeping," Kai said. "I gave them healing potions. They aren't badly hurt."

"Oh … that's good."

I settled into my seat, and dull pain flared through my arm. I frowned at it where it rested across my thighs. A chain hung from my fist, and I uncurled my fingers to find the Vh'alyir Amulet. Bile rose in my throat and I threw the artifact onto the floor between my feet. Pain flashed through my arm with the motion, and I pushed my sleeve up. A vibrant purple bruise in the shape of Russel's hand had darkened my wrist.

"You okay, Tori?" Aaron asked.

No. Not one tiny little bit of me was okay. "Just a bruise. Where are we?"

"Idaho." His hands tightened on the wheel. "I don't think anyone from the Keys followed us, but we don't want to hang around and find out."

"There's no way to know what the fallout will be," Kai added from the back. "Assuming Blake survives, he can tell them what happened—but will they believe him? He has no proof that Russel and the others were traitors. We may be facing murder charges in a few days."

Fear pierced the numb despair that had settled over me. "What do we do now?"

Aaron rubbed the back of his neck. "We go home."

My throat constricted until I couldn't breathe.

"With everything we've learned about the cult and its sects, and not knowing how the Keys' will react ... this is more than we can handle alone. We need to go back and tell Darius."

"What about Ezra?"

His gaze flicked to my feet, where the amulet lay. He didn't say it. He didn't need to.

The amulet, upon which Eterran and I had hung all our hopes, hadn't saved a demon mage. It'd killed him.

Its magic worked on regular contracts. I'd seen that. I knew it. But whatever magic went into a demon-mage ritual was different, and the amulet had only broken part of the binding. It hadn't been enough. It was worse than nothing.

Even if a better understanding of the ritual that bound Ezra and Eterran would allow us to make the amulet work, how would we get a cult grimoire? Havh'tan had tried to tell us what he knew, but his broken description of the location was meaningless. And even if we could figure it out, should we? Every secret we'd uncovered since Enright had led to an even darker cesspool of deceit and danger. Assassins. Demon mages. Corrupt guilds.

There was nothing else we could do.

I buried my face in my hands, sobs fighting to escape my chest. I gulped them back, breathing hard, but I couldn't stop the silent tears from streaming down my face. As anguish swamped me, the flame in my heart, the desperate hope I'd clung to since learning of Ezra's impending fate, flickered and died beneath the flood.

22

I WALKED THE MOTORCYCLE down the alley so the engine's rumble wouldn't alert my babysitter for the night—assuming he was here without me. When I hadn't returned home for the evening, he might've left. My phone was on silent, tucked in my pocket.

Thoughts and emotions whirled in my head like a maelstrom, and Eterran was quiet, giving me space. Or he was retreating as far as he could from the chaotic human feelings he so despised.

The bike's tires splashed through the puddles dotting the empty parking pad. The rain had let up as I'd neared the house, but I'd still gotten drenched. Rubbing my sleeve over my forehead, I pushed the motorcycle into the corner by the fence. As I threw the cover over it, I wondered what Kai would say if he knew I was borrowing his bike. With my limited depth perception, it was a better choice than an enclosed vehicle; I could sense the air currents around me, giving me a slight edge.

Still, not particularly safe.

I headed for the backyard gate, and with aero magic on my mind, I absently stretched my senses out, checking for movement. My hand closed over the gate latch.

The breeze wasn't the only air movement nearby.

Eterran snapped to attention and power surged through us. The temperature plunged as demonic magic flashed over my arms and into my hands.

My arm shot up, reaching for an object I could sense swinging toward me, and I caught a limb clad in cool leather—but I couldn't see it. The air shifted all around me, frenzied input, too much to track, but my eyes saw nothing except the parking pad and fence.

Phantom claws, six inches long, formed over my fingers and I struck with my free hand. The talons sank into the wooden fence with a muffled crunch.

Something sharp dug into my lower ribs. Something else, blunt and hard as steel, pushed into my spine, and yet something else pressed against my side, just above my left kidney.

Like a light switch flipping on, a man appeared in front of me. I held his wrist, preventing his silver dagger from reaching my throat, but his second blade had cut through my shirt, the tip stinging my flesh as he angled it to pierce between my ribs. My talons were buried in the fence beside his head, and one had grazed the side of his face.

Blood trickled down Darius's cheek as his steely gray eyes stared into mine.

On my blind side—that would be Girard. I couldn't see him, but the weapon he was ramming into my side would be his enchanted pistol, loaded with bullets that were more alchemy than lead. And behind me could be none other than Alistair, his steel-tipped staff wedged into my spine so that, with one powerful thrust, he could shove my vertebrae through my spinal cord.

Eterran's thoughts rippled as he considered and discarded a dozen plans of attack in a heartbeat. We could probably kill one of them, but we'd die anyway.

Eterran, I thought.

Bitterness flashed, then the demon receded. The demonic power coursing through me thinned and faded. As the talons piercing the fence post dissolved, I noted the difference in my response to an attack now as compared to only a few days ago. The demonic power, once my last resort, had risen to my command instantly.

There were as many disadvantages to allowing Eterran this much autonomy within me as there were advantages.

"I thought you were going to wait," I said quietly.

Darius's emotionless gaze searched my eyes. "That was the plan ... until your behavior changed." His dagger parted my skin above my lowest rib. "Your demon has already learned to control you in your sleep."

"He isn't controlling me."

"Would you even know anymore, Ezra?"

My eyelids hooded as I considered that. "Ask Robin Page."

Surprise flickered over Darius's stony features.

"I've been working with her." I studied him. "You know about her, don't you?"

The dagger eased out of my flesh. "I know."

244 ● ANNETTE MARIE

He said nothing more about Robin, and I didn't ask. That was the thing with Darius. He was the ultimate keeper of secrets, and for better or worse, he would never reveal one of his guilded's secrets without permission—even when it might save someone's life. If it wasn't his secret to share, then Darius wouldn't so much as drop a hint.

"And what are you working on with Robin?" he asked neutrally.

"A way to survive."

Another flash of surprise. "What brought on your change of heart?"

I grimaced.

"Ah." Darius smiled faintly. "Our fiery bartender inspires us all."

He pulled his dagger away from my ribs and I released his wrist. As his blades slid into the sheaths belted to his hips, Girard and Alistair retreated a step. I shifted out from their lethal circle and turned to bring all three men into view.

Black leather, cold eyes, deadly experience, and enough magic to defeat almost anyone. The mythic world was lucky these three could be counted among the good guys.

Darius flipped the latch on the gate, and I followed him into the yard. The other two waited in the alley.

"Are you in control, Ezra?" my GM asked.

Again, I considered his question carefully. "I think so." I let out a slow breath. "Eterran wants to survive too. Tori allied with him, and I ... I've done the same."

"That's a dangerous line to walk."

Ice blanketed my mind as Eterran pushed me aside. "As dangerous as the line you walk with the demon of Vh'alyir?"

Wariness flared in Darius's eyes, and I quickly resumed control.

"One way or another, this will end soon," I said. "I want to try."

The former assassin assessed me for a long moment. "Imminent death does strange things to the mind, Ezra. It brings out the best in some, and the worst in others. I've feared all along that, when the time came, we would have to face your worst."

I opened my mouth to protest.

His hand closed around my shoulder, gripping tightly. "You can't rise above your worst if you've never faced it." He turned away. "We'll be keeping an eye on you, but I expect updates as well."

I watched him stride to the gate. He swung it closed, and as the latch dropped into place, he looked back at me, Girard and Alistair behind him.

"I've waited six years for you to commit to the fight, Ezra. Don't disappoint me."

Their footfalls crunched across the parking pad, but when they walked onto the asphalt of the alleyway, the sound of their steps went silent. They faded from sight, disappearing as Darius's magic bent the light around them.

I pressed a hand to my ribs, where blood had soaked through my shirt.

Inside the house, I showered, dabbed a healing potion on the shallow cut, and dressed in comfortable clothes. The rooms echoed, painfully empty, as I walked through the house. In my bedroom, I pulled my guitar from its stand, sat on my bed, and plucked each string to check it was in tune.

Too many secrets. Mine. Tori's. Robin's.

My eyes closed as I let my fingers slide across the strings and press into the frets, the quiet notes scarcely heard.

Aaron and Kai had only given up because I'd asked them to stop. Darius had been waiting for me to fight for my life. Tori had risked everything to keep me alive long enough to take up the fight on my behalf.

Why did I wait this long to try?

Eterran stirred, his mind more calm than usual, the sharp cut of his bitterness dulled. *Do you want to know?*

My fingers hesitated on the guitar strings.

He just told you.

Who?

Darius.

What do you mean?

The memory replayed—Darius's hand on my shoulder, his murmured words. *You can't rise above your worst if you've never faced it.*

I ran through the words again, and understanding drove in my chest like a twisting knife.

My guitar went silent under my hands. I drew in a deep breath, then let it out. Memories rose inside me—shattered homes, abandoned possessions, the obliterated temple with its gray stones stained red. Emptiness where there had once been family. Agony where there had once been happiness.

My fault. All my fault—and any attempt at escaping my predetermined end felt like an evasion of my rightful punishment for the damage and death I'd caused.

I didn't deserve to be happy. I didn't deserve to be loved or protected. I didn't deserve to have a normal life—as normal as my life could be while concealing that I was a demon mage.

Setting my guitar on the bed, I reached for my nightstand. In the top drawer, a leather-bound album. I pulled it onto my lap and opened the cover. Slowly, I flipped through photo after photo of me, Aaron, Kai, and Tori. Especially Tori.

I stopped on the last photo. My and Tori's selfie from the Christmas party, taken as I'd laughed at her attempt to get a more flattering picture. Mere minutes later, in a back hall of the manor, she'd kissed me under the mistletoe.

With the album balanced on my lap, I slid my phone from my pocket. The screen glowed too brightly for the dimly lit room as I opened our text conversation. Her last message waited, unanswered. She hadn't sent any more.

I didn't deserve to be loved …

My thumb tapped her icon, bringing up her contact info. I selected her number.

… but somehow, it had happened anyway.

I pressed the call button and lifted the phone to my ear as it rang.

23

WEST YELLOWSTONE was a town in southern Montana. Yeah, Montana. We were heading home, but Aaron had detoured off the main road so we could all get a proper night's rest in an out-of-the-way location.

Food, showers, clean clothes, sleep. They should have been my top priority, but while the others were in our motel room, taking turns in the bathroom and finishing off several bags of takeout, I wasn't with them.

Instead, I was back in the passenger seat of Aaron's SUV. With the chair reclined as far as it would go, I stared dully at the roof, my bruised, aching arm resting on my stomach.

I hadn't been able to handle the others' quiet discussion of the cult—the *Court*, as Daniel's demon had called it. The Court, which seemed to be the cult's top level that controlled the smaller "circles" like the one in Portland. An interconnected system both hidden and powerful, and insidious enough to ensnare not one but *four* members of the Keys of Solomon. Who knew what other guilds or groups the cult had wormed into?

The Court knew the Portland circle had been discovered, and they would make it disappear—if they hadn't already. The Praetor had vanished, and he was probably the only member of that group who knew anything of consequence.

And without the Portland circle and its Praetor, we had nothing but a dying demon's nonsensical description.

North. West. Capilano. Among the *thāitav*. By the river.

Google hadn't revealed a town or city called Capilano, but it was a common name for everything from neighborhoods to streets to shopping malls. "By the river" narrowed the options slightly, but *thāitav* wasn't a word in any language we could figure out, meaning it was probably demonic.

Maybe, with weeks or months of careful investigation, the Crow and Hammer could expose the Court. Maybe our guild could even bring it down, though Aaron thought it would require MPD oversight and a coordinated multi-guild effort to truly stamp out.

But none of that would save Ezra.

Somewhere at my feet, the Vh'alyir Amulet lay where I'd dropped it. How many deaths had I caused with this naïve expedition? I'd deceived and hurt my friends. Dragged Aaron and Kai away from Ezra when he most needed them. Put Justin's life in danger. Gotten Blake horribly injured—or maybe fatally injured.

All for nothing.

Swallowing a miserable groan, I sat up and studied the amulet between my feet. I lifted it by the chain, then popped open the glove box to toss the amulet inside. As the plastic door dropped open, the cult scepter rolled out.

I caught it. The amulet in one hand and the scepter in the other, I stared at the two artifacts. Why had I thought a lost talisman could save Ezra? Why had I thought I could find a way when no one else could? Why had I thought I could change anything?

I was just a magic-less human pretending she was special.

Jaw clenched, I wrapped the amulet chain around the silver scepter handle and shoved both into the dark compartment. Flopping back onto the reclined seat, I stared upward as tears slid sideways down my face and into my hair.

My phone buzzed against my butt cheek.

I jumped half a foot off the seat, then dug my phone out of my pocket. Expecting a call from Aaron telling me to come inside and shower, I glanced unenthusiastically at the screen.

Ezra's picture filled it, a crop of him staring with extreme seriousness into the camera while he had paintball goggles perched on top of his plastic helmet and pink paint splattering one cheek. My heart stalled.

Ezra was calling me after days of silence.

Why?

Panic wrapped its icy claws around my lungs as I brought the phone to my ear and whispered, "Hello?"

"Tori?"

Ezra's voice washed over me, soothing the open wounds in my soul. I'd missed his voice so much. I'd missed *him* so much.

"What's wrong?" I asked, my panic unabated. "Are you okay?"

"I'm okay."

252 ♠ ANNETTE MARIE

More than just the words, he *sounded* fine, and that's all it took for relief to flood me.

"What about you?" he asked with a hesitant pause. "You don't sound like yourself."

My mouth was open to speak, but I couldn't say I was fine. Nothing was fine. Everything was wrong, broken, disintegrating as I desperately tried to hold it together. I'd promised myself I would save him, and I'd failed.

I burst into tears.

"Tori, what's wrong?"

I shook with sobs as anguish and guilt and regret pummeled me. "I'm so sorry, Ezra. I'm so sorry. I lied to you and I put everyone in danger and I knew it was important to tell you about Eterran but I—I was so afraid. I couldn't lose you. I couldn't handle it."

"Tori—"

"And then I dragged Aaron and Kai out here." The words spilled out, trembling and barely coherent. "I thought I could do this, and I got their hopes up too, but it's been a complete disaster and I—I—I screwed up everything, Ezra, and I'm so sorry."

"It's okay," he said softly. "I'm sorry too. I'm sorry you had to fight for me."

My hand tightened on the phone, pressing it hard into my ear. "I should've listened. You all told me it was impossible and there was no way to s-save you, but I didn't want to believe it. I thought you guys just hadn't tried hard enough, and that was stupid and wrong and just—just *wrong*. All I did was make everyone suffer more because I didn't trust you and Aaron and Kai."

"That isn't true. You have more trust in us than we deserve." A rustle as he shifted the phone. "Tori, what's been happening?"

I rubbed my damp cheeks. "We went to Enright and found a lead and we followed it, and everything went up in flames. We're all okay, more or less, and we're coming home." Gulping back another sob, I added quietly, "And so you don't get your hopes up, we're coming back empty-handed."

The line was silent as he absorbed that.

"I know I'm being vague," I mumbled miserably, "but the details ... I think I should tell you in person. Is ... is that okay?"

"Yes," he said without a hint of the disappointment and despair he must have felt at my failure. "That's okay."

I closed my eyes tightly. "Ezra ... I'm s—"

"Stop apologizing, Tori. You've put yourself through hell for me, and you never should've had to do that."

"I had to try," I whispered, and as I said the words, the weight on my lungs eased slightly. "It ended up being pointless, but I had to try."

"I should've been trying too." An unexpected note of steel slid into his voice. "I'm sorry, Tori. I'm sorry it took me so long, but I'm ready to fight now too."

My eyes flew open, staring at the blank roof of the SUV.

"So you can't give up on me, all right? I need your help."

"You ... you want to fight?"

"I want to live. I've always wanted to live, but I have more reasons now than I did before." A pause. "I don't have any dreams for the future. I've never allowed myself to imagine a future. But I want to change that. I want you to be part of my future."

Throat closing, I clutched the phone. "Ezra ..."

"If whatever you went to Enright to do isn't working, then get back here so we can try something else. I have a couple of ideas."

"You do?"

"Mhm. Maybe your leads will help as well."

I grimaced. "Not unless you can tell me what place could be described as 'north, west, Capilano, among the *thay-tav*, by the river.'"

A short, disbelieving laugh escaped him, and the sound warmed my entire body.

"We're doing riddles now?" he asked bemusedly. "What does *thay-tav* mean?"

"No idea. It's a demonic word, I think."

"Demonic?" A pause. "*Thāitav*? Is that the word?"

"Oh ... right, yeah."

"Eterran says *thāitav* means someone who's died or 'the dead.' So 'among the dead, by the river' ... and Capilano?" He muttered to himself. "Are we talking local spots? Because there's a cemetery by the Capilano River in West Vancouver."

Gooseflesh prickled my skin from head to toe. *North*—a northern city. *West* Vancouver. A cemetery *beside* Capilano *River*.

It couldn't be. The Court couldn't be in Vancouver.

The Court ... moves. He moves it where he wants it. If Havh'tan was right, then it *could* have moved to Vancouver—but why? Why on earth would the Magnus Dux move the ruling sect of the cult there? What was in Vancouver that would attract a cult?

"Did I get it right?" Ezra asked.

"Maybe—but don't even think about going there! Do you understand? I need to tell you the rest—but once we're back."

Pinching the phone against my ear with my shoulder, I yanked the handle on the side of my seat to straighten it. "I'll explain everything once I see you, so please wait for us."

"All right."

"We're in southern Montana right now—"

"*Montana?*"

"—but we'll return as quickly as we can. Tomorrow afternoon, I think." Scooching forward, I opened the glove box again. "I need to talk to Aaron and Kai and get everyone moving. Just hang on until we're back, okay?"

"I'll be waiting. Stay safe, Tori."

"I will. I have to go. Bye for now, Ezra."

Only after I'd ended the call did I realize neither of us had brought up the text I'd sent him. My mouth quivered, but I shoved the hurt and anxiety away. This wasn't the time for that kind of stuff anyway. Fierce hope burned in my chest again, and I wouldn't let anything dim it.

As I pulled the amulet-scepter tangle out of the glove box, my phone chimed. I tapped the screen, and my text conversation with Ezra popped up. A new message had appeared beneath my last text.

I love you too.

My heart swelled until it choked off my air. Tears standing in my eyes, I shoved the car door open with my elbow.

When I burst into the motel room, Aaron and Kai leaped to their feet in alarm. Justin, sitting at the built-in desk beside the tiny motel TV, gawked at me.

"Guys," I gasped. "I think I know where the Court is. We have to get back to Vancouver right away."

Aaron's and Kai's jaws dropped to match Justin's.

My hand clenched around the scepter's handle, the amulet hanging from it. "And if we're lucky, we can steal the cult grimoire out from under those bastards before they realize we're coming—and before we sic every guild in the city on them."

AFTER ENDLESS HOURS driving down endless highways, I should've been delighted to be back home. Aaron's home, technically, but still home.

We hadn't made great time. Halfway across the Columbia River Basin, the SUV had blown a tire. Aaron and Kai had swiftly swapped it out for the flimsy spare, and we'd limped into a town, but between finding a service shop, waiting for it to open, and having the tire replaced, we'd lost several hours.

But we'd made it, and I now stood in the center of the living room. Aaron and Kai stood with me, and together we formed a triangle, facing each other.

"Ezra texted us an hour ago that he'd be out for a bit," I said, bouncing my phone on one hand. "He wants to know when we're back in town. Should I call him?"

Aaron rubbed his stubbly chin. "Can we dump the reveal of the cult's survival on him, then immediately drag him into their stronghold—or whatever we find in that cemetery?"

"He said he wanted to fight."

"But he doesn't know who or what we're going up against."

I bit the inside of my cheek.

"Let's not risk it," Kai murmured. "We almost lost him a week ago. That isn't much recovery time."

Relenting, I nodded.

Aaron brushed his hands together decisively. "Let's gear up, then. The Court probably doesn't know we're on to them, but we shouldn't waste any time. Who knows how long it'll take them to pick up and move again?"

Kai agreed, then hastened for the basement where Makiko had disappeared—to freshen up in the bathroom, probably—while Aaron marched up the stairs, heading for his room to change and weaponize himself. I watched them go, my chest tight and hands clenched. My only set of combat clothes was in my suitcase in the SUV, and as for weaponizing myself . . .

Two alchemy bombs and Hoshi. That was all I had left to contribute.

Swallowing the nausea building in my gut, I swept through the kitchen and out the back door. The chilly January air bit into my cheeks as I crossed the yard and passed through the open gate. The unhitched trailer we'd used to haul Kai's and Makiko's bikes dominated half the parking pad.

Beside the trailer, the SUV was lit up, rear hatch open. Justin stood beneath it, sorting through his duffle bag to ensure he had all his stuff before heading home.

He glanced up when I joined him. A purple bruise darkened one temple from his encounter with Daniel and Anand outside the Keys guild.

"Hey." He haphazardly folded a wrinkled shirt and tucked it in his bag. "I thought you were getting ready for battle with a demon cult."

I plucked the shirt out and refolded it. "I'm not sure I'm going."

"What do you mean?"

Frowning at my folding job, I shook it out and tried again. "What good have I done this whole time? I'll just get in their way."

Justin faced me, but I kept my attention on the shirt as I carefully smoothed the sleeves out.

"I've been useless." I tugged on the shirt's collar. "I didn't stop a single mythic we came up against—except for when I accidentally killed Russel. How awful is that? Hoshi has been more useful than me. I should just send her with the guys and stay home."

Sliding the shirt into his bag, I stared at my all too human hands. "You've been asking questions about whether I was qualified to do these things, whether it was safe or a good idea ... I was never qualified. It was always a bad idea, and I just kept telling myself I could handle it."

"Tori," he murmured.

My fingers closed into tight fists. "You asked Aaron if I can play in his league. I can't. I'm not a combat mythic or a bounty hunter. I'm just a bartender."

Justin sat on the bumper. "You know that's bullshit."

My gaze snapped to him.

"You don't do things all neat and tidy, Tori. You're a messy person. You storm around and shake things up and cause chaos. You've always been like that."

I frowned at him. "If that was supposed to be a compliment, it sucked."

"You didn't neatly arrest anyone, but you found answers, escaped danger, and got your friends into and out of all that alive." He grimaced. "I may have had several heart attacks along the way, but you survived it all."

"That was just luck, though. If anything had—"

"Surviving by the skin of your teeth *once* is luck. Doing it over and over again is something else." He squinted at me. "You know you aren't useless, Tori. What's the real problem?"

I stared back at him, then sank down to sit on the bumper beside him. My chest had tightened again, familiar insecurity settling deep in my bones.

"I wanted to be a mythic so badly," I whispered. "I wanted to be special and kick ass and do things other people can't do. But then I lost almost all the magic I'd collected, and I realized I can act like tough shit all I want, but when the cards are down, I'm just a human."

"So am I. Is that such a bad thing?"

I twitched like he'd jabbed me in the ribs.

"You could kick ass and do things other people couldn't before you ever heard the word 'mythic.'" He arched his eyebrows. "Magic doesn't make you an invincible superhero. If I'm useless because I couldn't stop Russel's men, then so is Makiko. She was captured too."

He tilted his head back, staring through the hatch's window at the evening sky. "When I joined you for this trip, I thought you'd need my protection. But you didn't. You knew when to jump in—and you knew when to stand back and let your friends take the front line."

I frowned.

"Are you worried you'd be endangering your friends by going with them to that cemetery? Or are you afraid you're too human to be there?"

My lungs constricted. "I don't have any magic, Justin."

Twisting toward his bag, he dug inside it. When he turned back to me, he held his pistol by the barrel.

"Then take this," he said quietly. "And instead of being 'just a human,' you'll be a tough-ass human with a gun."

I stared at him. "Are you, uh, allowed to loan that out?"

He shrugged mysteriously. The cold handle pressed against my hand, and I realized I'd reached for it. My fingers curled around the grip.

Headlights flashed at the end of the alley. Glancing toward the vehicle, Justin pushed to his feet. "That's my ride."

I watched him collect his bag. Slinging it over his shoulder, he gave me a long, assessing look—then smiled. It was a familiar smile that had soothed my fears since I was sixteen.

"Whether you go or not, Tori, I know you'll make the best choice for you and your friends."

I clutched the gun, my voice muted by a surge of emotion.

He started down the alley. "And if you need me, all you have to do is call. I can be a tough-ass human too."

I grinned through the tears filming my eyes. "I know it."

The car waiting at the end of the alley gave a short beep, and Justin waved as he hurried toward it. A car door opened and closed, then the vehicle pulled away.

For a long moment, I studied the gun in my hand, then set it down in the back of the SUV. Riffling through our luggage, I found my combat belt. The alchemy bombs clinked as I wrapped the leather around my waist and buckled it.

Retrieving the gun, I weighed it in my hand, then slid it into the empty holster at my hip.

My grin widened, baring my teeth. I heaved my suitcase out, shut the hatch, and sped back across the yard to the house. We had a job to do, and no time to waste.

24

THE CAPILANO VIEW CEMETERY was a twenty-minute drive from Aaron's house—across the downtown core, through Stanley Park, over the Lions Gate Bridge, and into West Vancouver.

As I climbed out of the SUV, parked in the cemetery's small lot, I peered toward the out-of-sight harbor. How unbelievable—and infuriating—that the heart of the Court could be this close, and we'd had no idea.

Darkness had fallen, and I checked for the flashlight clipped to my belt. With a final peek at my phone—no updates from Ezra, who was still out on whatever errand had lured him away from home—I switched it to silent and tucked it in the belt pouch that used to hold the Queen of Spades. In another pouch was the demon amulet, and hanging from a loop opposite my flashlight was the cult scepter.

I didn't have any real use for it, but you never knew when a stolen artifact might come in handy.

Aaron joined me, adjusting the baldric on his shoulder. No zippered case this time—Sharpie was on full display. Black combat clothing covered him from head to toe, from his fireproof shirt and protective vest to his strategically padded leather pants and steel-toed boots.

With near-silent footfalls, Kai circled the back of the vehicle. He was in full combat gear as well, his slim, SWAT-style vest loaded with throwing weapons and two katana sheathed at one hip. He'd added a black knitted hat for warmth, which only slightly detracted from his Absolute Badass Level.

Makiko followed him, her delicate features somber. She'd tied her hair back in a high ponytail, which swung with each step, and a fitted black jumpsuit covered her like a second skin. Her only weapons were the two metal fans clipped to her belt.

"Okay," I whispered, glancing around the otherwise empty parking lot. "We need to find the Court's … uh … hideout? Evil lair? Demon-worship temple? I dunno, but we need to find *something* here."

"We can skip over most of the cemetery," Aaron murmured. "Too public and way too many visitors. Let's head for the northern portion."

Via satellite view, we knew the northern reaches of the cemetery were heavily treed—an untouched forest that would eventually be chopped down to make room for more graves. Kind of a waste, I mused, as we jogged along a paved path, fields of flat headstones on either side of us. I didn't want any beautiful old trees dying so my corpse could lie beneath mowed grass.

"Hey guys," I whisper-called. "When I die, put me down for cremation, 'kay?"

"You're not gonna die," Aaron called back grumpily.

"I just meant in general."

"Oh. In that case, fine—but I'm not doing the cremating."

"Why not? Isn't that what a good pyromage friend would do?"

He grumbled something under his breath.

The cemetery grew darker as we jogged away from the developed sections. A wall of trees rose in our path, and we came to a halt. Plucking my flashlight off my belt, I shone it at the forest. Several types of conifers were jammed so tightly together that my light wasn't penetrating more than a few inches into the foliage.

"That's … extremely dense," I muttered. "Anyone bring a machete?"

Kai shook his head. "Even if we could bushwhack our way through there, we shouldn't have to. The cultists need access to the location too."

"It'd help if we knew what we were looking for." Aaron scrubbed his hand through his hair. "This could take all night."

I cast a sidelong look at Makiko. "Can you just, like, fly up in the air and look around?"

"Levitation is more draining than combat."

"Oh." I puffed out a frustrated breath—then snapped straight as I realized we didn't need Makiko to get an aerial view. "Hoshi!"

She uncoiled from my back pouch. Undulating through the air as if it were as thick as water, she dipped her head to sniff at my braided hair.

"Hey girl," I murmured. "Can you help us out? Will you fly around this place, then come back and show me what you saw?"

With a snap of her long tail, she soared upward, fading from sight as she went.

Aaron and I headed one way to search for paths into the forest, and Kai and Makiko moved in the opposite direction. The minutes ticked by, and my skin prickled with growing nerves. The longer we wandered around, the greater the chances were that someone might notice our suspicious activity. Getting the cops called on us would be annoying, but a spy alerting the cult could be disastrous.

As I squatted on my heels and shone my flashlight under the boughs of a conifer to check for a hidden path, Hoshi appeared in a swirl of endless tail and bobbing crystal antennae. She bumped her nose against mine and a dizzying maelstrom of images filled my head.

"Whoa, whoa," I gasped. "Slow down, Hoshi."

With an apologetic flicker of rose-streaked violet, she replayed her surveillance flight at a more sane speed. She'd soared over the trees, finding several dirt tracks and one gravel pathway. Trees, trees, more trees, a clearing with a small structure, then—

"Wait, what was that last thing?"

She showed me the image again: a vaguely gazebo-shaped structure constructed of gray stone, with a domed roof supported by pillars. It sat alone in a small clearing of overgrown grasses and weeds.

"Well, *hel-lo*," I breathed. "Guys!"

Aaron had already backtracked to join me, and Kai and Makiko jogged out of the darkness.

"There's a mausoleum-ish thing back there," I said, rising to my feet with Hoshi hanging off my shoulder. "All alone in a little clearing. Seems like a good place to check out."

Kai and Aaron nodded.

I patted Hoshi's nose. "Can you lead us there?"

She nuzzled my palm, then undulated straight into the trees. Guess we'd be doing some bushwhacking after all.

Thank goodness for all my leather clothes, otherwise traversing a hundred yards of woodland would've left me in a worse state than our recent battles. My flashlight flickered wildly as I wrangled past bushes and boughs with dead leaves clinging to them.

Just when it seemed it would never end, I burst out into the clearing. The guys and Makiko tumbled out after me, and we spent a moment picking leaves and twigs out of our hair and clothes before focusing on the structure in the center of the treeless glade.

Far smaller than the remains of the temple in Enright, it looked like a fairly generic stone monument with carved pillars, a peaked roof, and an octagonal base.

Aaron and Kai followed behind me as I cautiously approached and shone my flashlight between the pillars. Several steps led to a raised floor, where a life-sized statue of an angel stood, weathered and crumbling.

Her wings had broken off, leaving rough stumps running down the folds of her simple dress, and the delicate features on her upturned face were so worn down they were almost indiscernible, giving her a mask-like visage. She held a bronze chalice in one hand, the metal blackened with age, and her other hand was curled as though she'd once been holding a second item.

Keeping on the grass, I circled the structure until I was facing the angel.

"Look," I murmured. "On her head."

Atop her flowing hair was a delicate stone crown with three points—just like the symbol on the Praetor's tapestry.

Gulping down my nerves, I placed my foot on the first step of the mausoleum. Hoshi clutched my jacket collar as though ready to pull me away. I braced for an explosion or spewing fire or some other horrific booby trap, but after twenty seconds, I relaxed and ascended the three steps. The others followed me.

"This isn't a recent structure," Kai murmured, brushing his palm over a pillar. "I seriously doubt the cult built this."

I studied the angel's weathered face, a foot above mine with the short pedestal under her bare stone feet, then lifted my gaze to her crown. Eyes narrowing, I tapped a fingernail against one point, then tapped the side of her face, then poked at the crown again.

"The statue is original," I decided, "but I don't think the crown is. It feels more like clay—like I could break it pretty easily if I tried."

"I think the cult might've broken the wings off, as well." Makiko, standing behind the angel, touched one of the wing stumps. "The damage doesn't look as old as the rest."

"That makes a twisted sort of sense," I said. "Breaking her wings makes her a *fallen* angel—in other words, a demon. The Christian version, at least."

Aaron stepped to my side. "Then this is likely a cult-ified mausoleum. How—"

"Cenotaph," Kai interrupted.

"Huh?"

"A mausoleum has a body interred in it. This is a cenotaph—a monument."

Aaron shook his head. "Okay, how is this *cenotaph* going to lead us to the cult lair? Could there be an underground room again?"

We all looked at the very solid stone floor.

"Maybe there's a secret entrance," Makiko suggested. "Do you see a hidden button or lever?"

Aaron peered around. "If this were a video game, there'd be a clue to solving the puzzle."

I shot him a withering look, then returned my attention to the angel. This was the part of the structure the cult had marked. My gaze drifted to the chalice she held—and a vivid memory of the Praetor raising a silver chalice hit me. There'd been chalices in the hidden room in Enright too.

Grasping the angel's stone shoulders for balance, I stepped onto the pedestal and peered into the bronze cup. The inside was far smoother than the outside—except for the bottom, where a geometrical shape had been carved, a spiky rune in its center.

I dropped back to the ground, my face scrunched with displeasure. Of course it couldn't be a nice, simple "open sesame." Oh no, the cult had to make it all weird and creepy.

"Theoretically speaking," I began unhappily, "could blood be used to trigger a spell?"

Aaron shrugged, while Kai and Makiko exchanged uncertain looks.

"Possibly," Kai said. "Alchemy and sorcery can be blended in many ways. None of us are experts to say for sure, though."

"Then I guess I'll try it. Can I borrow a knife?"

"What for?"

"I'm going to bleed in that chalice and see if anything happens."

Everyone stared at me.

"You saw their blood-drinking ritual." I held out my hand impatiently. "It's worth a shot."

"Then I'll do it—" Kai began.

"You're more likely to need all your blood, so let me do it."

He shook his head, jaw set—then swore when Makiko held out a tiny knife. I blinked as I accepted it. Where the hell was she hiding knives under that skintight leather?

I clipped my flashlight to my belt, tugged my left sleeve up, and set the blade against my skin. Teeth gritted, I sliced the blade down, opening a shallow cut. As blood welled, I held my wrist over the chalice.

No one spoke as my blood dribbled into the bronze cup. I really hoped a magic word wasn't required as well, or I was bleeding for nothing.

A crimson glow flared inside the cup, the light casting eerie scarlet shadows over the angel's face.

My heart leaped in anxious excitement. I stepped back quickly, holding my breath, and waited for something else to happen. Running out of air, I inhaled and waited again.

The chalice continued to emit that eerie glow, but otherwise ... nothing.

"Oh my god, seriously?" I snarled. "Why is nothing happening?"

"There must be an incantation," Makiko murmured. "Or some other trigger."

Swearing under my breath, I dug into the first-aid pouch of my belt and used a potion to stop the bleeding. Opening a vein for no reason. Ugh.

As I reached back to replace the potion vial, my arm bumped the scepter hanging from my belt. I peered down at it, then looked back at the angel—at her empty hand, fingers curled.

Could it be ...?

Shoving the potion in its pouch, I unhooked the scepter. Heart in my throat, I reached up and slipped the handle into the angel's waiting grasp. It slid into place with a quiet clink—and the single red crystal set in the crown-like point on top lit with the same crimson glow as the chalice.

A third spot of scarlet light ignited behind the statue, and Makiko leaped aside as something made a hissing, grinding sound.

The glow faded, and we all peered around the statue. A panel of stone floor had lifted several inches.

Cautiously approaching, Kai and Aaron took hold of the panel and heaved it up. It rose on thick hinges, helped by shiny metal pistons that definitely didn't go with the weathered stone of the cenotaph.

Inside the hole, wooden stairs descended into the earth.

We'd found the Court's lair.

25

AARON WENT FIRST, holding a palmful of fire to light his way. I followed with my flashlight in one hand, the other resting on the holstered gun at my hip. Makiko descended on my heels, and Kai brought up the rear, his hands bristling with throwing knives ready to fly.

Hoshi was standing guard—or floating guard?—at the entrance. She didn't like underground spaces, but she could warn me if anyone approached the cenotaph. The last thing we needed was to get trapped down here. That'd be the opposite of fun.

My heart thumped in my ears as we descended deeper, the rough wooden stairs creaking underfoot and tree roots dangling from the earthen ceiling like spiderwebs. The stairs turned, then kept going. We were at least three stories beneath ground level before Aaron's warm light danced across a damp stone floor.

We walked out of the rough stairwell and into a much larger space with stone walls, the arched ceiling supported by smooth, round pillars streaked with water stains. The rectangular shape of the room, about fifty feet wide but so long I couldn't see either end in the darkness, confused me until I spotted the dark openings high in the walls.

It was an old storm-water reservoir.

And now it belonged to the cult. They'd gone right ahead with customizing their damp, echoey lair into a new "temple."

The summoning circle in the center spanned twenty-five feet, each precise line filled with silver inlay. At the top of the circle, a stone lectern with an imp-like demon carved into its base faced the circle, and behind it, a long wooden altar held candelabras, ornamental boxes, and other ritual paraphernalia. Hanging from each of the six pillars was a scarlet tapestry displaying the cult's sigil of a crown within a circle.

I gestured at the others. "Come on."

My quiet whisper echoed off the walls, and I cringed at the sound of our feet slapping the damp floor. My muscles quivered with tension as we crossed the expanse toward the altar. This was it. This was our last chance to save Ezra. If there was no grimoire—or no additional clues on where to find one—then we were done.

My pace quickened, anxious hope driving me forward. Rushing ahead of the guys, I dashed to the lectern and spun toward its angled top, facing the summoning circle the way the Praetor—or in this case, the Magnus Dux would when he led his brainwashed flock through a ritual.

The lectern wasn't empty.

LOST TALISMANS AND A TEQUILA ♠ 273

Sitting atop it was an ornate wooden box, perfectly sized to hold a large book, carved and painted with the cult's emblem. An intricate clasp held it shut, its glossy surface unmarred by a speck of dust or dampness.

My heart hammered. *Please don't be empty. Please, please, please.* I clipped my flashlight back on my belt, relying on Aaron's fire for light. Using my sleeve to shield my skin, I nudged the box's clasp open and hooked my fingers under the lid's edge to lift it.

Maybe it was the tiny voice in the back of my head whispering that this was too easy, but instead of flipping the lid open, I looked up—across the summoning circle, past the tapestry-decorated pillars, past the rough hole in the wall that we'd entered through.

I looked straight to the three figures standing at the edge of the darkness.

My gasp brought Aaron, Kai, and Makiko to attention. They whipped around, and we all stared across the echoing reservoir at the intruders.

Except *we* were the intruders.

The trio moved forward, their scarlet cloaks sweeping along the water-streaked floor. Deep hoods hid their faces, but guessing by their stature, two were broad-shouldered men. The third was either a slender man or a tall woman.

They stopped between the first of the tapestry-adorned columns. The centermost man took one more step and held his arms out, his cloak rippling dramatically.

With his gesture, scarlet light bloomed through the space. Fixed high on the columns, large crystals radiated the eerie glow.

"Welcome," the man intoned in a deep voice, "to the Court of the Red Queen."

My grip on the lectern box tightened.

"Are you here to pledge your souls to the service of the Queen? Have you come to join us in joyous worship of the mother of magic, the beautiful and all-powerful being known as the Goddess?"

When we didn't respond, his low chuckle echoed through the reservoir.

"I didn't think so." He lowered his arms. "You would be the ones who defiled the temple ruins in Enright, the site where so many of the Goddess's beloved children lost their lives. And you would be the voyeurs who spied upon a sacred gathering of the circle in Portland. *And* you are the fools who slaughtered my loyal subjects in Salt Lake City."

I swallowed to get some moisture in my mouth. "And you would be the Magnus Dux," I announced. "That's a stupid name, by the way."

Makiko shifted closer to my elbow. "At least one is probably a contractor," she whispered, her lips scarcely moving. "We should run for the exit."

I flicked a glance to my other side, but Kai and Aaron were several steps away—too far to consult with.

"You've come farther than any other," the Magnus Dux mused. "And I would like to know how you managed it. That information in exchange for your lives seems fair, wouldn't you agree?"

Yeah, right. Like he'd let us leave if he could help it.

"Well, we outnumber you, in case you can't count that high," I blustered. "So maybe we'll spare *your* lives in exchange for information about your creepy cult."

"Hmm. Fair point, Miss Dawson."

Makiko sucked in a sharp breath beside me, and my blood ran cold. He knew my name. Did he know who we all were?

"Shall we even the numbers, then?"

He raised his hand, and I flinched, expecting a flash of red light and a horned demon to appear. When nothing happened, I frowned, my panic ratcheting even higher.

"Kai?"

At Aaron's surprised gasp, I whipped around—and saw Kai plant his hands on Aaron's chest.

Saw Aaron's eyes widening in shock.

Saw Kai's eerily vacant expression as flickering crackles ran over his arms and the air sizzled with power.

The assassin was here. The realization hit me and Aaron at the same time, and he lurched backward—but no human or mythic was faster than electricity.

White light flashed as Kai unleashed a blast of power straight into Aaron's chest. Aaron went rigid as stone, arcs of power racing down his body and leaping from his fingers toward the ground in bluish-white lines. The tang of ozone hazed the air.

"No!" Makiko whipped her fan out.

The blast of wind hit the two mages, flinging them off their feet. They crashed down side by side, and Kai lunged back up.

Aaron didn't. He didn't move.

I was frozen. Paralyzed. As long as Aaron didn't move, neither could I. My whole attention was locked on him, every iota of my being waiting for him to twitch, to gasp, to groan in pain because being electrocuted hurt like a bitch and he shouldn't be silent right now.

But he was silent.

Makiko shoved me aside, and a throwing star whipped past my face. Kai, his stare devoid of emotion, pulled two more blades and flung them at his fiancée. She whacked them out of the air with her fan and leaped toward him.

She was screaming something, but all I could hear was Aaron's silence.

I stumbled forward a step—then I was running. My knees hit the floor beside him and I grabbed his head, turning his face toward me. His half-open eyes were blank, pupils dilated.

Was he breathing?

I pressed my hand to his nose and mouth, but not the faintest hint of moving air warmed my hand.

Oh god. He wasn't breathing. *He wasn't breathing!*

Fuzzy high-school first-aid classes spun through my head, and I fumbled at his throat, pressing into the skin under his jaw, searching for his pulse. Why couldn't I find it? I groped my own neck, easily locating the hammering pulse in my throat, then pushed on the same spot in his neck.

Nothing. I couldn't feel anything.

"Aaron!" I gasped, my voice cracking. "Aaron, please!"

Tears spilled down my cheeks as I scrabbled for the buckles on his protective vest. I flipped it open, put one hand over the other on his sternum, and shoved down. Pain exploded through my bruised arm.

Clenching my jaw, I shoved down again. "Two," I gasped. Shoved again. "Three. Four. *Five. Six!*"

Somewhere nearby, Makiko's shouts and scuffing footsteps echoed, but I kept going. Kept going until my head spun, muscles burned, and my bruised arm was on fire. What number was I on? Fifteen? Twenty? I was supposed to do thirty, wasn't I?

Choking on sobs, I took hold of his face. Sucking in the deepest breath I could, I clamped my mouth over his and exhaled hard. I filled my lungs again, locked our mouths, and exhaled a second time.

I pressed both hands to his sternum. Stats about CPR success rates beat against the inside of my skull. If Aaron was in full cardiac arrest, he needed a defibrillator. Chest compressions wouldn't bring him back to life!

Tears dripped off my chin as I shoved down on his sternum again. I wouldn't lose him. Wouldn't let it happen. We needed our superhero pyromage, the one who'd brought us all together and made us a family. *We needed him!*

My limbs trembled with mounting fatigue. A pop sounded as one of his ribs cracked. Panic shot through me. Was that normal? That happened with CPR, didn't it? Why hadn't I paid more attention in that high school class!

Fifteen. Sixteen. Makiko kept yelling Kai's name. *Seventeen. Eighteen.* She was trying to snap him out of the mind-control trance. *Nineteen. Twenty.* He was in the grip of the assassin's psychic power, and—

The assassin.

She was nearby. She was one of those cloaked figures.

I pulled my hands off Aaron's chest, knowing every second without compressions was a second too many. I drew Justin's gun from my holster, spun on my knees, and opened fire on the three robed figures watching Kai and Makiko battle.

The gunshots split my eardrums, the cacophony echoing off the concrete walls. Two of the three robed figures dove to the side, while the third thrust a hand toward me.

"*Ori—*" he began to shout.

I pulled the trigger twice more.

This time, my limbs weren't shaking from a recent electrical shock. Blood splattered from the man's chest and he keeled over backward.

"Kai!" Makiko screamed.

I jerked around. Kai was sprinting toward me, dirt smudged over his black gear, but I knew he was himself again—the anguish and horror in his face was so terrible it ripped my heart in two.

He dropped to his knees, put a hand on either side of Aaron's chest, and discharged a bolt of electricity. Aaron's torso jumped.

"*Aaron!*" Kai yelled, voice breaking. "Come on!"

Pushing down on Aaron's chest, he sent another shock into his friend—and Aaron's whole body spasmed. He gasped in a violent breath, then shook with a wheezing cough.

"Oh my god," I whispered. "Is he—"

The air in the reservoir shivered strangely.

A blast of wind hit me and Kai. It flung me backward and I slammed into the long wooden altar. A candelabra landed on my head as I slumped against it, diaphragm locked.

Kai, who'd fallen into the altar beside me, yanked out two bladed stars, one in each hand. He flung them.

They whipped through the air on either side of Makiko as she bore down on us, her face wiped of thought or emotion and her steel fans extended toward us. She flicked them, blowing Kai's blades away from her.

He snapped his hand out. Electricity lit the flying stars and arced between them, catching Makiko in the middle. She shrieked as she dropped to her knees.

Kai lunged up. Five long steps carried him toward her, and as she slashed a fan down, he tackled her around the middle. One of her fans skittered away as they tumbled to the floor.

Gun clutched in one hand, I reached for my hip with the other, adrenaline numbing the pain in my arm. My fingers found a cool sphere, and as Kai wrestled Makiko, trying to pin the viciously struggling aeromage down, I hurled my second-last alchemy bomb into the empty center of the summoning circle.

It shattered, unleashing a blinding flash and a bang even louder than the gun. As the two cloaked figures flinched, I smashed the final glass orb a few feet away.

Smoke boiled out of the crushed glass, engulfing us in a gray haze.

Fighting back a cough at its peppery scent, I crawled through the fog, praying that the mentalist's ability required a direct line of sight; she'd been unnecessarily close to us at Blake's hotel otherwise. If she couldn't see us, maybe she couldn't control us.

The shadows of Kai and Makiko appeared, and they weren't struggling. They were both leaning over Aaron's prone form. As I scuttled toward them, Kai looked up. That terrible anguish twisted his face.

"He's breathing," he whispered. "But he needs a healer right away."

I crawled to Kai's side and touched Aaron's cheek. His eyelids fluttered but didn't open.

"We have to get out of here," I whispered back as smoke drifted around us, obscuring everything. "How do we get past the mentalist?"

"I don't know," Kai rasped. "If she takes hold of me again— I can't fight it. I don't even realize what I'm doing until her control breaks."

Makiko nodded, her lips pressed together so tightly they'd turned white.

Somewhere beyond our smoke screen came faint rustling and murmurs. The words "punctured lung" reached my ears and I realized our enemies were using the respite to check on the mythic I'd shot.

I sucked in air. "How long does it take her to switch her control from one person to another?"

"Twenty seconds," Kai answered. "Give or take five. That's about how long it took her to make Makiko attack us after she'd lost control of me."

My hands squeezed into fists. "Carrying Aaron, can you make it to the exit in twenty seconds? Once you're out of her sight, you should be safe."

"Maybe, but we'd have to run right past them. If she gets control of me—"

"If she gets control of either of you," I whispered as I pushed the release button on my gun's grip, "it'll be a disaster. But if she wastes effort taking control of me …"

The magazine dropped out of the gun and into my waiting palm. I passed the magazine to Kai, then turned the gun upside down and pulled the slide back. The final round fell from the chamber.

"… then she won't have enough time to take control of you two."

Clutching the magazine, Kai shook his head. "But then you'll—"

"I'll run after you as soon as she releases me," I interrupted. "And she won't have time to get me again. It's the only way." I shoved to my feet, the unloaded gun in my hand. "Grab Aaron and let's do this!"

His face white, Kai pocketed the magazine, then heaved Aaron up and over his shoulder. I gave him a nod, not allowing myself to show any terror, then spun to face the fading mist—and the two cultists beyond it.

Gun clutched in both hands, I charged out of the smoke. The scarlet lights high on the pillars bathed the silver etching of the summoning circle that lay between me and the assassin, the Magnus Dux at her side.

Screaming like a banshee, I charged straight at them. My stare locked on the woman's shadowed hood, and as she turned to me, the dim light caught on her lower face, illuminating that same smile I'd seen as she'd forced Kai to kiss me before electrocuting me.

Controlling people wasn't enough for her. She wanted to rip out their hearts too.

I aimed my gun for her chest.

My steps slowed, then stopped. Adrenaline burned in my blood, but fear was a distant fizzle in the back of my brain. I turned, my stare finding Kai as he charged past, Aaron over his shoulder and Makiko right behind him. I raised the gun, tracking Kai's movement, then pulled the trigger.

Click, click, click.

At the hollow clack of the empty weapon, the mentalist hissed angrily—and terror flooded back into my brain. As I wheezed from the sudden onslaught, the mentalist turned her hooded face toward Kai and Makiko.

Whirling, I sprinted after the others, my legs pumping. If we could get out of here and into the trees, we might have a chance. Up the stairs, through the cemetery, to the car—

Crimson light blazed.

282 ♦ ANNETTE MARIE

A streak of red power launched past us and hit the ground in front of the rough doorway out of the reservoir. The light pooled upward into a shape over seven feet tall. A demon manifested—gangly-limbed with skin like armor plates.

As Kai skidded in a frantic attempt to stop, Makiko leaped forward, thrusting her hand toward the demon. His glowing magma eyes flared as he swung his long arm.

The air boomed, and the lightweight aeromage hurtled backward. She crashed down and curled into an agonized ball, arms wrapped around her ribs.

The demon swung his other arm, and Kai could only twist so that the blow hit his side and not the unconscious pyromage he carried. He crumpled, barely keeping Aaron's head from cracking on the concrete.

Halfway between them and the cultists, I could do nothing. I had no magic in my belt and no bullets in my gun. The only thing I had left was the Vh'alyir Amulet, and I was too far to use it on the demon.

The assassin pressed a fingernail to her smiling lower lip. "We only need one to question," she murmured in a throaty contralto voice. "Who would you prefer?"

"Miss Dawson should suffice, I think," the Magnus Dux replied.

Her smiled widened.

The demon lifted his arm, his two-inch claws extended as he aimed for Kai. Gasping, I ran toward them, even though I was too far. Even though I had no magic. Even though there was nothing I could do.

With a flash of crimson, a rune-marked circle appeared around the demon's upper arm. He jolted, his arm immobile inside the hovering circle.

Another ring flashed around his other arm. A third blinked into existence around the demon's waist. He jerked against the spells, trapped in place.

"What—" the Magnus Dux began.

Scarlet light blazed from the doorway behind the demon— and his chest burst apart in a spray of dark blood.

A ring of crimson spikes jutted from the creature's torso. With a final flash, an even thicker spear erupted from the center of his chest, ripping through his sternum. The immobilizing spells dissolved, and the demon dropped like a marionette with cut strings.

Standing in the doorway behind the fallen demon, crimson magic snaking over his outstretched arm and his left eye glowing with fierce power, was Ezra.

26

EZRA WAS HERE.

He had just slaughtered a demon with a single attack, and all I could do was stare.

Lowering his arm, he stepped out of the doorway. Dressed in combat gear with his steel-plated gloves covering his arms, he carried no weapons.

His gaze slashed across Kai and Aaron, then shot to me. The relief and terror filling my head battled for dominance with such violence that it made me dizzy—or maybe I was dizzy because I'd forgotten to breathe.

We'd decided not to tell Ezra where we were going because it would've been too much of a heart-rending, trauma-inducing trial to face the cult that had ruined his life, caused his parents' demise, and condemned him to an early death. We'd thought he wouldn't be able to handle it … but here he was, and his face was a calm, eerily emotionless mask—except for his blazing left eye.

And I didn't know whether that was a good thing.

"Well," the Magnus Dux breathed. "Well, well, well."

The crooning pleasure in the man's tone made my stomach heave.

Ezra turned toward the two cultists.

The Magnus Dux opened his arms as if to embrace Ezra from across the forty feet between them, his cloak rippling. "It's been such a long time, Enéas. You've grown from a talented boy to a powerful man."

For a moment, Ezra's expression didn't shift. Then he smiled—and it was the coldest smile I'd ever seen. Ten years of loathing had chilled it beyond the coldest depths of the Arctic Ocean.

"Xever. If I'd known you were alive …"

I shuddered. There was as much undiluted hatred in Ezra's smooth voice as there was in his smile.

The Magnus Dux pushed back his deep hood. As fabric pooled over his shoulders, the scarlet light from the pillars illuminated the face of a man in his late forties, with brown hair and a square jaw. His visage was entirely forgettable except for the ugly scar that ran up his chin and into his lower lip, permanently twisting his mouth.

"So calm, Enéas. Your control is superb, as always."

"Is that what you think?"

Xever arched his eyebrows. "Are you suggesting your control is inadequate?"

"That's an interesting question." Ezra walked past Aaron and Kai, his steps slow and steady. Crimson light crawled up his left shoulder and streaked the side of his face. "If my demon and I both want the same thing, which of us is in control?"

The slightest twitch of confusion touched Xever's face.

As the red light formed a pair of horns above his left temple, Ezra raised his left arm, palm aimed at Xever. "If we both plan to kill you, does control even matter?"

A pentagram flashed around his wrist, twisted runes flaring inside and around it.

"Xanthe!" Xever barked, not taking his eyes off Ezra. "Take him!"

"I did!"

Power blazed over Ezra's arm—and a hint of crimson gleamed in his brown, human eye.

"Whose mind do you have in your grasp, though?" he asked, his voice deeper and the words tinged with a guttural accent. "Not *mine*."

Xever's eyes widened.

Magic pulsed across Ezra's palm—and he swung his arm, pointing it at the mentalist instead. A blast of power exploded outward.

She sprang away, but not fast enough. Her scream echoed for an instant before the magic struck the reservoir wall and a thunderous crash of stone drowned her out.

Xever was on his feet, but the assassin was a scarlet-cloaked heap on the floor, unmoving. He glanced at her, then back to the demon mage.

"Interesting, Enéas," he remarked calmly. "I've been watching you for months, waiting for your inevitable collapse into madness. After all, it's been ten years." A crimson glow lit on his chest, shining through his shirt. "But I never imagined you would have found a way to evade that fate. Shall we test your new approach against another old friend?"

Crimson light streaked off his chest. It struck the floor halfway between the Magnus Dux and the demon mage, pooling upward—and outward.

The light solidified into a demon six and a half feet tall, his huge wings spread wide. His black hair was tied back, revealing a sharp-featured face that, aside from the glowing magma eyes and horns rising above his temples, was the most humanish demon countenance I'd seen aside from Robin's demon.

Crimson snaked up Ezra's arms, and power blazed in his eyes.

"Nazhivēr," he snarled. "*Vulanā vh'reniredh'thē īn Ahlēavah, karkis dahganul.*"

As the demon's lips pulled back in an answering grin, I stared at the radiant scarlet that had overtaken Ezra's brown iris. Eterran was in full control—without any sign of resistance from Ezra.

The demon—"Nazhivēr," I was assuming—and the demon mage faced each other, unmoving. With a crackling sizzle, red power lit Nazhivēr's hands and swept up his arms—and my terror increased tenfold. This wasn't a demon mage against a contracted demon puppet. It was a demon mage against a demon *with magic.*

They sprang for each other.

Phantom red talons sprouted from their fingers, and they slammed together. Eterran gave way to the demon's superior strength, evading the claws that would do horrific damage to his human host's body. Magic flashed. They broke apart—and crimson power exploded.

They leaped backward, opening a gap. Circles flashed over their arms, each demon conjuring a different spell. Blazes of light, shrieking explosions.

Rubble rained down from the ceiling, and I stumbled backward, retreating from the danger zone. By the door, Kai and Makiko were pulling Aaron up, the unconscious mage's arms over their shoulders.

Eterran cast his hands wide, and a dozen spells appeared on the floor all around Nazhivēr. The demon snapped his wings open and vaulted upward while gesturing at the floor. His magic swept down as Eterran's spells erupted—and when the two forces collided, an even more violent explosion ripped through the room.

I scrambled behind a pillar as chunks of concrete shot past like fist-sized bullets. The altar shattered and the lectern toppled, breaking into pieces.

The book-sized wooden case that had been resting on the lectern tumbled to the floor and the lid flipped open. Inside, the glossy black cover of a large, leather-bound tome reflected the flickering ruby glow of the demons' magic.

"I'm disappointed, Enéas." Xever's low voice echoed as quiet fell. "Your demon is very skilled, yes. I dare say he's evenly matched with Nazhivēr. But to let him fight for you … After surviving ten years, you would surrender your mind so easily?"

"Surrender my mind? I don't remember doing that."

Peeking out from behind the pillar, I froze in confusion. That—that was *Ezra's* voice.

He stretched out his hand and power blazed over his palm. "I told you, Xever. Eterran and I want the same thing."

Runes flashed over and around his hand. A red streak shot up from his palm, and as he closed his fingers around it, it solidified—forming a phantom blade in the exact shape of Ezra's long-destroyed short sword, with its foot-long handle and equal-length blade. He stretched out his other hand, and with another flare of light, the twin sword, made of glowing crimson power, formed in his grip.

My breath caught, disbelief flashing through me. In the same way a demon could shape his magic into phantom talons to tear into enemies, Eterran had created phantom *swords*—and Ezra, who'd been fighting at a disadvantage for so long without his switches, was armed with familiar blades.

Both eyes gleaming with demonic power, he stretched his arms out. He inhaled, shoulders shifting, and from fifteen feet away, Nazhivēr curled his talons in readiness.

Ezra slashed his phantom blades sideways, crisscrossing them in front of his body. The air rippled out from him, and Nazhivēr snapped his arms up to shield his head and upper chest.

Blood sprayed from the demon's forearms as two slicing wounds in the shape of an X cut deep into his flesh.

Ezra launched for the demon. Nazhivēr dropped his arms and slashed—and with a flick of Ezra's sword, wind slammed into the demon. Crimson runes spiraled up Ezra's other arm, and he thrust the blade. A blast of demonic power flung Nazhivēr backward.

Ezra was using aero magic and demonic magic *at the same time*. He and Eterran—they were fighting together. Not Ezra borrowing Eterran's power. Not their two minds switching back and forth.

Seamless, shared control of two magics and one body.

As he lunged for Nazhivēr, phantom blades flashing, I crawled out from behind the pillar. Light flickered, the ceiling trembled, debris showered down. With an ear-splitting crack, the concrete floor split. Dust hazed the air, obscuring the battling demon and demon mage.

Ignoring the grit peppering me, I scuttled through the rubble to the broken lectern. I scooped the ornate grimoire from its box, unzipped my jacket halfway, and shoved the large book down the jacket's front. I zipped it back up to my throat, then snapped the lid shut and shoved the box into the rubble where Xever might not notice it right away.

The floor shook.

Ezra spun past Nazhivēr's slashing claws, his swords whirling. Blades of air caught the demon and blood splattered. A punch of red power blasted off his wrist, then one of those short swords thrust out.

Ezra drove it into Nazhivēr's gut. The blade pulsed—then exploded.

Nazhivēr reeled back, blood spilling down his stomach. His second sword dissolving, Ezra slammed both palms into the demon's chest and the air boomed. A concussive blast of wind hurled the demon twenty feet and into the concrete wall with bone-breaking force.

As the stunned, bleeding demon sagged against the wall, Ezra whirled on the Magnus Dux. I looked at the cult leader too—and my gaze stuttered. The mentalist's body was gone from where she'd fallen.

"I am impressed after all, Enéas."

My attention shot to Xever, and even from across the room, I could see his smile.

"I knew from the moment I laid eyes on you as a child that you were gifted."

For the first time, Ezra's calm, steely façade cracked. He bared his teeth, hatred twisting his face.

"A greater success than your other experiments, Xever." Xanthe strolled out of the dusty haze to join her fellow cultist. Her hood was off, revealing raven hair and her sweetly mocking smile. If Ezra's attack had injured her, I couldn't tell. "Had Enright gone differently, he would've been a magnificent asset."

A low sound rasped in Ezra's throat—an enraged snarl more demon than human.

Xever stroked his cleanshaven jaw. "He's an even greater success than we imagined. I'm excited to discover what makes him and his demon so special."

"If only you could thank his parents for giving him to you," Xanthe purred. "But really, you should thank me. I acquired so many pretty toys for your experiments. Like sweet little Lexie, our first female demon mage."

Xever's gaze locked on Ezra. "An instant failure, as I'd expected."

Ezra lunged toward them. Magic blazed over his arms—and shimmered across his back as phantom wings and a snaking tail took form. Power rippled off him, shimmering, twisting.

He was losing control.

"Hoshi!" I yelled. "*Hoshi!*"

She appeared beside me, tail quivering with fear and little paws gripping my sleeve.

As Ezra charged the cultists, Nazhivēr shot at his blind side. Ezra pivoted on one foot and his swinging fist smashed into the demon's waiting palm. A blast of wind pushed Nazhivēr back a step.

Behind Ezra, Xever slid his cloak up his arm. Silver bands encircled his forearm, and he extended his hand toward Ezra's back.

"Hoshi, I need a diversion!" I gasped.

Her sickly green fear swirled in my mind, streaked with dark blue determination. The sylph rose into the air. Her tail lashed, and all the crystals that adorned her small body—the ones tipping her antennae, the one in the center of her forehead, the one on the end of her tail, and her crystalline eyes—glowed with fierce pink light.

Nazhivēr smashed a fist into Ezra's chest, throwing him backward.

"*Ori nov*—" Xever began.

Hoshi snapped her insect-like wings open—and a shrieking whirlwind erupted inside the reservoir.

The howling wind picked up all the loose debris and flung it in every direction. Dust turned the gale brown, and I ducked as a rock flew past my head. Scrambling up, I bolted for the exit, Hoshi hanging off the back of my jacket.

"Ezra!" I yelled. "This way!"

The dark doorway appeared in the gray wall—and a shape filled it. Kai, a hand outstretched toward me. Leaping over the demon corpse in front of the exit, I grabbed for his hand. He steadied me as I twisted to look back into the violent whirlwind.

"*Ezra!*" I screamed.

Crimson light flashed in the hazy tornado, then a shadow appeared. Ezra sprinted through the wind, his aero magic deflecting the airborne projectiles. As he reached us, Kai turned and dashed up the stairs. I ran on his heels, and Ezra followed right behind.

Up, up, up. Light flicked ahead—a flashlight at the entrance, beckoning us to safety.

Kai shot out of the hidden staircase, and I bolted after him and onto the grass, Hoshi clinging to me. Ezra flew out after us, then whirled around. Crimson blazed up his arm, and a corresponding circle of light appeared on top of the cenotaph, circling the weatherworn angel with her false crown.

Runes popped up across the tangled lines inside the spell, then it flashed. The stone floor shattered and caved inward. The pillars toppled and the heavy ceiling tumbled down. It all sank into the collapsed underground staircase with a hideous grinding of rock.

Panting, I looked from Ezra to Kai, then to Makiko, who was bracing Aaron's side, a flashlight in her other hand. Aaron was standing under his own power—mostly—but his face was tight with pain.

Wordlessly, I pointed toward the trees. Together, we fled.

Despite our best efforts to hurry, it took us longer than it should've to reach the parking lot. Kai's motorcycle—not the red one he'd driven down into the States, but the one he'd left at Aaron's house when Makiko had forced him to move out— was parked beside the SUV.

And on the vehicle's other side was a monstrous black SUV that dwarfed Aaron's.

As we approached, the driver's and passenger's doors opened. Two men in suits leaped out and bowed.

"Miura-*dono*," they said in unison. "Yamada-*dono*."

"I called them," Makiko said breathlessly, limping beside Kai. "They'll take us to my family's healers."

The attendants opened the back doors and helped Kai get Aaron inside. Makiko slid in after him, and Kai took the next spot. As I stepped toward the open door, I realized Ezra was hanging back.

I turned. "Ezra?"

"There's something I need to do," he said quietly.

"What?" My eyes widened. "You can't go back for them. You—"

"Not that. Something else." He stepped closer. "I'll take the SUV and meet you guys back at the house."

"But—" I broke off, staring at him. Really seeing him.

He was back to his non-demonic self, with no more glowing veins or magma eyes. But something was different. Something had changed.

His softness, that gentle kindness that had warmed me from the moment I'd met him, was still there. That hadn't changed. But it had been joined by ... by ...

Fire.

That was the only word to describe the light in his eyes. The burn in his gaze. It was as though the Ezra I'd known for eight months had been half asleep.

Suddenly, I was looking at an Ezra who was wide awake.

As I gawked at him, that Ezra strode up to me, cupped my face in his hands, and kissed me.

Like, *really* kissed me.

And the fire I saw in him—I felt it in his kiss. An inferno of desire incinerated my innards, and I clamped my arms around his neck. Plastered against him, I kissed him back with every flame of intensity I possessed—my fire meeting his, and it was like I'd never kissed him before.

The burn of passion and fear and need and desperation and determination combined until I was scorched from the inside out, until the shape of me was burning into something new.

Then someone cleared their throat loudly.

I tore my mouth off Ezra's and looked over. I was standing at the open car door, and everyone in the vehicle was right there, staring at us. Including the two Miura attendants.

Cheeks flushing, I unclamped my arms and stepped back.

Kai leaned out and tossed something to Ezra. The aeromage caught the object—Aaron's car keys.

"Thanks." Ever the poker-face champion, Ezra gave me a calm smile. "I'll see you soon."

"Y-yeah."

I blinked repeatedly as he strode to Aaron's SUV, climbed into the driver's seat, and shut the door. I was still staring as he reversed into the middle of the parking lot, then peeled out, tires squealing. The taillights flashed, then the SUV disappeared.

And I still stared, because *holy shit*.

When Ezra had said last night that he was ready to fight, I hadn't realized that wasn't a mere change in attitude. It went *way* deeper than that.

I lifted my fingers to my tingling lips. So far, I had zero complaints.

27

THE MOMENT I WALKED into Aaron's house, I might have run straight for Ezra, dirty shoes and grimy gear be damned. And I might have thrown my arms around him all over again, and I might have kissed him with a ridiculous amount of desperation.

I also might have cried a little. The last few days had been really tough, okay?

Three hours had passed since we'd parted ways in the cemetery parking lot. Aaron, Kai, and Makiko were with the Miuras' healers. I'd waited until they were in better shape, then called a cab to take me home so Ezra wouldn't have to wait alone all night.

At least, I'd tried to call a cab. Makiko had plucked the phone out of my hand, ended the call while the operator had been in mid-sentence, informed me her driver would take me home, and stared at me stonily until I'd agreed.

Then, even more bizarrely, she'd hesitantly patted my shoulder and murmured something that sounded sort of like, "It'll be fine," before walking back into the room where a healer had been examining Kai.

Weird.

But now I was home, and Makiko wasn't getting another thought tonight.

I desperately needed a shower, but after prying myself off Ezra, I shed my shoes and jacket, then returned to the living room where he waited for me. Rubbing the evidence of tears from my cheeks, I dropped onto the sofa. He sat beside me, and I leaned into him, my astounded gaze flicking across his face. That new intensity in him wasn't as obvious now that we were safe, but it was definitely there.

"So …" I drawled, smiling wanly. "Guess we have some catching up to do."

He arched his eyebrows. "The first thing I want to know is whether you knew that was the Court of the Red Queen when you went in there. Because if you did …"

I cringed. "I didn't know the full name, but we did know it was the home base of the cult …"

"A *demon-worshipping* cult." His expression hardened. "And you didn't think going in there unprepared to battle *demons* might be a mistake?"

"Honestly, we didn't think there'd be anyone there, but … yeah." I slumped into the cushions. "It was a mistake for sure. We were in a hurry. We wanted to get in and out before they realized we'd killed their moles in the Keys of Solomon."

His jaw dropped. Recovering quickly, he leaned back beside me. "Maybe you should start from the beginning."

Resting my head on his shoulder, I ran through the events of the past few days, from our investigation of Enright, to the "circle" in Portland, to our trip to Salt Lake City, where we'd fallen into the trap at the Keys guild. When I reached the part where Daniel had thrown me down on the table to interrogate me, Ezra brushed my cheek.

I realized tears were trickling down my face.

"What's wrong?" he murmured.

I shoved my hand into my combat belt, still buckled around my hips. The chain jingled as I pulled out the Vh'alyir Amulet.

Faint crimson lit Ezra's left eye.

"Russel grabbed it," I whispered, staring at the metal disc. "His demon took control and started to tear free from Russel. And—and it …" My fingers closed tightly over the medallion, squeezing so hard it hurt. "It killed them both. Russel and his demon."

Ezra inhaled sharply.

"It didn't break whatever magic imprisons the demon inside the human. When the demon tried to get out, Russel's body … it ripped apart. The demon couldn't break free, and he died when Russel died."

My fingers spasmed, and I flung the amulet onto the coffee table. It bounced off and clattered across the hardwood floor.

"*Useless.*" I gasped back a sob. "It works so well on regular demon contracts. I was so sure—I was counting on it so much, but it'll kill you, not save you, and—"

Ezra captured my hands, pressing them between his warm palms. "But you were searching for something else. You went to find a grimoire."

I nodded, sniffling. Sliding my hands from his, I pushed off the sofa and crossed to the front door. After taking off my jacket, I'd left the textbook-sized grimoire on the closet shelf. I carried it back to Ezra and set it on his lap.

He stared at the emblem inscribed on the black leather cover.

"What does it mean?" I asked, sinking onto the sofa beside him. "The symbol."

With one finger, he traced the circle. "The Court." He touched the crown. "The Red Queen who rules it."

"Their Queen is this 'goddess'?"

He nodded. "Have you ever noticed that all demons are male?"

I blinked, then shrugged. "I guess, but I'd never thought about it."

"They're all male because only male demons can be summoned. Female demons can't be called into this world. The cult says that's because demon males are servants of the one true Goddess who created magic, and she sends her servants to this world to aid and protect her followers."

His mouth quirked in a humorless smile. "Eterran says females are never summoned because they would obliterate anyone who summoned them, contract or no contract."

"Huh. Um." I swallowed. "Speaking of Eterran … your fighting style has changed."

Real amusement softened his smile. "We came to a truce. It's been interesting. We should last a bit longer now that we aren't constantly fighting each other."

Fear jumped in my chest at the reminder of his dwindling time, and I looked down at the grimoire. He ran his thumb along the cover's edge, then drew in a deep breath. Holding it in his lungs, he opened the book.

I squinted. "It's written in … Latin?"

"Most spells are in Latin or another ancient language." He turned the pages, flipping past precise Latin printing and ink flourishes. "I remember a book just like this during the ritual."

I leaned closer as he continued to peruse the tome. The walls of text morphed to diagrams of spells and detailed drawings of Arcana circles. Demonic runes marked other pages. He kept going, and illustrations of humans appeared, their bodies marked like a disturbing mockery of a medical text.

He stopped on an ink illustration of a face, the man's mouth open to reveal long fangs. His eyes had the colors reversed—the sclera pitch black, with a white pupil in the center.

"That's a vampire," Ezra muttered. "Why is there a drawing of a vampire in here?"

I'd never seen a vampire in person, and judging by that illustration, I didn't want to.

Ezra flipped to a detailed drawing of the vampire's creepy inverted eye, paused to scrutinize it, then continued. More diagrams. Another drawing of a human, marked up with illegible Latin text. He turned to the next page and stopped again.

A drawing of a wolf. But if the book had a vampire in it, then I was willing to bet that wasn't a regular ol' *Canis lupus*.

"Werewolf," Ezra whispered.

My hand was already diving into my pocket. I pulled out my phone, and in seconds, I was speeding through my gallery of photos, racing back in time to December.

A photo filled my screen. I'd snapped it the day after Ezra and I—and Eterran, if I were being fair—had stopped apprentice alchemist Brian from kidnapping Sin, who'd been bitten by a mutant werewolf. We'd gone back the next day to clean up, gather evidence, and write our report for the MPD.

The picture I'd taken showed a square piece of paper lying beside a steel box with a foam insert, the cutouts in it suggesting it had held vials or test tubes. We'd turned all that evidence over to the MPD, but I'd stolen a few photos beforehand.

The crisp handwriting stood out sharply against the white paper.

> Brian,
>
> Please find enclosed your final stock. I hope to receive a completed sample by the end of the month.
>
> Yours most sincerely,
> — X.

"It's signed 'X.'" I croaked the words. "And that metal case … what if it contained …"

Ezra had gone rigid beside me. "Demon blood. It contained demon blood—a conduit of demonic power, according to the cult."

My gaze flicked between the photo and the grimoire.

"And vampires," he muttered. "There was something about a surge in vampire activity last November. Drew was talking about super-powered vamps."

I swallowed hard and gestured at the book. "Keep going."

He flipped through the pages. More diagrams. Drawings of strange creatures began to appear—not demons, but other things … beasts that vaguely resembled animals. He kept turning. Now we were into a section on infernus spells, and then …

I pointed at the page he'd halted on. "That looks like a golem."

My voice was remarkably calm, but internally, I was shrieking, "*Golem!*" over and over like a madwoman.

"A golem," he agreed, staring down at the man-shaped behemoth of steel drawn in careful detail.

"The liquid that came out of Varvara's golems," I said, again sounding far calmer than I felt. "Aaron said it smelled like burnt blood."

My gaze met Ezra's, and we said in unison, "Demon blood."

I swallowed against the panicky ringing in my ears. "Ezra, just who is Xever?"

"He's the cult leader, and the summoner who created all the demon mages in Enright. His demon, Nazhivēr, is very powerful and only loosely contracted. When I was a teenager, Xever used Nazhivēr as an example of a loyal *Servus*, and claimed all demons could serve us like that if our faith was strong."

His jaw clenched. "Nazhivēr killed Lexie when she lost control."

I rubbed his shoulder, sympathy softening the tension in my jaw as I waited for him to push through the flare of old grief.

"Xever didn't live in Enright. He visited every couple of months, but even though he was rarely there, everyone was blindly loyal to him. He was so ... composed and perceptive, and he seemed all-knowing to me." A faint frown turned his lips down. "I'm more familiar with Xanthe. Seeing her tonight was a bigger shock than seeing Xever."

"Wait. You know the assassin?"

"Assassin?" He blinked. "*Xanthe* is the mentalist assassin you described?"

My mouth had gone dry. "How do you know her?"

"She's the *Magna Ducissa*—the cultist ranked just below the Magnus Dux. She spent more time in Enright than Xever. A few days every month, at least, helping settle in new members and working with the demon mages."

I studied the cold bitterness in his gaze. "You tried to kill her first."

"Xever made me a demon mage, but she's the one who convinced my parents I should become a protector."

Cold settled deep in my limbs. A mentalist with the ability to make her victims do whatever she wanted … Had she used that power against the cultists without their knowledge? Her control didn't seem to have had any lasting effects on us, but were there other ways she could use her ability?

Had she influenced Ezra and his parents into accepting the cult's dogma?

"All along," I muttered, "was Enright just an experiment on how to create a perfect demon mage? Experiments on living people … just like Brian was experimenting on living werewolves?"

"Xever, Xanthe, and the cult helped create those enhanced golems, too. They may have done something with vampires as well, if Drew was right about an unexplained surge in their strength."

My hands clenched around my knees, squeezing. "Ezra, just how big is the Court of the Red Queen?"

"I don't know." He gazed at the golem illustration, and for a second time, crimson glimmered across his left eye. "But whatever Xever and Xanthe are doing … whatever they want golems and werewolves and vampires and demon mages for … we need to know."

Reaching across him, I flipped the grimoire closed and said fiercely, "But before anything with them or the Court, we need to save *you*." Noting the lingering red gleam in his pale eye, I added, "And Eterran, I guess."

A faint, un-Ezra-like smirk twitched his lips before his expression smoothed again.

I rubbed my sweaty palms on my leather pants—which just smeared the moisture. Ew. "You said you had some leads of your own."

"I do." He set the grimoire on my lap and rose to his feet. "Xever and Xanthe have destroyed a lot of lives and made a lot of enemies. We aren't the only ones working against them."

Circling the coffee table, he picked up the Vh'alyir Amulet, letting it dangle by its chain without touching the medallion.

"We have potential allies right under our noses— surprisingly powerful ones." Returning to the sofa, he lowered the amulet onto the grimoire's cover. "And I know how to convince them to help us."

I stared up at his sudden grin, mesmerized by the fire in his eyes—that spine-tingling intensity born of his newfound desire to survive. To *live*.

Shaking off my trance, I squinted at him. "Who are you talking about?"

His grin widened. "Just wait and see."

28

"I DON'T UNDERSTAND why this needs to be a surprise."

"Don't you enjoy a little mystery in your life?"

"Not at the moment, no."

Standing between Aaron and Ezra as they bantered, I rolled my eyes and rubbed my cold hands together. The last night of January was as unpleasantly cold as the rest of the month had been, and I hoped February would pick up the slack. We desperately needed a sign of spring.

It didn't help that we were huddled in a grove of trees in a park. The same grove, in fact, where the Crow and Hammer's witches had repaired my bond with Hoshi just over a week ago—which was in the same park where we'd fought Burke and his demon hunter cronies in one of our first Keys of Solomon encounters.

Seeing as it was the nearest park to our guild, I supposed it made sense that multiple members would use it, but it was still kind of weird how we kept coming back.

"How much longer?" I asked, stuffing my hands in my pockets.

"They'll be here any moment," Ezra replied.

I didn't bother asking who we were waiting for. Whether Ezra was being mysterious for kicks or he had a reason for keeping Aaron and me in the dark, I didn't know. Maybe Kai could've gotten an answer out of him, but the electramage was stuck with Makiko again, catching up on whatever criminal business they'd missed while we were jaunting around the western United States.

An icy breeze slid through the trees, rustling their bare branches. The orange glow of streetlamps scarcely penetrated our hidden clearing, and my eyes strained to pick out shapes among the dark shrubbery as I scanned for our unknown guests.

Another minute ticked past. Then another.

The back of my neck prickled. I rolled my shoulders uncomfortably, peering side to side. Ezra glanced behind us, then faced the dirt path that wound into our hidden nook. The breeze gusted, bending the boughs overhead and blowing a swirl of dead leaves past my legs. I glanced up at the creaking branches.

When I looked down again, we were no longer alone.

Two women stood on the trail, wrapped in leather jackets. One was tall and willowy, with blond hair in messy waves. The other was slim and petite, with shoulder-length hair that appeared black in the darkness and glasses perched on her small nose.

Robin Page, our guild's only demon contractor, and her cousin Amalia.

I blinked repeatedly. *Robin* was the mysterious "ally" we were waiting to meet?

"You're late," Ezra observed, his smooth voice blending with the darkness.

Robin shot an annoyed look at her blond cousin, then took an uncertain step into the clearing, studying me and Aaron carefully. Had she known we'd be part of this rendezvous?

"Why are we meeting here?" she asked.

Ezra shrugged. "Some of us prefer room to maneuver."

I hid a frown. Who was "some of us" supposed to be? Because I'd been in enclosed spaces with Robin before with no problem.

"I see." She folded her hands in front of her, waiting expectantly. "We're ready to hear your trade."

A fresh twist of uncertainty unsettled my gut. Why did I get the feeling I was way out of the loop here?

Ezra gestured toward the bag I carried over one shoulder, and I passed it to him. He reached inside and pulled out the glossy black cult grimoire.

"Robin," he murmured, "it turns out we share an enemy, except I know him as Xever." He extended the grimoire toward Robin. "This belongs to him."

She approached the book, gingerly taking it as though it might morph into a beast and bite her arms off.

"This is what you want to trade?" she whispered.

"No, not that." Ezra gestured to me. "Tori?"

I'd already passed him the bag with the grimoire, and there was only one other thing he'd told me to bring.

Doubt flickered through me—but I wouldn't second-guess him now. I slid my hand into my back pocket and took hold of a fine chain, warmed by my body heat. Lifting it out, I held up the swinging talisman.

Robin's eyes went saucer-wide as she tracked its motion, her whole attention focused on it like it was the key to the universe.

"The amulet," she breathed, disbelief feathering the words. "Vh'alyir's Amulet."

"*That*," Ezra said, "is what we're here to trade."

Her stunned gaze snapped to him. "And what do you want in exchange?"

"I want you to use that grimoire"—he pointed to the book—"and find a way to break the demon mage contract binding me and Eterran so he can leave my body."

My heart screeched to a halt, and it took my brain a moment to catch up.

I whirled on Ezra, the amulet swinging from my fist, and shrieked, "She *knows?*"

Amalia cocked her hip. "Well, duh."

"Since when?" I blurted.

Crimson flared across his pale eye. "Since you went to Enright," he rumbled in a guttural accent, "leaving Ezra and me to find out what she knew about the amulet."

I backpedaled away from him, and Aaron recoiled in the opposite direction with a breathless curse. Eterran had taken control? Just like that? But *how*—

Eye still glowing, he turned to Robin and Amalia—and they didn't so much as flinch. No fear, no surprise, no confusion. They'd seen this before.

What had Ezra said to Xever? *If my demon and I both want the same thing, which of us is in control?*

Holy freaking shit.

"We have made our offer," Eterran rumbled. "Will you accept it, or will we finally spill each other's blood, Zylas?"

Silence fell across the park.

I held my breath, confusion buzzing in my head and my nerves prickling with inexplicable apprehension. Stillness lay heavy over us, and even the breeze had died down. Then an almost inaudible sound rolled out of the darkness behind me.

Low, husky laughter.

I whipped around. Pulse hammering, I scanned the darkness, seeing only the black shapes of foliage and shrubbery.

"Escaping your *hh'ainun* prison ..." The voice, suffused with a throaty accent, floated out of the night. "... does not mean escaping the *hh'ainun* world, Eterran."

My head snapped back, gaze flashing upward.

In the branches of a tree, a pair of magma eyes glowed. A dark shape uncoiled, then dropped from the high boughs and landed with a soft thump in front of me. His thin tail lashing, the demon straightened, glowing eyes fixing on mine.

Not all that long ago, I'd taken a good long look into this demon's eyes. His lithe, humanoid shape was strangely unnerving, and something about him had never sat right with me. All demons were frightening, but this one had made me twitchy in a different way.

Looking into his eyes now, I knew why he'd unsettled me—because staring back at me was a pair of demon eyes bright with cunning intelligence and lucid ferocity.

This demon was no mindless puppet.

His lips curved up, revealing sharply pointed canines. Terror flashed through me and I lurched backward in a frantic scramble. The demon glided after me with prowling steps more graceful than any contracted beast.

My back thumped against a warm body—Ezra. His heady scent filled my nose as he laid a hand on my waist.

"Tori, Aaron," he murmured, "meet Zylas."

The demon's sharp smile widened, and his tail snapped against the ground. I trembled, instinct screaming at me to flee from the predator standing almost on my toes.

From somewhere on my left, a soft female sigh fluttered through the quiet. "Zylas, could you *try* not to terrify her?"

At her exasperated question, the demon slid back half a step, and I took a couple small, gasping breaths.

"No fun," he growled quietly. "When do I get to scare *hh'ainun, na?* Never."

"At least you don't have to pretend to be enslaved right now," Robin retorted.

Another snap of that barbed tail.

Pretend? Had she said he *pretended* to be enslaved in a contract? All those times I'd seen him out of her infernus, his stare blank and motions wooden, he'd been *pretending?*

I inhaled again, battling a wave of lightheadedness.

"Well?" Ezra's voice rumbled against my back—except that guttural accent had returned, meaning I was leaning against Eterran, not Ezra. "Do you accept the trade, Zylas?"

The demon's eyes narrowed. Robin walked to his side, the grimoire cradled against her chest, and he flicked a glance at her before refocusing on Ezra. "One condition, Dh'irath."

"What is that?"

"When you are free, you will bring no harm on me or my *hh'ainun.*"

Ezra—or Eterran—nudged me aside so I was no longer between him and Zylas. Facing the demon, he raised his left arm, and crimson veins raced across his hand and up his wrist.

Zylas lifted his left arm, and the same magic snaked up the demon's hand.

They pressed their palms together, outstretched fingers aligning. One hand bronze-skinned and human, the other reddish toffee with dark claws tipping his fingers. The scarlet magic radiating from their skin sizzled on contact and the air around them chilled, electric with deadly power.

"*Enpedēra dīn nā*," Zylas said, the alien words flowing with the cadence of a chant.

"*Enpedēra dīn nā*," Eterran answered.

The crimson light flared, then died away, and the demon and demon mage lowered their hands.

Great. Just *wonderful*. Robin's demon was not only uncontracted enough to walk and talk under his own power, but he had control of his magic too. My gaze snapped between her and Zylas, and I wasn't sure which I wanted to do more: demand answers in a hysterical shriek or run screaming in the opposite direction.

Off to one side, Aaron stood two steps away from Amalia. They were watching us—Amalia with an impatient arch to her eyebrows, and Aaron with an expression somewhere between shell-shocked and grimly resolved. I knew how he felt. When I'd walked into the park, I'd been confident that no matter what "allies" Ezra had in mind for us, I could handle them—but now, I felt so far out of my depth I might as well have been swimming the Mariana Trench.

I froze as magma eyes turned to me. Zylas extended his hand again, palm turned up expectantly.

"Give it to me, *hh'ainun*."

I realized I was clutching the demonic amulet against my chest, the medallion hidden under my hands. Sucking in a wild breath, I glanced questioningly at Ezra.

A faint red gleam lit his pale left eye, but it was the human who spoke. "It's okay. You can give it to him."

"But he's …"

"It belongs to him, Tori." He glanced at the demon. "*Zylas et Vh'alyir*, King of the Twelfth House. The Amulet of Vh'alyir is his."

My stare shot to Robin. That's why she'd been searching for it? That's how she'd come to have a perfect drawing of its front and back?

Cradling the cult grimoire in her arms, she nodded, a small, reassuring smile on her lips. The timid girl I'd first met, who'd flinched and stammered through every conversation, was nowhere in sight as she waited beside her lethal and—as far as I could tell—completely out-of-control demon.

Even though I was intimidated as hell, the hope that had rekindled in my heart, so fragile after we'd stumbled and faltered and failed so much, flared bright and steady. Refocusing on the demon, I straightened my spine and unclamped my hands from my chest.

The medallion, its center marked with the same sigil etched on Zylas's armor, swung gently from its chain as I extended my hand.

Shrewd crimson eyes assessed me, then a triumphant grin flashed across the demon's face. The expression was at once disconcertingly human and savage in a way that only a demon could be. Somehow, he had become our ally? Were this deadly being and his contractor Ezra's only hope? Did we dare trust them?

I had no answers, and it didn't matter anyway. This was Ezra's life, Ezra's fate, and Ezra's decision. The deal was done ...

Zylas's hand closed around the amulet, pulling the chain from my fingers.

... and there was no going back.

TORI'S ADVENTURE CONCLUDES IN

DAMNED SOULS ᴬᴺᴰ SANGRIA

THE GUILD CODEX: SPELLBOUND / EIGHT

Once upon a time, I was your average spunky redhead with the lamest employment history ever, a shaky relationship with my only family member, and no idea what I was doing with my life.

Now, I'm a pseudo mythic with the best bartending job in the world, the most amazing (and hot) best friends I never knew I needed, and a guild of misfit magic-users who've become my extended family.

And I'm about to lose it all.

In my desperation to save Ezra, I stumbled into a web of ruthless deception—and seriously pissed off a sleeping hydra. Now its every murderous head is turned toward me and my guild, and I don't know how to stop it. I'm not sure I can.

I'm not sure *anyone* can.

But if I don't, we're all doomed—Ezra, Aaron, Kai, and my beloved guild.

www.guildcodex.ca

ABOUT THE AUTHOR

Annette Marie is the author of YA urban fantasy series *Steel & Stone*, its prequel trilogy *Spell Weaver*, and romantic fantasy trilogy *Red Winter*.

Her first love is fantasy, but fast-paced adventures, bold heroines, and tantalizing forbidden romances are her guilty pleasures. She proudly admits she has a thing for dragons, and her editor has politely inquired as to whether she intends to include them in every book.

Annette lives in the frozen winter wasteland of Alberta, Canada (okay, it's not quite that bad) and shares her life with her husband and their furry minion of darkness—sorry, cat—Caesar. When not writing, she can be found elbow-deep in one art project or another while blissfully ignoring all adult responsibilities.

www.annettemarie.ca

SPECIAL THANKS

My thanks to Erich Merkel for sharing your exceptional expertise in Latin and Ancient Greek. Any errors are mine.

THE
GUILD CODEX
SPELLBOUND

Rule one: Don't hit first, but always hit back. Rule two: Don't get caught. Rule three: Any rule can be broken. But when the Court of the Red Queen turns its gaze on the guild, they'll need a new rule: Survive—at all costs.

Welcome to the Crow and Hammer.

THE
GUILD CODEX
DEMONIZED

Robin Page: outcast sorceress, mythic history buff, unapologetic bookworm, and the last person you'd expect to command the rarest demon in the long history of summoning. Though she holds his leash, this demon can't be controlled.

But can he be tamed?

THE
GUILD CODEX
WARPED

The MPD has three roles: keep magic hidden, keep mythics under control, and don't screw up the first two.

Kit Morris is the wrong guy for the job on all counts—but for better or worse, this mind-warping psychic is the MPD's newest and most unlikely agent.

STEEL & STONE

When everyone wants you dead, good help is hard to find.

The first rule for an apprentice Consul is *don't trust daemons*. But when Piper is framed for the theft of the deadly Sahar Stone, she ends up with two troublesome daemons as her only allies: Lyre, a hotter-than-hell incubus who isn't as harmless as he seems, and Ash, a draconian mercenary with a seriously bad reputation. Trusting them might be her biggest mistake yet.

CPSIA information can be obtained
at www.ICGtesting.com
Printed in the USA
LVHW041743011020
667692LV00004B/733

9 781988 153490